R-B.

08

|

0

2011

A COIL OF ROPE

A young journalist and his girlfriend visit a small island to investigate rumours about a Baron Grevas and his disciples who are believed to practise a new peace cult. David and Susan stumble on a murder, and then find themselves involved in a series of curious incidents, and finally, the death of Baroness Grevas. There are many tense moments and intriguing situations before David finally gets to the bottom of it all and provides his paper with a first-class 'scoop'.

Books by J. F. Straker
in the Linford Mystery Library:

A CHOICE OF VICTIMS
SWALLOW THEM UP
DEATH ON A SUNDAY MORNING
A LETTER FOR OBI
COUNTERSNATCH
ARTHUR'S NIGHT
A PITY IT WASN'T GEORGE
THE GOAT
DEATH OF A GOOD WOMAN
MISCARRIAGE OF MURDER
SIN AND JOHNNY INCH
TIGHT CIRCLE
A MAN WHO CANNOT KILL
ANOTHER MAN'S POISON
THE SHAPE OF MURDER

J. F. STRAKER

A COIL
OF ROPE

Complete and Unabridged

LINFORD
Leicester

First published in Great Britain in 1962

First Linford Edition
published 2004

British Library CIP Data

Straker, J. F. (John Foster)
  A coil of rope.—Large print ed.—
  Linford mystery library
  1. Journalists—Fiction
  2. Cults—Fiction
  3. Detective and mystery stories
  4. Large type books
  I. Title
  823.9'14 [F]

ISBN 1–84395–207–6

Published by
F. A. Thorpe (Publishing)
Anstey, Leicestershire

Set by Words & Graphics Ltd.
Anstey, Leicestershire
Printed and bound in Great Britain by
T. J. International Ltd., Padstow, Cornwall

This book is printed on acid-free paper

1

'I wouldn't know about travel broadening the mind,' Susan said. She wriggled uncomfortably on the worn seat, in which the springs had long since ceased to function. 'Not in trains, I wouldn't. But it certainly broadens the behind. Mine feels like a slab of overdone steak.'

'Tough, eh?' said David. 'Sort of leathery?'

'How delicately you put it, darling! No; it just isn't resilient any more.' She wriggled again. 'How long before we reach Littleport?'

'Twenty minutes if we're on time,' he told her. 'And that's highly improbable.'

He continued to frown at the rain-soaked countryside slowly unfolding beyond the window of the compartment. Susan's pretty face and plump, well-rounded figure did not interest him; in any case, he had had a surfeit of Susan the previous evening. His head ached, his eyes were red and sore and hot, his tongue felt like coarse sandpaper, his stomach was queasy. He wanted to close his heavy eyelids and sleep. But Susan's constant chatter, the hard seat, and the uneven motion of the train were against him. And they did nothing to ease his headache.

'This is the slowest, dirtiest, uncomfortablest train I've ever been in,' the girl complained. Since she rarely travelled on land other than by car (Susan's male acquaintances were handpicked) this was not such a severe indictment of British Railways as it sounded. 'I just hope the Baron's worth it.' She snapped open her handbag and peered anxiously into the mirror. Reassured that all in her shop-window was as it should be, she settled back in her corner with a resigned sigh. 'It's always been my ambition to meet a real live baron.' She lingered over the title, savouring it. 'Much more romantic than dukes or earls or any of that lot. A baron sounds kind of medieval and feudal and — and wicked.'

'He's wicked, all right,' David said sourly. 'That's for sure. He's also elderly and married and hasn't a bean. Doesn't that damp your enthusiasm?'

She had supposed he must be married; it would be hard for a baron to stay single. And experience had taught her that married men (and elderly married men in particular) were even more appreciative of her charms than the young and unmarried. Poverty, however, was always a handicap. She was no gold-digger, she hoped, but without money even a baron lost much of his appeal. Unless, of course, he were sufficiently young and attractive to outweigh material disadvantages.

'There's a castle on the island, isn't there?' she asked hopefully. A castle seemed to indicate substance. 'Or is it a château? I saw a picture of it once. It stands on a hill overlooking the sea, I think, and it's got turrets and ivy and things. Terribly romantic.'

' 'Terribly' is the *mot juste*,' David said. 'No castle; just a barrack of a mansion that is practically in ruins. No water, no electric light, no sanitation. Pure palæolithic.'

Susan wriggled uneasily, uncertain how much of this was truth and how much the invention of a warped sense of humour. On the previous evening David had eulogized both the island and its baron. Had he been holding out a carrot to entice her into accompanying him on his mission?

'And no servants,' David added. 'I forgot that.'

'Don't be silly, darling. He couldn't have all those people in the house with no one to look after them.'

'They look after themselves. And him. That's his gimmick.' He took his eyes away from the rain-spattered window and grinned at her maliciously. He was fond of Susan, but in his present ill-humour her cheerful expectancy was an affront. 'If you've been dreaming of a brief interlude of luxury and romance you can forget it. It won't be like that at all. Show willing, and before you know where you are you'll be washing his linen and cooking his food and making his bed. That's all the romance you can expect.' He snapped his fingers. 'No! I tell a lie. He'll probably try to tumble you into bed after you've made it — if you can call that romance. He likes his home comforts, does Baron Grevas, and I'm told that the one he married doesn't ring bells for him any more.'

Susan eyed him thoughtfully. That the Baron might try to tumble her into bed did not trouble her greatly; she had faith in her ability to cope with such a situation. But she wondered yet again what it was about David Wight that had made her forsake her otherwise firmly held precept that men without money didn't matter. He was such a scarecrow of a man. No one would believe that his unruly mop of black hair had ever been smoothed by brush or comb; his loosely knotted tie was half-way round his neck, one wing of his collar projected awkwardly, his suit looked as though he had slept the night in it — and not too tranquilly at that. He never remembered her birthday, never paid her compliments, and more often than not treated her with the casual, next-door-neighbourly air that had characterized his attitude towards her ever since they were children together in Watford. All that could be said in his favour was that he looked clean and reasonably wholesome. Yet he had only to ring her up and suggest an evening out (for which, more often than not, she would find herself paying), and she would cheerfully abandon a more splendid date in order to be with him.

It doesn't make sense, she told herself. David's a sentimental luxury that a girl in my position simply can't afford. One of these days I shall have to do something about him.

'You're a real comfort, darling.' She smiled at him, refusing to be drawn. 'You make it sound just too marvellous for words. But aren't you rather overdoing the syrup? After all, you've never actually met the Baron. And you've certainly never been to his island. You're just repeating what your nasty old editor told you. He could be wrong.'

'Editors are never wrong. Not to cub reporters, they aren't.'

He returned to the window. But Susan

was right; he had no first-hand knowledge of the Baron. He had never even heard of him until the newspapers had reported that a man had been drowned off the island, and old Snowball had sent for him and told him to go down to Littleport and get the story. 'I'm not interested in the drowning,' Snowball had said, 'but it's brought Grevas and his island into temporary prominence, and we may as well cash in on it. The Baron's always good for a story.' *Topical Truths* was a weekly journal purporting to give its readers 'the intimate background to the news,' and the more intimate and sensational that background could be made to appear the greater the circulation. 'He's skated over some thin ice in his time.'

Snowball should know, thought David. Snowball was quite a skater himself. Few editors had skirted the laws of libel and obscenity more narrowly or more skilfully than Snowball.

'What's his racket?' he asked.

'Anything likely to show him a profit. At present it's religion.'

'Where's the profit in that?'

'I don't know. That's why I'm sending you down there. There must be a profit, or Grevas wouldn't touch it.' A trace of enthusiasm had shown faintly on the editor's normally dead-pan face. 'We could be on a winner here. There are some things one just can't exploit in this country; the blind, for instance, or dumb animals, or children. The dear old British Public won't stand for it. I'm hoping religion falls into the same category.'

'Is he a real baron?'

'Real enough. One of those mid-European titles that families hang on to for their snob value.'

David had nibbled his nails in doubt, aware of his rawness. Although not entirely new to journalism, was he adequately equipped to handle the story? Perhaps Snowball had sensed his doubt, for he said, 'Don't worry about Grevas. He may be crooked, but I suspect he lacks brains, or he'd have made his pile and got out by now.'

'Any convictions?'

'Not even a prosecution.' The editor

had hesitated. 'Maybe I've exaggerated a little. There have been rumours a-plenty, but the only swindle I can actually swear to was way back. Even then it was his associates who collected most of the loot.'

Despite his chief's attempt at reassurance David had still had his doubts. That was why, after his fifth whisky later that evening, he had invited Susan to accompany him. He had never considered the possibility that Susan might have a brain, but there was no disputing that she had a body. Susan would make an admirable foil. The Baron might resent a reporter, but he could not resent Susan.

'There's the sea,' Susan said briskly, sitting up and reaching for her bag. 'And am I glad to see it! It's been a pig of a journey.'

'It'll be damned rough. And wet.' David was filled with gloom. He was a bad sailor, and with his stomach in its present unstable condition he viewed with dismay the prospect of the sea-crossing. 'If we don't drown we'll probably get pneumonia.'

Susan refused to be discouraged. As the

fields and woods gave place to the outskirts of the town, and the train began jerkily to slow, she put the final touches to hair and face. For a few seconds David watched her. Then he stood up and started to tug the suitcases from the rack.

2

Littleport was a small fishing-town, built in a semicircle round the bay. Because it had proved difficult and expensive to extend laterally it had grown vertically, clinging to the cliffside until it had debouched on to the moor beyond, with each succeeding layer of shops and houses more modern than the last. Down by the quay they stood in terraced rows, slate-roofed, their walls of mellowed grey stone. These were the homes of the fishermen; there were walled backyards for gardens, the streets were narrow and cobbled. Half-way up the hill the houses grew larger, still of stone, with gardens and garages, and with pavements to the streets. Up on the moor were the new estates, bungalows and semi-detacheds, bricked and tiled and squarely uniform, with neat little gardens abutting on to wide macadamed roads, and neat little allotments behind. Here were the few big stores, the one cinema, the bus depot, the railway-station. Here were modernity and progress.

To the student of architecture, a stroll down one of the steep streets that led to the quay was a stroll back through history. But not to David or Susan; neither history nor architecture interested them then. The wind blew fiercely in from the sea, and with bent heads and watering, unseeing eyes they fought it down the hill, with Susan's light raincoat billowing behind her. As they came on to the quay one of the girl's high heels caught in the cobbles, and she stumbled, clutching at her companion. David held her while she rubbed her ankle, but he had little sympathy to spare. His mind was concentrated on the sea and the crossing ahead. Though the water in the bay was not exposed to the full force of the wind, to David's jaundiced eye the waves looked menacingly high.

Susan put her foot to the ground, tested her weight on it, and sighed with relief. 'I thought I'd sprained it,' she said. 'But it seems O.K.' She released David's arm and stood upright, shielding her eyes against the stinging rain as she peered round the bay. 'I don't see any island.'

'Beyond the point, probably. Not that it matters; we can't cross in this weather. Look at those damned waves! And it'll be rougher still outside the bay. You don't catch me risking my neck in that.'

He had expected wholehearted agreement. Instead, she laughed.

'Call that rough? Don't be such a cissy, darling; of course we're going. After that awful train it'll be a picnic. And having come all this way to meet your mysterious baron I'm not letting a few waves stop me.' She looked along the quay. 'There are some men down there by the steps. Let's ask them.'

'Ask them what?'

'To take us to the island, of course.'

In the train David had begun to doubt the wisdom of having brought the girl with him. Now he was sure it had been a mistake.

'They won't do it,' he said. 'They're not daft.'

But Susan was already on her way.

Scowling, he followed her reluctantly. He could only hope the men would confirm his judgment.

There were two of them — an elderly grey-faced man in oil-skins and a bare-headed youth wearing a stained duffle-coat. As David and Susan approached they turned from the rail on which they had been leaning and eyed the newcomers gravely.

'Good afternoon,' Susan said briskly. 'Can you tell us where Shere Island is, please?'

'T'other side of the point,' the man said, jerking a thumb over his shoulder. His eyes were hard. 'Why?'

Susan hesitated. This was David's affair. She had broken the ice for him, but he might resent her further interference. And it was against her principles unnecessarily to arouse resentment in men.

David said genially, 'We'd thought of taking a look at it. But obviously that's out of the question in this weather. We'll have to put it off till to-morrow.'

'That'd be best,' the man agreed.

David smiled at him gratefully. A sensible chap, he thought; no stupid heroics for him. His gratitude increased when the man gave them a curt nod and walked away. The youth, with a lingering glance at Susan, followed him.

'Keen, aren't you?' Susan said. 'I thought you had a job to do.'

Just looking at the tumbling water had made David feel sick, but now that the prospect of trusting himself to it had gone he felt better. 'It'll keep,' he said. 'Let's look for a hotel. I'll put you on the expense account.'

Susan had been a part of too many expense accounts to enthuse over this announcement. She turned to the rail and gazed down at the boats bobbing and splashing below. Some of them certainly looked frail enough to warrant David's timidity. But not all. That big one just beyond the steps, for instance. She had been out . . .

A voice behind her said, 'If you don't mind a wetting I'll take you across to the island.'

It was the duffle-coated youth. Susan

smiled at him, and looked hopefully at David. But David was not smiling. He said quickly, before she could involve him further, 'Thanks very much, but we do mind. It's a damned sight too rough. We'll wait till to-morrow.'

''T'ain't all that rough,' the youth said, his eyes on Susan.

'Of course it isn't.' Susan laid a hand on David's arm. 'He must know, darling. He lives here.'

'So does the other chap,' David retorted. 'And he's older and more experienced.' But arguing with Susan was seldom profitable, and he decided to take a firmer line. 'Meet us here at ten to-morrow morning,' he told the youth. 'If the wind has dropped you can take us across then.'

The youth shook his head. 'That'll be worse to-morrow,' he said. 'Reckon you'll have to wait two-three days if you don't go now.'

'No!' David shouted the word, but the wind snatched it away, and its impact was lost. Controlling his annoyance, he said, 'Your friend didn't think the weather would worsen, or he wouldn't have advised us to wait.'

'Tom Gelly?' The youth grinned. 'It ain't the weather he's agin, it's the island. Him being a lay preacher, he don't like the goings on. Right sinful, he says.'

'What goings on?' asked Susan, intrigued.

'Husbands and wives,' the youth said. 'Always chopping and changing. Or that's what they say.' But when she pressed him further he shook his head. There was talk in the town, and no lack of rumours, but he'd never been on the island himself. 'Visitors ain't welcome,' he explained.

'But you must meet them,' she persisted. 'They shop here, don't they?'

'Oh, ay, we meet them,' he agreed.

David had been indulging in second thoughts. They had given him no pleasure, but he realized that the youth might be right about the weather; and, much as he disliked the prospect of trusting himself to such a sea in an open boat, he had a job to do. Snowball wouldn't stand for a heavy expense account; not unless the story justified it.

And could he be sure that it would? If Susan and the youth were prepared to risk the crossing he could hardly do otherwise.

He hoped his stomach would co-operate.

'How much?' he demanded.

'Two quid,' the youth said promptly.

'That's a lot of money.' It was a feeble attempt at procrastination, a postponement of final decision.

The youth shrugged. 'Please yourself, mister. That'll be three quid come morning, if'n you can find some one as'll take you.'

David looked at the sea, at the youth, at Susan. The last provided the more pleasing prospect, but his scowl did not lessen. He was looking for comfort, not beauty. And of comfort he saw nothing.

'Very well,' he said curtly.

The youth turned and went down the steps to the stone jetty. As they followed him David eyed with mistrust the cluster of boats, dipping and rolling as the waves passed under them to break angrily against the quay. In his opinion all of them looked too frail for the trip; and the one the youth untied and skilfully manœuvred alongside the rusted iron steps looked frailest of all. But he could not draw back now. Susan was already standing on the bottom step, one hand outstretched to the youth in the boat.

The youth shook his head. 'You'd best take off them shoes and stockings, miss,' he said. 'She ain't no pleasure-steamer. There's allus a drop of water in the bottom.'

Susan retreated up the steps with a squeal as a bigger wave barged its way between boat and jetty in a lather of spray. As the boat rocked to it David saw that there was indeed water in the bottom. It had an oily look. No doubt the engine leaked as badly as the boat itself.

'Hang on to me, darling,' Susan said, lifting her skirt. 'Standing on one leg in a gale like this just isn't on. I'm no flamingo.'

From his vantage-point below the youth watched her with an enthusiastic glint in his eye. Unaware of his interest, Susan was in no hurry. But David was.

With a deep scowl at the gaping youth, he snatched at the shoes and stockings she held out to him, cramming them into his raincoat pocket.

'Careful,' Susan admonished him. 'I can't meet the Baron with ladders in my stockings. Do we take the suitcases?'

'Of course we take them. We can't just dump them here, can we?'

'No.' She giggled. 'He'll think we're converts come to stay.'

The youth helped her into the boat. He had shed his dufflecoat and laid it, Raleigh fashion, across the wet seat. He was so long in settling her that when he eventually turned to David the latter, impatient at the delay, ignored the proffered hand, and put one foot firmly on the gunnel. As he did so the boat began to slide away from him. Slowly the gap between boat and steps widened; David found himself being stretched as on the rack, but there was nothing he could do to save himself. He would have fallen into the water had not the youth grabbed him and jerked him forward. Stumbling, he landed on his knees in the bottom of the boat.

The youth helped him up. David grabbed at him as the boat rocked wildly.

'Belt up, mister! Waltzing around like that you'll have us over.'

Susan giggled. David scowled at them both, and sat down beside her in the stern. He seemed perilously near the water, and as the bows rose and fell to the waves he gripped the seat and the gunnel tightly and shut his eyes. He felt sick and undignified and angry.

The sudden splutter of the engine made him look up. Skilfully the youth cast off and headed out into the bay. The rain had ceased, but the wind was still strong. The bows crashed down on the waves, sending up a shower of spray; the wind caught it and flung it back, so that in a short while they were wetter than any rain could have made them. But it was the motion, not the spray, that was David's agony. Every fresh lurch sent his stomach soaring into his mouth. And once round the point he knew it would be worse.

It was worse. Worse than ever he

imagined it could be. His few previous outings in an open boat had been on the river; even on a cross-channel trip he had not known weather like this. Or so it seemed to him now.

'The island!' Susan shouted the words at him. And when he did not look up, 'There's the island, David!'

But David was no longer interested in islands. The purpose of his journey was already lost to him. Why he was sitting in that unstable craft on that unstable sea no longer mattered; he was concerned only with his unstable stomach. One hand held it firmly, the other gripped the gunnel. Spray smacked into his face and trickled down it unheeded, filling his eyes with salt and wetting his tightly closed lips; he could not spare a hand to wipe it away. Never for a moment was the boat on an even keel; if it was not pitching wildly it was rolling, and for most of the time it was doing both.

Any moment now I'm going to be sick, he told himself, gulping at the unpleasant taste in his mouth. And I don't care. I just don't care. Nothing could make me feel worse than I do now.

In that he was wrong. The burbling sound of the exhaust had been with him throughout the journey, accompanied by the faint smell of oil. Now, with a quick veering of the wind, the smell was no longer faint. Its pungent heaviness filled his nostrils, completing his nausea. Clapping one hand to his mouth, he almost threw himself over the side, and allowed his rebellious stomach to have its way.

For how long he lay there, with Susan holding him and her anxious little voice coming to him faint and meaningless, he did not know. It seemed to him that all his intestines had erupted into the sea, yet when the spasms were over he knew that they had not. They were still with him, still threatening trouble. But for the moment they were only threats, and with Susan's help he dragged himself back into the boat. Weak and miserable, he sat with his eyes half closed, gripping the stern and the gunnel, the girl's arm around him.

'Better?' she asked. With her free hand

she pushed back the damp hair that had fallen lankly over his face.

David shook his head. Apart from his stomach, his head seemed to be strung with taut wires, on which little hammers beat relentlessly.

'We're nearly there,' she told him. 'You'll be all right once we get ashore, darling.'

Privately he disagreed with her. He thought he would never be all right again, that the journey had so mangled his inside that neither time nor dry land could unravel it. Only when the arm behind him suddenly tightened and he heard the urgency in her voice did he open his eyes.

'Bob, what's that? Look! Over there!'

Bob, he supposed, was the youth who was primarily responsible for his present wretchedness; it was typical of Susan to have discovered his name. Wearily he followed her pointing finger, screwing up his eyes against the pain of the relentless hammers. The island was less than a hundred yards away; he could see the gravel beach and the grass and woodland beyond, with the roof and chimneys of a house showing distantly above the trees. A stone jetty protruded from the gravel, and by it a launch, swathed in a dark-green cover, rocked gently in the more sheltered water.

But it was not at the island that Susan was pointing. Unscrewing his eyes, David saw something floating in the water; almost under the water, it seemed to him. Then he lost interest. The youth suddenly opened the throttle and spun the wheel, so that the boat rocked and shuddered under the strain, and David's stomach revolted in sympathy.

'It's a corpse, miss,' sang out the youth. He sounded exultant. 'A corpse, that's what that is.'

3

Only the feel of the gravel under his feet told him that he was once more on dry land; the motion of the boat was still with him, and he found difficulty both in walking and in standing. Keeping his back to the sea (not only because of the torment he had suffered from it, but because of the thing that lay on the foreshore, the water lapping its feet), he stumbled farther up the beach to a ledge of rock, sat down, and fumbled under his raincoat for a cigarette. Its taste was unpleasant in his mouth, but he hoped that the smoke might steady him.

Susan came gingerly up the beach behind him, uttering squeals of protest as the gravel bit into her bare feet. With a sigh of relief she plumped herself down on the rock and began to rub them.

'Give me a cigarette, darling,' she said. And then, 'Feeling better?'

'A little. At least I'm still.'

'Inside as well as out?'

'I think so. Temporarily, anyway.' He fumbled in his pockets and produced her stockings. 'Do you want these?'

She took them from him. 'It's funny about seasickness, isn't it?' she said, delicately smoothing a stocking up one leg. 'There you were, heaving your heart out, and me enjoying every minute of it. The trip, I mean. Well, perhaps not every minute,' she added, remembering the corpse. Standing up, she fixed the stocking to her suspender-belt and then put her hands up to her hair, smoothing and patting it into place. 'But it was quite a breeze, wasn't it? Do I look absolutely ghastly?'

He eyed her casually. Her hair was a rich auburn, short and straight except where it curled at the neck and under the tiny ears. Only the single, carefully trained lock that hung down over her forehead, and which had escaped the protection of the plastic hood she had worn for the crossing, had been darkened by the spray. Her cheeks were flushed from the wind, the grey-green eyes under the thinly pencilled brows were shining. Her make-up looked immaculate. It's probably waterproof, he thought.

'You'll do,' he told her.

'Such enthusiasm! I think I'll check for myself.'

While she busied herself with the contents of her handbag David looked about him. He was beginning to feel better; his interest in the job was reviving. So this was Shere Island. From where they sat he could see nothing inland but the trees; even the roof of the house was now hidden. Gravel stretched for about thirty yards in each direction, to end in outcrops of rock that shut off further view of the island. From the cursory glance he had given it as they approached, he estimated it to be about a mile in length, running parallel with the coast; he did not attempt to guess its width. Despite the trees and the rocks there was no impression of height, yet he knew there was height. As Susan had said, the house stood on a hill over-looking the Channel. Snowball had shown him a photograph of it.

The youth came trudging up the beach and dumped the two cases on the gravel. He eyed David with interest, but made no comment on his appearance. 'What'll us do with him?' he asked, jerking a thumb at the sea.

Susan shuddered. Those last few yards to the beach, with Bob towing the body by means of a boathook caught in its clothing, had been horrible. It had been even more horrible when he had handed the boathook to her while he brought the boat alongside the jetty. She had held it with her eyes averted from its grim catch, which in consequence was soon lost. The youth had waded out to retrieve it after landing them.

'Can't it stay where it is?' she asked. 'Let the people here deal with it. They could telephone the mainland.'

'No telephone,' the youth said. 'And us can't leave 'un there. That'll be washed out agin.'

For the first time David turned and looked back at the sea. The little cove in which they sat was sheltered from the wind, the waves that licked at the gravel were gentler than their fellows farther out. Yet he knew that the youth was right. The tide was coming in; probably at its full the whole beach would be covered, for it shelved only gradually. Certainly they could not leave the body where it was.

He stood up. His stomach revolted at the thought of what had to be done, but he could not leave the youth to tackle it alone.

'We'll fetch it up above the water-line,' he said, surprised at the firmness of his voice. 'And the police will have to be informed. We can't expect the people here to cope. It's not their pigeon.'

'Could be,' the youth said. 'One of 'em was drowned Friday. Looked for 'un all night, we did, till the storm come up.'

David had temporarily forgotten the tragedy that had sparked off his mission. But it made no difference. 'It's still the responsibility of the police,' he said. 'You'd better get cracking.'

'Am't I to wait for you, then?'

David shook his head. When he had hired the boat it had been with the intention of spending an hour or two on the island and then returning to Little-port for the night. He had said so to the youth. But that was before he had known what the crossing would be like. It was an experience he had no intention of repeating. Nothing and no one could force him into that dreadful boat again until the sea had relented of its anger.

'We'll stay here,' he said firmly.

'But, David, we can't,' Susan expostulated. 'We can't descend on these people uninvited, and calmly announce that we're spending the night. It's a private house, not an hotel.'

'I don't care. Now I know what seasickness is like I'm not risking it again. Until I can see my face reflected in the water with complete clarity, I'm stopping right here on dry land. If you want to go back with Bob you can. But not me.'

Susan did not argue. David was the only man she knew whom she could neither coax nor manage. Perhaps that was why she loved him. If she did love him. That was something on which she had yet to make up her mind.

'O.K. We stay,' she said. 'For some days, if Bob is right about the weather. I just hope the Baron likes us, that's all. *And* our friend down there by the water. I wonder which will be the least welcome.' She shuddered. 'Well, at least they won't have to feed *him*.'

David did not answer. Slowly and rather unsteadily he walked down the beach to the water's edge, the youth following. The body lay on its stomach, for which he was thankful; it was naked except for a tight-fitting jersey of indeterminate colour. The flesh was a dirty grey, dotted with splotches of pink and white. The hair, thick for a man, might once have been fair. Now it was matted and discoloured.

'They allus lose their trousers,' the youth said. 'I've seen 'em before. Must 'ave been in the water some days; the fishes 'ave been nibbling. Want to see?'

'No.' David shuddered. 'Do we carry him, or do we drag him up the beach.'

The youth shook his head.

'That don't matter to me, mister. Don't matter to him neither, I reckon.'

In the end they carried him; it seemed irreverent to do otherwise. Bob took the feet, for which David was thankful; he could not bring himself to touch the naked flesh. Even the feel of it under the greasy jersey made his nausea threaten to return; it was soft and spongy to the pressure of his fingers. Was that the beginning of putrefaction, or was it his imagination?

He kept his eyes averted from the lolling head.

They laid him down gently on the narrow strip of coarse grass between gravel and woodland. David would have liked to cover his nakedness, but there was nothing with which to do so. He went down to the water's edge and washed his hands, and then returned to Susan.

'Let's get started,' he said.

They stayed to watch the youth leave. It was a relief to David to see him go. He had liked neither Bob nor his boat nor anything connected with them. With their going he was safe from the sea.

They had no difficulty in finding their way. The path through the wood was well-defined and short; they came out from among the soughing firs to a field of pasture in which a few lonely cows were grazing. Beyond was another field, dotted with hens and hen-coops, and beyond that again the ground rose gradually to the house.

They put down their suitcases and looked at it. Of grey stone, it sprawled low over the top of the hill. At that distance, and in that murky light, it looked bleak and unattractive.

Susan sighed. 'It's not like the photograph,' she said. 'Not from this side. I hope I'm going to like it here.'

'It's more important that they like us,' David said.

He looked about him. The island was wider than he had expected; the hill hid most of the southern shore, but from where they stood it seemed to be roughly circular in shape. To the west, pasture gave place to what appeared to be bracken and rock. To the east, the trees spread in a wide arc, thinning into lonely clumps until they disappeared from view behind the hill.

He grunted, and picked up the suitcases.

'There's a couple of the natives over there. Let's go see how they react.'

'Over there' was the western end of the chicken-run, where a man and a woman were working. Susan, for all her courage on the sea, was terrified of cows; as they crossed the pasture she kept skipping from one side of David to the other in her efforts to keep him between her and the nearest animal, knocking the suitcases against his legs as she moved. David said irritably, 'For heaven's sake stop rabbiting around! Why be afraid of cows? They're only mammals like yourself. Though I must say their behaviour is a lot more dignified.'

Susan was too frightened to retort. But when the gate into the chicken-run was safely closed behind her she regained her courage, and made a face at the nearest cow, shooing it away. The beast eyed her levelly and then turned and trotted off, udders swinging.

Susan watched it with distaste. 'They may be more dignified,' she said, 'but at least I'm more decent.'

The islanders stopped work and watched them come. As they drew near David saw with surprise that the woman was a Negress. She was young and lissom and tall, small-breasted and with a slim waist. Her nose was too squat, her mouth too full, for facial perfection; yet with her large liquid brown eyes and high cheek-bones, the white, even teeth which flashed when she smiled (and she smiled freely), she looked a vital and handsome creature. She wore a figure-hugging grey jersey above a vivid orange skirt, but her legs and feet were bare.

'Good afternoon.' David addressed himself to the man, but his eyes kept wandering to the girl. 'Are you Baron Grevas, sir?'

'I'm Andrew Mackay.' He was short and stocky, a square box of a man beside the slim pole of the young Negress. Although obviously not much over forty, his hair was a startling white, arresting in its profusion and curliness, and spreading down his cheeks to a short, bristling beard and moustache that were streaked with greys and browns. 'This lady is Mrs Myerson. What did you want with the Baron?'

His voice was cultured, with a faint Scots accent. David liked the look of him. So did Susan. After a prolonged and puzzled, but not entirely friendly, look at Mrs Myerson, she eyed the bronzed, rather solemn face of Mackay with approval. David had seen that expression on her face before. It was almost predatory, and without giving her time to speak he hurriedly introduced themselves.

'A reporter, eh?' Mackay frowned. 'You may not be entirely welcome, Mr Wight. It depends on why you're here. If it's sensationalism you're after you'll get short shrift from the Baron.'

David hastily disclaimed any such purpose. Nor had he any. All he wanted was the facts. What Snowball made of them was his affair.

'Facts, eh? Well, I can supply those,' the Scot said. 'No need to trouble the Baron. I'll walk back to the boat with you, and we can talk as we go.' He looked up at the grey sky, beneath which heavy black clouds were being swept along by the wind. 'I'm surprised you had the nerve to cross in this weather. If you take my advice you'll waste no time in getting back. The wind's freshening.'

David shuddered at the thought. Susan said, 'We can't. There isn't any boat. But there is a body. David forgot to mention it.' She smiled seductively. It was difficult to be seductive over a corpse, but she did her best. 'We left it on the beach.'

'A body?' the girl and the man exclaimed in unison. And Mackay added, 'Whose body?'

'I don't know whose body, except that it's male, and has been in the water some days. We picked it up on the way over,' David said. Susan had been wrong. He had not forgotten their tragic catch, but it had seemed unwise to clutter up the main purpose of their visit with side-issues. For that was what the body was to him. 'I've sent the boy back for the police.'

The man and the girl looked at each other; there was dismay on both their faces. The girl said softly, 'Jan!'

Mackay nodded. For a moment he

seemed undecided. Then he said, 'I'd better explain. Three days ago one of our friends was drowned. A man named Jan Muzyk. You may have read about it in the newspapers.' David nodded. 'At least, we assume he was drowned. He went out fishing in the evening, and that's the last we saw of him. Neither his body nor the boat was recovered.' He frowned. 'I'd better take a look at this body of yours. It could be Jan. In the meantime, Mrs Myerson will take you up to the house. I presume you'll be staying the night; you said you'd sent the boat back.' He glanced down at the suitcases. 'You've come prepared, I see.'

Susan nodded cheerfully. Back on the beach it had been she who had urged the conventions; now she had conveniently forgotten them. Though there had been neither sarcasm nor annoyance in Mackay's tone, David flushed guiltily. But he did not deny their preparedness. The suitcases were too concrete a confirmation.

'See you later,' Mackay said. He turned to the girl. 'Make sure the gate's shut,

Bessie. I can't believe anyone here would open it on purpose, but it's damned mysterious. Damned annoying, too. We must have lost at least a dozen.'

'Maybe we'll find them later,' the girl said.

'Maybe.'

David had been fearful that the man might ask him to accompany him. He had no wish to revisit the corpse. He might even have been expected to handle it, to help turn it over so that the other might identify it. He greeted Mackay's departure with relief.

'You come with me,' the Negress said, smiling at him.

David smiled back. There was such warmth in the rich, husky voice that she might have been inviting him to an assignation. Susan said, 'Do you always go barefoot?'

'Not always,' the girl said. 'But often, yes.'

They followed her out of the field, waited while she fixed a chain round the gatepost, and took the track that led up to the house. The girl walked smoothly and effortlessly, her body erect; she seemed to glide over the ground, her bare feet never far from it but touching it only lightly. David watched her with admiration, delighting in the suppleness of her body. He had always thought of Negresses, even young ones, as fat and ungainly, with fuzzy hair and shrill, sing-song voices. Bessie Myerson's only resemblance to that image was in her hair. And even there it was not complete. Though her black hair was a mass of tight little curls, it was fine and glossy.

Susan noted his admiration, and frowned. But she had no breath to spare for the comment she might otherwise have made. The track was steep, and their guide moved along it swiftly, humming to herself as she went, turning now and again to give them an encouraging smile, but never pausing. They passed through an iron gateway into what was obviously the beginning of the garden — a garden overgrown with weeds and nettles and creepers, with here and there a cultivated plant or shrub to bear witness to a former glory.

To their left were fruit-trees, apples and pears and plums, the old trunks grey and knotted and heavy with fungus, their spread branches intermingling to form a green canopy of leaves. A dank smell mingled with the odour of rotting vegetation and whiffs of smoke from a smouldering bonfire. The path was overgrown with weeds. Soon David's shoes and the turn-ups of his trousers were soaking wet.

He began to wonder about Mackay. What would it be like to turn over a drowned, almost nude body, and look into the dead, disfigured face of a friend? How deeply had their friendship been rooted? Perhaps Mackay had used the word loosely. Although surprised, neither he nor the girl had seemed greatly distressed by the news.

He shook off the unpleasant memory and turned to grin at Susan. 'How are you making?' he asked.

Susan grimaced. She had long since ceased trying to pick her way. Her shoes were ruined, her feet wet, and her stockings laddered. Neither the island nor the house now held any charm for her. Even anticipation of meeting the Baron had temporarily lost its appeal.

'Bloody,' she said succinctly. 'I preferred the sea. It was drier underfoot.'

Yet she said it with what gaiety she could muster. She would not let David see the mood that was on her. He liked her to be gay and provocative and charming (although sometimes, as in the train that afternoon, he had not seemed responsive to her gaiety), and gay and provocative and charming she would be. Particularly with that black panther bounding ahead.

'But less stable,' he said. 'This may not be dry, but at least it's land.'

They went on up; past a walled garden where the walls had crumbled, and in which patches of cultivated earth showed among the rampaging weeds; along a broad pergola, where the roses rioted over their heads and the grass grew thick between the flagstones under their feet; across a wide expanse of lawn, scythe-cut for the most part, and mown only in patches; and so up wide stone steps, flanked by heavy balustrades surmounted by grinning gargoyles, to a broad terrace that ran the length of the house. Here Susan and David paused; partly to recover breath, and partly to look back down the way they had come. But the young Negress did not allow them to pause for long. With her beaming smile and a gay wave of the hand, she beckoned them on, and rather wearily they followed.

'You should have warned me this was a hiking holiday,' Susan complained. 'I'd have brought my rucksack.'

They went round to the front of the house. Here the ground fell sharply, in a series of grassy terraces, to an uneven stretch of gorse and bracken and rock that sloped gently down to the line of tall trees hiding the high cliffs. The grass on the terraces was coarse but freshly mown, the box hedges trimmed, the flower borders gay with colour. It was clear that more care was lavished here than at the back.

'Andrew,' the Negress said, noting their interest. 'He does the garden.'

'And very nicely too,' David said, smiling at her.

The house looked taller at the front. The first floor was on a level with the crest of the hill, projecting over the stone terrace below, and supported by columns that appeared too slender for the task. It gave protection from the sun (when there was sun) to the rooms on the south side of the ground floor, and to the terrace itself.

To David the house was a monstrosity. The different levels, the apparently haphazard way in which additions had been made to the original building, offended his rigid taste. There had been no respect for architectural style, no conformity of material; gables and turrets and grey stone fused unhappily with flat roofs and red brick. But Susan was delighted with it. Gloom was never more than fleeting with Susan, and she pattered up and down the terrace, peering in at the large windows and up the wide steps at the massive arched doorway, set well back in a recess; stroking the slender pillars, and pausing to gaze in fascination at the white-capped rollers beyond the tree-lined cliffs.

'It's absolutely terrific!' She beamed at David, her smile even including the Negress. 'So unusual.'

'Unusual, I grant you,' he said. 'I doubt if there's another like it. But terrific — ugh!'

'Why did you tell me it was a ruin? It's nothing of the sort.'

'It was. Some one's been patching it up. Now it's just a monstrosity.'

The hall was a disappointment, even to Susan; it was small and low-ceilinged for such a large house, and the staircase that led up to the gallery above was narrow and ugly. But the spacious study into which the Negress showed them was comfortably, if too lavishly, furnished. Even on that dull day it had a cheerful look, with its gay curtains and chair-covers, and the deep red carpet on the floor.

'The Holy of Holies, no doubt,' David said, looking around him when Bessie had departed. 'The sanctum of the Prophet Grevas himself. Well, he doesn't do too badly. Too many bits and pieces, of course. But at least they coalesce.'

Susan nodded absently. She was wondering about the Baron. Would he be all she had anticipated? She had endured much to meet him; that dreadful train journey, and David being sick, and that disgusting corpse (she shuddered at the memory), and David's eyes popping at the sight of that black lamp-post, and her feet soaking, and her stockings laddered. Could the Baron possibly compensate for all that? He would have to be quite something if he could.

But she was not to meet the Baron yet. When the door opened it was to admit a small, thin-faced woman with grey hair drawn tightly back from a receding forehead into a bun at the nape of her neck. She wore a long wrap-over dress of black satin, clasped tightly at the waist by a belt of the same material. The full sleeves were buttoned at the wrists, a black-velvet band encircled her neck. Tied up like a ruddy parcel, thought David. Modesty gone wild!

The eyes that looked at them through

rimless spectacles were challenging and hostile. 'I am the Baroness Grevas,' she said, with no word of greeting. 'What do you want with my husband?'

She spoke clearly and distinctly, with no trace of a foreign accent, yet David knew she was not English. There was little modulation to her voice; the words came out from between her thin lips as tightly compact as was her meagre body. Susan disliked her on sight; the woman was too severe, both in manner and in dress, to be comfortable. She knew that the dislike was mutual. There was no mistaking the frosty disapproval in the other's eyes.

David had a quick temper, and the Baroness's curt, almost contemptuous, reception had angered him. So he wasted no time in preliminaries, but told her briefly why they were there, his curt tone matching her own. She listened without interrupting, her lips compressed into a tight line, her bright beady eyes darting from one visitor to the other.

'You have no appointment, then?' she asked.

No, David said, he had no appointment. He had not thought it necessary.

She asked him about the journal he represented, and he told her what he could without damning his cause completely. The description would have surprised Snowball, he thought. From it Snowball would have had difficulty in recognizing *Topical Truths*.

'And Miss Long? She is also a reporter?'

'A friend,' he said.

The Baroness seemed undecided. David took heart from that. Her manner had not thawed, but he knew that had her rule over the island been absolute she would have dismissed them without further parley, boat or no boat, storm or no storm. That she did not do so implied that she had no such authority.

'Please wait,' she said eventually. 'I will speak to my husband.'

As the door closed behind her Susan grimaced.

'The motherly sort, eh? I see what you mean, darling, about her not ringing bells for the Baron any more. She wouldn't ring them for any man. Not even if he were the most sex-starved creature alive.'

'How sex-starved can you get?' David asked. 'I wouldn't know.'

'I believe you,' she said, pouting. 'And from the way you were leering at Black Bess I'd say you don't intend to.'

He laughed. It did not occur to him that Susan might be jealous.

'We're only here for one night. Not that long if the Baroness can get us out before. You think I work that fast?'

She shook her head. It had seemed to her that David did not work on women at all; it was they who worked on him. And Bessie Myerson, she suspected, was a quick and capable worker. She said, 'Well, anyway, having seen the Baron's wife, I don't blame him if he prefers to sleep out occasionally. Her body looks as hard and uninviting as her voice. Or do you think Bob had it wrong? About the chopping and changing of partners, I mean?'

David shrugged. 'That's what the lad said. Thinking of muscling in?'

'Not if he's anything like his wife.'

David smiled to himself. Susan was like

50

one of those fruit-sweets, he thought; hard-boiled and glittering on the outside, but with a soft, syrupy centre. For all her glib, sophisticated chatter, that hinted at promiscuity and a disdain for convention, she was a romantic little idealist at heart. Any man who accepted her at face value was in for a disappointment.

The Baroness, he suspected, had nothing to fear from Susan.

The Baron was not like his wife. He came into the room a few minutes later — a man in the late fifties and above average height, who carried himself so well that he looked taller. His features were firmly chiselled, his eyes grey and penetrating, his ears set close to his head; the nails of his long, tapering fingers were carefully tended. Like Mackay, his hair was snowwhite, but cut short, and with a parting at the side. Though he wore a brown sports-jacket above buff-coloured twill trousers, Susan instinctively visualized him in tails. He would look magnificent, she thought. So distinguished and — and right.

'So you're from the Press, are you?' he

said genially. He spoke quietly, but the warmth that had been lacking in his wife's welcome was there in his. His hands too were warm as he shook each of theirs in turn; warm and moist, so that afterwards David surreptitiously wiped his palm down the seat of his trousers. But Susan did not appear to find his touch unpleasant, although the Baron held her hand longer than he had held David's. He was still holding it, apparently unconscious of the fact, as he went on, 'How can I help you? We're not used to being thus honoured.'

After Mackay's doubts and the Baroness's coolness, this friendly reception was as unexpected as it was welcome. David was delighted. He said eagerly, 'We just want to know something about this new religion of yours, sir.'

Grevas shook his head.

'Like many other people, Mr Wight, you are under a misconception. There is no new religion. What we are trying to do here is to create an ideal within existing religions; something that will appeal to all and conflict with none. With the world as

52

it is to-day people must learn to live amicably together; not just with relatives and friends, not just with those in their own town or country, but with the world. We need a real internationalism.' He sighed. 'There's nothing new in the ideal, of course. What is new is that here we are trying to do something practical to bring it about.' He had been pacing steadily up and down the room. Now he paused in front of David. 'There are twelve people living on this island, Mr Wight.' He frowned. 'I beg your pardon — eleven. They are of different religions and social standing, different nationalities, different degrees of education and culture and wealth. But we think of ourselves as being equal. We are learning to ignore the differences, and to concentrate on the one factor that unites us. A desire for peace. Our concept of life is that we should love one another — that we *must* love one another if the world is to survive.'

Grevas paused. For breath or comment? wondered David. But he could think of no suitable comment. To say that he too was for peace would be like the bishop who said he was against sin.

He contented himself with an approving nod of the head.

'You may say that twelve people in a little island like this form so minute a fraction of the world's population that their influence can only be infinitesimal. But in a few months' time we shall be branching out. The people here will be leaving to form their own little communities, and those communities in turn will do the same.' Grevas smiled. 'I'm no mathematician, but Maurice Hunt, who is an accountant and at home with figures, tells me that if each group splits into not less than six other groups, and allowing two years for indoctrination (I don't like the word, but it is reasonably apt), within twenty years there could be over sixty million people dedicated to a life of peace. That's a large number; too large to be disregarded. And it can be multiplied by six for each further period of two years.'

He paused again. Susan, whose eyes had never left his face while he was speaking, gave a deep sigh, her lips parted. She was uncertain whether it was the man or his ideals that she admired, or just the magic of his voice. Everything that David had said to the Baron's detriment was lost to her now. She could see only the good in him.

'It's a wonderful idea,' she breathed, her eyes shining. 'Absolutely wonderful.'

He smiled at her. 'We think so too. But it won't be easy. People are too apathetic; they pay lip-service to peace, but few are prepared to take positive action to achieve it. It will be our job to educate them to our way of thinking. And that doesn't mean noisy demonstrations or ban-the-bomb marches. It means teaching them to appreciate that peace can come only through love, and that it is as easy to love a black man as a white, a Jew or a Mohammedan as a Christian.' He sighed. 'As I said, it won't be easy. Those sixty millions I spoke of depend on one hundred per cent. success with each little community. We're unlikely to achieve that. But we'll succeed eventually. Not in my lifetime, perhaps. But in yours or your children's.'

David was more sceptical than Susan. The scheme was too spacious, the man's background too dubious. Even granted that Grevas was a reformed character, that he was sincere in his beliefs and aims — and certainly he had sounded sincere — history and human nature were against him. Greater men than he had preached the same gospel. Could Grevas expect to succeed where they had failed?

'The idea's fine, sir,' he said. 'But impracticable, surely? Do you really expect it to work?'

'Why not? It's working here.'

'Perhaps. But presumably these people were hand-picked. There wouldn't be the inherent mistrust and differences between them that you would normally expect to find. They were ready-made converts, imbued with your ideals even before they came here.'

'Of course they were. So are most of the peoples of the world. In theory, that is. But how many have the opportunity or the will to put them into practice? Well, I'm giving them that opportunity, and I hope the will will burgeon as a result. As for being hand-picked — oh, no, Mr Wight. Among us we have a Jew — an embittered Jew, at that — and the daughter of a man who was a prominent Nazi; a woman from the Deep South, an aristocrat, and a West Indian Negress. Would you call them natural mixers? There was friction at first, but it's disappearing. Or it was until — ' He broke off, frowning at some thought. Then the frown changed to a smile. 'But you'll see for yourselves. Bessie tells me you'll be staying the night. Fine. Stay longer if you wish. Who knows; you may finish by joining us.'

Susan glowed back at him. But David was worried. Snowball hadn't sent him down to Shere Island for a basinful of ideals, and if Grevas were sincere, then ideals seemed all he was likely to get. There had to be more than that; something for Snowball to get his teeth into, something more in keeping with what was expected of *Topical Truths* by its readers. And noting the way Grevas was looking at the girl, remembering how he had hung on to her hand in greeting, he said diffidently, 'There's a rumour, Baron, that marriage is taken lightly here. The lad who brought us across mentioned it — husbands and wives always chopping and changing, he said. Any truth in it?'

The Baron continued to smile. But now the smile was more mechanical, as though he had switched it on and had forgotten to switch it off.

'There are always rumours,' he said. 'I am sorry to disappoint you, Mr Wight, but the answer is No.'

Andrew Mackay came into the room. He was accompanied by another man, tall and bronzed, with the broad shoulders and narrow hips of a boxer. Grevas introduced him as Maurice Hunt.

'What about the body, Andrew?' Grevas asked. 'Was it Jan?'

'Yes. We've brought him up here, and put him in the cellar. We couldn't leave him down by the beach, the tide was coming in. Besides, it didn't seem decent.'

'Poor fellow.'

It was all he said. But to David's

suspicious ears the sympathy did not ring true; it was expressed because it was expected, not because it was felt. The Baron could still be a phoney. There might yet be a good story to come out of Shere Island.

'I doubt if the police will be over this afternoon,' Mackay said. 'There's quite a gale.'

Grevas nodded. 'It may blow itself out during the night. In the meantime we have two visitors to entertain. You might start by showing them over the house, Maurice.' He turned to David. 'If you have any further queries, Mr Wight, ask Maurice. He'll do his best to answer them. We want your report to be as accurate as possible. It may help to dissipate some of the wilder rumours.'

David thanked him. Susan said, 'It's terribly kind of you all. David's here on business, of course, but I'm just a hanger-on. I hope you don't think I'm a nuisance.'

They assured her earnestly that they did not.

The inside of Shere House was as

undisciplined as its exterior. The two upper floors were a warren of passages on varying levels, with no regard for the necessary juxtaposition of bedrooms and bathrooms and lavatories. The same lack of planning existed on the ground floor and in the basement, where the kitchens were a long way from the dining-room and the storerooms a long way from the kitchens. But although the passages were dark, most of the bedrooms were bright and well furnished, and had recently been redecorated. Susan was delighted with the room that had been assigned to her; it was on the first floor and overlooking the sea. David's was smaller and on the second floor, but it too faced south.

'You've done us proud,' he told Hunt. 'Much more of this V.I.P. treatment and you'll find us hard to dislodge.'

Hunt grinned. He had a wide mouth, and the grin stretched it and the small moustache above it to the full. It also seemed to make his large ears stick out even farther from his head.

As they toured the building he gave

them a brief word-picture of its occupants. Mackay, married to a German girl, was a large landowner in the South of Scotland; he was probably the most dedicated of the Baron's followers. 'Apart from my wife, that is,' Hunt added. 'But then she's Welsh. And the Welsh are always so wholehearted in their causes, don't you think?'

It was lightly said. But was there a hint of sarcasm in the comment? David wondered.

Harold Myerson was an English Jew. He had made some quick money on the Stock Exchange, since when he had spent his time in travel. But apparently neither money nor travel had brought him much joy. They had, however, brought him a wife — the West Indian girl, Bessie. 'Difficult to know why he married her,' commented Hunt. 'They've nothing in common, and she's much the younger.' He grinned. 'Quite a girl, too.'

'I believe you,' Susan said, 'So does David. He's met her.'

'And haven't you?'

'Oh, yes. But I didn't get the same impact.'

Tom and Edith Hampson were cockneys, Hunt went on; both in their early sixties, and the oldest members of the community. In her younger days Edith had been in domestic service. 'I don't think she ever recovered from the experience. You'll see what I mean. She's too quiet, too self-effacing; always doing more than her share of the work. As for Tom — well, he's quite a character. Used to be a docker. Now he likes to think of himself as a farmer. That's Andrew's doing; the two of them run the farm here. Or what passes for a farm. A few cows and chickens, plus the vegetable-garden.'

To David this seemed a good opportunity to probe the finances of the community. If Grevas was running a racket there had to be money in it somewhere. And big money at that.

'How can the Hampsons afford to live here?' he asked. 'It isn't for free, is it?'

'Hell, no! But Tom's well off. He won a packet in some football pool.'

'Lucky chap.' David hesitated. But the

Baron had told him to ask questions. 'What does it cost you each per week?'

'Twenty quid.'

It was a large but not an exorbitant sum. With no staff to maintain it would provide the Baron and his wife with a good living, but little more than that. There could be no fat bank balance salted away.

David would have liked to probe further, but Hunt had not looked too pleased at the question. So he said, 'What about the chap who was drowned?'

'Jan Muzyk? He was a Pole. Young and rather moody, but charming when on his best behaviour. Olive, his wife, advanced most of the money for this place to be repaired. She's a Virginian; wealthy, and typical Deep South. They hadn't been married long, but she's taken his death surprisingly well.'

'How did it happen?' asked Susan.

'He was out fishing. There was an old boat, a home-made affair, that he kept at the south jetty.' He moved to a window and pointed. 'You can just see the end of the jetty above the trees. Most fine evenings he went fishing before dinner. And last Friday he didn't come back.'

'Didn't you look for him?'

'Of course. There were boats out from the mainland most of the night. Unfortunately, the weather worsened. It hasn't let up since.'

It was a stilted account of the tragedy. Both Susan and David were puzzled by his reticence. He was obviously reluctant even to discuss it at all.

'And that's the lot,' Hunt said, turning away from the window. 'You've met the Baroness. She's French, but you'd never guess it.'

'And you?'

'Me? Oh, I'm as English as they come. And as ordinary. No story for you in me.'

Glumly David accepted this pronouncement. At that moment it seemed to him that there was no story anywhere. Certainly not the sort of story Snowball was expecting. His main hope must lie in the wealthy American widow. Just how much money had she invested in the Baron?

As they descended the stairs a woman

came out of a room on the first landing — a room which Hunt had previously told them was the Baron's private study. But it was not the Baroness. The woman was tall and dark. She gave them a startled look, and then hurried away down one of the passages.

'Who was that?' Susan asked.

Hunt took his time in answering. He was standing on the step below her, lighting his pipe, and gazing thoughtfully after the retreating woman. Then he turned, smiling.

'I'm sorry.' He blew out a cloud of smoke. 'That? Oh, that was Beryl. My wife.'

4

The rain had started again, and the wind hurled it against the south windows with considerable force. Their tour of the house over, Hunt took them into the library. This was a big room, its furniture consisting mainly of armchairs and settees. Paint and paper looked fresh and new, and there were thick Axminster rugs on the pine-block floor.

A hefty young woman, dressed in a yellow turtle-neck sweater and tartan slacks that seemed to be stretched perilously near to bursting-point by her plump thighs, lounged in a chair by the empty hearth. She looked up as they entered, pushing back her untidy fair hair to scrutinize them the more closely. There was a slight squint in her blue eyes.

Hunt introduced her as Olive Muzyk.

'My goodness, but you've chosen a fine day for your visit, haven't you?' she said, the words pouring out from between thick, pouting lips in a fussy stream. 'It sure does rain here.' She scrambled untidily from the chair, releasing the pressure on the tartan slacks, and shook each of them warmly by the hand; to David it felt like squeezing a dry sponge. 'So you're a reporter, are you? Well, it's good to know that folks are becoming interested in us. I guess the dear Baron can do with a little publicity.'

To David she sounded more American than anyone he had met. He wondered whether he should condole with her on the recent death of her husband. She did not look like one in need of condolence.

Susan had no such doubts. Olive Muzyk accepted her sympathy with cheerful matter-of-factness. 'It sure was a tragedy,' she agreed. 'But I can't say I was surprised. Many's the time I've told him it wasn't safe to go out in a rickety old boat like that — and him not able to swim, too.' A shake of the head dismissed the subject. 'You must call me Olive. We use only given names here. The Baron prefers it.'

To David her cheerful garrulity

augured well; if there were disclosures to be made she might be persuaded to make them.

He wondered if she had heard that her husband's body had been found.

A grey-faced, grey-haired woman limped into the room and stood waiting for the conversation to cease. She was fat and elderly and diminutive, and the sleeves of her faded and shapeless blue dress were rolled up to expose plump, knotted forearms and toil-worn hands.

'I'm sorry,' she said, her voice low, almost apologetic. 'I was looking for Tom.'

Maurice Hunt introduced her as Edith Hampson. She acknowledged their greetings awkwardly, and did not offer to shake hands. Susan half expected her to curtsey. Clearly she was ill at ease in their company.

When Edith had gone — and she went as unobtrusively as she had come — Susan said, 'She doesn't look very cheerful. Is she always as glum as that?'

Olive nodded. 'Most always. But she's a real nice person.'

Maurice looked at his watch. 'Half an hour to dinner,' he announced. 'I'm going up to wash.' He sucked at his pipe, found it empty, and slipped it into a trouser pocket. The trousers were stained and baggy. 'Can you two find your own way, or would you like a guide?'

Susan accepted the offer. She was always ready to be shown anywhere by a presentable male. David said, 'Look out for her, Mr Hunt. She's a man-eater.'

Hunt laughed. 'Thanks for the warning. I'd be easy prey. And the name's Maurice. As Olive told you, we don't use surnames.'

When Susan and Maurice had gone David said, 'Seems a decent chap,' and sat himself down opposite Olive, who had returned to her chair. 'Most helpful. He tells me you put up most of the money for this project, by the way. That was generous of you.'

'Close on sixty thousand dollars,' she volunteered. 'I figure it's an investment in peace. And there can't be a better investment, can there?'

'Perhaps not. But do you honestly

believe it can come this way? Isn't it all rather an airy-fairy dream?'

For a few moments she did not reply. The rain-filled clouds had brought dusk early to the room, and he could not see her face clearly. Then she said, 'Sometimes it does one good to dream. Particularly if one's dreams are insured.'

'Are yours?'

'They certainly are.' She stood up. 'We shall be late for dinner, David. The Baroness won't like that. She's a very punctual person.'

What insurance, he wondered, could cover her in such an abstract scheme? But he was wise enough not to pursue the subject. Clearly she had had enough of it for the present.

At dinner the Baron sat at one end of the long table, with his wife at the other. They were thirteen in number; a fact which Susan remarked with some foreboding, but which seemed to leave the others unconcerned. Even such a large party as this was dwarfed by the room itself. On the opposite side of the hall to the library, it was easily the biggest room in the house. It was also an ugly room; a huge rectangular box with little to relieve its bareness. Susan wondered if that was why they ate by candlelight, so leaving the empty corners in darkness. When she asked Maurice, who sat next to her, he said it was to conserve the batteries.

'We make our own electricity,' he explained, smiling at her.

Susan smiled back. She liked Maurice. His brown eyes under the heavy brows were warm and friendly, yet the firm jaw hinted that he could be ruthless. A well-cut serge blazer hid the check shirt that had previously covered his muscular torso; but he wore no tie, and she could still see the tufts of dark hair that sprouted at his throat. It was a pity about his teeth, she thought. They were stained and uneven.

The cutlery and glass and plate were undistinguished, but the food was excellent. As she sipped her mushroom soup Susan, who sat on the Baron's right, inquired into the domestic arrangements of the household. 'My wife does most of the cooking,' he told her. 'She and Edith are the culinary experts. But we all do our share of the other chores.' He gave no details of how the shares were allotted, and Susan wondered whether she would later be expected to help with the washing-up. For such a large party it would be a monumental task. 'But we're not overworked. We still find plenty of time for discussion.'

'Discussion on what?'

'On what we are trying to do.'

Susan had temporarily forgotten the purpose behind the community. 'I wonder you don't employ servants,' she said.

He shook his head, his white hair gleaming in the candlelight. 'It would be against our principles. There can be no true equality when one group of persons is employed to wait on another.'

'But isn't that what most of us have to do? I mean, there are more employees than employers, aren't there?'

He smiled. 'Of course. Many more. And we have no quarrel with that. It is the personal, more menial service that we boggle at. Irrational, perhaps. But there it is.'

Maurice said, 'Principles apart, they wouldn't come. The island may suit us, but it wouldn't do for them. No telephone, no mail until we collect it, no shops or cinemas, no mechanical amusements other than steam radio, and communication with the mainland dependent on the weather. Can you see them sticking that?'

Susan could not. She doubted if she could stick it herself for long. It would be fine for a week or two, but after that it would certainly pall. 'Is there no place in your community for a single person?' she asked. 'You're all married, aren't you?'

'Mere coincidence,' Maurice assured her. 'We don't insist on matrimony.'

It was an ambiguous remark, and he was looking at Grevas as he made it. But if the Baron saw the look he disregarded it. 'We would, for instance, be delighted to have you join us,' he said, smiling at Susan.

Susan believed him. Not only that — she wanted to believe him. He might be elderly, but he was undeniably handsome. He was also attentive. If David could amuse himself for a day or two with his assignment, that would be fine with her.

In the look she gave the Baron was concentrated the full force of her considerable charm.

From across the table Olive said in her plaintive voice, 'I'm not married. Not now.'

She spoke easily, with a slight smile on her pleasant, lightly freckled face; but to Susan it sounded like a challenge. Or was it a warning? Had the newly made widow now got her sights on the Baron? Susan looked down the long table to where the Baroness sat — still in the black satin, her only concession to colour the thin line of her lips and a touch of rouge on her cheeks. Baroness Grevas was no longer — might never have been — physically attractive, but she could be difficult to dislodge. There was an air of permanency about her that boded ill for any competitor. Well, she can count me out, Susan told herself. Admittedly I'd welcome a little attention — I might even encourage it — but I know where to draw the line.

She wondered if Olive were also a line-drawer.

Harold Myerson sat on Olive's left. He was small and thin, with what seemed like a permanent frown on his pinched face, and as Jewish in appearance as a caricature. He was a messy eater. Each time he lifted the spoon to his mouth some of the soup dribbled back into the bowl, there were stains on his tie and on the lapels of his light-grey jacket. So far he had not spoken. Now he said to Olive, 'I suppose you know they've found Jan's body?'

His voice was high-pitched and querulous. Olive said sharply, 'My goodness, no! Who found him?'

Spoon in hand, Myerson pointed across the table at Susan.

'Our visitors.'

Since no one but Olive evinced surprise at this news, Susan presumed they had already been informed. Olive was obviously annoyed that it had been kept from her. She said so forcefully.

'I intended breaking it to you later,'

Grevas apologized. He looked worried. 'I'm sorry you learned it so baldly. But no one fancied the task of telling you.'

This veiled reproof left Myerson unmoved; he returned noisily to his soup. But it brought a response from Jutter Mackay, Andrew's German wife, who sat opposite him. Up to now Jutter had taken no part in the conversation at Susan's end of the table, but had been talking quietly to the Hampsons. At the mention of Jan Muzyk's name, however, both she and the Hampsons had stopped talking to listen. Now she said sharply, 'No one except Mr Myerson, that is.'

Susan found herself gaping at her, and shut her mouth quickly. As she said later to David, it was not only the remark itself that startled her, but the use of the surname. It emphasized the contempt. Yet, although the Baron still wore his worried frown, no one else showed concern. Not even Myerson. Completely ignoring Jutter, he said, 'Even now we shan't know how Jan managed to tip the boat up and drown himself in a perfectly calm sea.'

Maurice leaned forward across the table, pushing his empty soup-bowl aside to make room for his elbows. He said quietly, 'It didn't tip up. You can take my word for that.'

'Can I? Suppose you tell us what happened, then?'

'I don't know. Perhaps it sprang a leak and sank, or Jan fell overboard, or he was taken too far out by the tide and was swamped before he could get back. But that boat wouldn't tip up.'

Myerson did not answer. His shoulders hunched, he stared at Maurice with a worried, almost a frightened look on his face. And Maurice stared back at him.

'Tell us about your work,' Grevas said to Susan. 'I understand you're an actress.'

At the other end of the table conversation was stilted. The Baroness concentrated on her food, her sharp, rabbity teeth nibbling incessantly, and spoke only when directly addressed. This gave David, who sat next to her, the opportunity to observe more closely his fellow-diners. On his right was Beryl Hunt. She was a dark young woman in the middle thirties; dark-haired, dark-skinned, with a dark, brooding look in her dark eyes. Neither beautiful nor plain, hers was the sort of face that a man might pass unnoticing in the street unless he chanced to look into her eyes and wonder at the intensity of her gaze. David could make no guess as to her figure. The shapeless beige dress hid it completely.

But Beryl was as uncommunicative as the Baroness, although she showed less interest in her food; she ate sparingly and mechanically, with no sign of appreciation on her square, sallow face. Mackay and Bessie sat opposite, chatting amicably together on farming matters. Standing, the girl had topped the man by several inches; seated, it was the man who was the taller — emphasizing, if emphasis were needed, the slender length of Bessie's legs and the shortness of Mackay's. The girl's slim body was sheathed in a simple dress of buttercup yellow, sleeveless and cut low at the neck, out of which her dark arms and throat erupted with startling vitality. Mackay, too, had changed his attire. Like Maurice, he wore a blazer; unlike Maurice, he had also donned a tie. At their first meeting David had thought him solemn and a little pompous; now, talking to Bessie, he looked neither. There was a twinkle in the deep-set hazel eyes, an animation in the weather-beaten bearded face, that reminded David of a more youthful Ernest Hemingway.

Next to Bessie sat Tom Hampson, a long, stringy man with a long, stringy neck and bony fingers. His face was brown and deeply wrinkled, his eyes a vivid blue under white bushy brows, his head a high bald dome fringed at the back by a few straggling, apathetic grey hairs that only accentuated the baldness. He was a rapid and gargantuan eater, yet managed to fire a stream of questions at David in broad cockney, his loose dentures clicking noisily.

David rather resented the questions. His eyes had strayed from the dark, exciting Bessie to the more placid beauty of Jutter Mackay, and he wanted quiet in which to contemplate it. He thought Jutter the loveliest woman he had ever seen. Her face was oval and softly curved, her features classically perfect. The dark eyes under the long lashes held, he thought, a hint of sorrow — or was it bewilderment? The arched eyebrows were unplucked, the jet-black hair, glossy and with the merest suggestion of a wave, had been swept back over her head to a gleaming coil that hung low on her slender neck. Like the rest of the women present, she wore no jewellery, but her woollen dress was a vivid scarlet, cut low to show the first faint curve of her breasts and the gentle slope of her shoulders. Yet it was her skin that fascinated David above all. It had a golden translucency, as though the sun that had touched and gilded it had shone from within. Only her voice was a disappointment. It was harsh and guttural, and he noticed that 'w's' and 'th's' still came strangely to her tongue.

Mackay and Bessie were discussing a dead fowl they had found that evening, and the mystery of the open gate. Bessie said softly, with a slight gesture of her hands that seemed to David wonderfully expressive, 'But they're not just yours and mine and Tom's, Andrew. They belong to all of us. Have you told the Lord?'

David had a vision of Andrew Mackay on his knees, reporting the loss of a chicken to the Almighty. Then Mackay said, 'Not yet. I didn't want to bother him,' and he realized that Bessie had been referring to the Baron.

Tom Hampson leaned across the girl and said, in a hoarse whisper that may or may not have been intended as confidential, but which was plainly audible to David, 'I reckon there's those as ain't exactly partial to 'ens. Nor cows nor human beings neither, come to that. Talk about bringing peace to the ruddy world! We could do with a bit of flippin' peace right here, if you asks me.'

The Baroness looked up sharply. There was anger in her bright little eyes, contempt in the set of her head and the long, aquiline nose. Edith Hampson said nervously, 'Hush, Tom! Don't talk so foolish,' and then glanced quickly at the Baroness in apology for her temerity, a slight flush on her grey cheeks.

All through the meal David was uneasily conscious of the Baroness's disapproving gaze, and it was only while she was absent from the table between courses that he felt able to talk freely. It was during one of these absences that he asked Mackay why Grevas laid such stress on equality. 'You won't get it in the outside world,' he said. 'So why insist on it here?'

Mackay admitted that he too had at first found that hard to understand. It was also hard to explain. 'Briefly, the idea is that inequality breeds envy, and that envy is the enemy of peace.'

'Fair enough. But what happens when you leave here?'

'By then, he hopes, we shall be too single-minded in our aims for envy to intrude on them.'

'I see,' David said, wondering if he did. 'But even here you aren't equal, are you? Surely some are wealthier than others.'

'Yes. But wealth isn't allowed to intrude. If we have it we don't have it here. And we certainly don't display it.' Mackay smiled, the creases deepening in his forehead, the twinkle back in his eyes. 'You won't see any Dior creations or expensive jewellery. It's important, you see, that if we aren't equal in fact we should at least appear to be equal.'

David switched to another line.

'All of you here have private means. Right?' Mackay nodded. 'But the majority aren't so lucky; they have to work for a living. How can they do that, and still join the various communities you hope to set up?'

Mackay smiled. 'We don't envisage every one living a life of idleness. Nor will the communities be in such isolated places as this. They'll be in towns and villages, with the members meeting in their own homes. Only for the community leaders will it be a whole-time job and no pay; it's they who must be well-heeled. And we, of course, are their nucleus.'

'And if there aren't enough well-heeled, whole-time leaders to go round? What then?'

'Then we'll make do with part-timers.'

David left it at that. The more he heard of the scheme the more impracticable it sounded. But he was not concerned with its practicability. It was its genuineness which mattered to him, and so far he had found little to disprove that.

At the end of the meal the Baron rose to say grace. He said it in Latin, speaking slowly and sonorously, and David suspected that even that brief, trivial moment of focused attention could be important to him. Whether he was a fraud, or whether he did in fact see himself as the Great Leader — a new Messiah, perhaps — he had to make these people believe in him, look up to him. He must take advantage of every opportunity, no matter how small, to impress his personality and authority on them.

In the brief silence that followed the end of grace the Baron took a handkerchief from his pocket, and something fell to the table with a dull, metallic clang. Startled, they all looked at it. It was a slender platinum cigarette-case, inset with diamonds that winked and twinkled at them in the candlelight.

Grevas picked it up, slowly turning it over and over in his hands as though wondering how to explain its presence. With Mackay's denunciation of expensive possessions fresh in his mind, David could appreciate his embarrassment.

The Baron cleared his throat.

'I meant to speak to you about this,' he said. 'I found it in my jacket pocket just before dinner. Some one, presumably acting under a generous but misguided impulse, must have put it there.' He looked round at their watchful faces, his composure returning. There was a grave smile on his face; the Great Leader, thought David, gently admonishing his disciples. 'While appreciating the impulse I must deprecate the deed. You know how I feel — how we all feel, I hope — about costly possessions such as this.' He held the cigarette-case up for all to see. 'Since the donor obviously intends to remain anonymous I have no alternative but to accept it. But I hope no one will be impelled by a similar impulse in the future.'

The Baroness was frowning. So was Maurice. Most of the others were either smiling or trying to look unconcerned.

But Olive was obviously upset; she was staring wide-eyed at the case, the colour drained from her cheeks so that the freckles showed more clearly. Several times Susan saw her open her mouth to speak, only to think better of it.

Into the silence piped the high-pitched voice of Harold Myerson.

'I hate to contradict you, Baron, but haven't you made a mistake? No one could have put that case in your pocket. It belonged to Jan. What's more, he had it with him Friday evening when he went fishing.'

5

'Harold's right,' Maurice said soberly. 'I saw it too.'

With the exception of the Baroness and Beryl and Edith, they were all in the library. Only Olive had sat down; the rest stood around uneasily, their eyes drifting inevitably to the cigarette-case in Grevas's hand. It was as though its twinkling shafts of light had mesmerized them. Susan could almost feel the tension; she was tense herself, held by the drama of the situation. She looked at David. His eyes were bright, darting eagerly from one anxious face to the next, and she knew that he too was keyed up, excited by the possibilities inherent in the mystery. Drama had suddenly erupted where he had begun to fear that only the commonplace existed. Even the elements appeared to have been affected. The wind had hushed, the patter of rain against the windows had ceased.

'I don't understand it,' the Baron said. His voice was almost a whisper. 'I took this jacket off after lunch and hung it on the hook on the study door. I can swear there was no cigarette-case in the pocket then. But it was certainly there when I put the jacket on for dinner. Yet if Jan . . . '

'There's no 'if' about it, I'm afraid,' Maurice told him. 'I met Jan as he was walking down to the jetty, and he pulled the case out of his pocket to light a cigarette. Harold joined us while we were talking.'

'And he didn't take it back to the house,' Myerson cut in. 'I went as far as the cliff with him, and watched him go down to the jetty.'

'Did you see him cast off?' Andrew asked. He looked suddenly older. The lines in his weather-beaten face were more clear-cut, the twinkle had departed from his eyes.

'You know I didn't. We went through that on Saturday.' Myerson sounded impatient. 'He was fixing his gear when I left.'

'So he could have come back,' Andrew said. 'He may have realized it would be foolish to take such a valuable possession on a fishing-trip.'

'He could. But it's a hundred to one he didn't. No one saw him, did they? And if he'd wanted to return it he'd have done so after talking to Maurice, not waited until he got as far as the jetty.'

Tom Hampson's deep voice boomed into the argument.

'Him knowing the ropes, you'd have thought he'd keep a thing like that out of sight, eh?'

'You would, wouldn't you? He must have pulled it from his pocket without thinking. He was obviously embarrassed when I pounced on it.' Maurice turned to the widow. 'Did you know he was carting it around, Olive? I'd never seen it before.'

Olive started, and looked at him vaguely. 'I'm sorry. I wasn't listening.' He repeated the question. 'Oh, no,' she said. 'I'm sure he didn't.'

'Then why take it fishing?' Tom demanded, the light gleaming on his bald pate, his voice challenging them to supply an answer.

No one did.

Olive got up from her chair, threaded her way through the still figures in the room, and went out. There was a deep frown on Maurice's face as he watched her go. She did not close the door behind her, and they could hear her footsteps on the stairs; slow at first, and heavy for a woman, and then breaking suddenly into a run.

Grevas too was frowning. He said anxiously, 'Poor Olive. I hope she isn't too upset. This will have come as a great shock to her.'

'It hasn't left the rest of us completely cold,' Myerson said. 'And it still has to be explained.' He pulled his stooping body erect, and fixed Grevas with an accusing eye. 'How about it, Baron? From where I'm standing it looks as though the ball is on your side of the net.'

There was a flutter among the women. Andrew said sharply, his beard bristling, 'Cut that out, Harold.' But they were all looking at the unhappy Baron, waiting for an explanation. However strong their faith in him, it seemed that for most of them it needed reassurance now. He might be Caesar, but he was not above suspicion.

And Grevas knew it.

It was David who came to his rescue, although not with that intention. He wanted to force out the truth before Grevas was allowed to smother it in a platitudinous pillow of words. Here was the first unbuttered crust for Snowball to bite on. He must insure that it would provide an adequate meal. There might be little or nothing to follow.

'I know it's none of my business,' he said pleasantly, pushing tobacco-stained fingers through his thick unruly hair. 'But if Jan took the case out of his pocket to light a cigarette, then presumably there were cigarettes in it. Are there any in it now?'

Relieved at this shift of interest, Grevas snapped open the case to reveal three cigarettes. He took one out and examined it. 'Senior Service,' he said. 'Is that what Jan smoked? I don't remember.'

'Yes.' Maurice sounded impatient. He was twisting a gold signet ring round and round the little finger of his left hand. Occasionally he would jerk it up against the knuckle, pause, and then continue the twisting. 'But what's all this in aid of? No one doubts that the case was Jan's, do they? Olive has identified it, and both Harold and I saw him with it.'

'Identification wasn't the point,' David said. 'It occurred to me that if you could remember how many cigarettes were in the case when you saw it we'd know how many Jan smoked before he was — well, separated from it. Couldn't that give us a rough time-estimate between the two events?'

Maurice frowned. The ring was still twisting. 'Maybe. Two or three, perhaps; I didn't really notice. He didn't offer me one; he knew I'm a confirmed pipe-smoker.'

Susan had listened with growing impatience to this discussion. It seemed to her quite childish. If this was a fair sample of intelligent male thinking, then no wonder there were so many unsolved crimes. But she had to handle it carefully. To flatten their egos with a burst of feminine ridicule would be disastrous, for her as well as for them. So she said, with an apologetic little cough by way of preface, 'I expect every one's thought of this ages ago, but it's only just occurred to me. And as no one has actually said it, I thought — well . . . '

'Oh, stop bleating, Susan!' David said impatiently. 'What are you trying to say?'

He did not see the baleful glance she gave him. He was watching Bessie, who stood by the window, away from the others. He did not watch her solely because he found pleasure in it — although that too. There was something wrong, something that involved her and her husband. Each time she looked at Myerson — and she looked at him often — there was an air of expectancy about her. And it was the expectancy of fear — or if not fear, then disaster. Occasionally her thick lips parted, and he saw the pink tip of her tongue and thought she was about to speak. But she did not speak. She just closed her lips tightly, and turned back to the window.

He wondered why.

'Mr Myerson went as far as the cliff-top with Jan,' Susan said. Christian names came easily to her lips, but not Myerson's. She did not like him and she did not understand him; or perhaps the first was the result of the second. 'And he saw him go down to the boat. So either Jan dropped the case on the way, or he left it on the jetty; he couldn't have given it to anyone, because there was no one else about, was there?' Myerson shook his head. 'But he didn't drop it in the sea, and he didn't take it in the boat with him. That's for sure.'

Her normally soft voice was sharp and decisive; David's jibe had maddened her into forgetting her original apologetic air. They looked at her with interest and some surprise, David among them. This was a new Susan.

'Is it?' he asked. 'Why?'

'The cigarettes would show it, wouldn't they? You know how they look when they've been in water. All brown and spotty.' Ignoring David, she smiled sweetly at the others. 'But don't tell me that hadn't occurred to you. I'm sure it had.'

Grevas smiled back at her. 'If it had it would be most ungallant of us to say so. The credit shall be all yours, my dear.' He looked from Maurice to Myerson, and back to Maurice. 'So where are we now?'

'Without wishing to belittle Susan's ingenuity, not much forrader, I'm afraid. We already knew Jan hadn't taken it into the boat, or how could it have turned up in your pocket?' Maurice paused as Olive came into the room. She seemed unaware of their watchful eyes; she went straight to her chair and sat down. David thought she looked more cheerful, as though she had successfully resolved an important problem. Susan's mind ran on more feminine lines. That turquoise-blue suits her, she thought, but not the short flared skirt. Not with legs and ankles like hers. And those perky little bows on the shoulders! They'd look sweet on a teenager. On Olive they just look silly.

Myerson's high-pitched voice broke the silence.

'I suppose you have now all reached the conclusion that it was I who pinched the case.' There was a half-hearted murmur of denial, in which David did not join; he for one had reached that conclusion. Since by his own admission Myerson had been with Jan or had had him under observation right down to the jetty, who else was there to suspect? 'Well, I'm sorry to disappoint you. I didn't. And if I *had* pinched it I certainly wouldn't have popped it into the Baron's pocket. I'd have found a better use for it than that.'

David could believe that last assertion, if not the first. He wondered what the others were thinking.

Andrew said quickly, 'Nonsense, Harold. We all know you and Jan were friends.' Was that true? David wondered. 'Either Jan lost the case and some one found it (only don't ask me how it got into the Baron's pocket), or — Olive, you ought to know. Did Jan come back to the house at all?'

She shook her head. 'Not to our room.'

'And he wouldn't leave a valuable thing like that anywhere else,' Myerson said.

'Not even in the Baron's pocket.'

Of the women, only Susan had so far contributed anything to the discussion. Jutter had been leaning against the mantelshelf, her dark eyes thoughtfully contemplating each speaker in turn, her scarlet dress a vivid splash of colour against the sombre background of the fireplace. Now she stepped forward so that she was directly in front of Grevas. She said harshly, 'Didn't anyone see Jan in the boat? Not even you, Baron? You weren't, for instance, at your usual observation-post among the trees?'

There was something here David did not understand; it was as though she were goading the man. And from the look on their faces the others were equally puzzled. But Grevas understood. There was a faint flush on his lean cheeks, and he avoided Jutter's eyes.

'I wasn't,' he said briefly.

'I saw him,' Edith said. She had brought in the coffee-tray, and with a sigh of relief she deposited it on a table near the door and put a hand to her ample bosom. She still wore the faded blue dress, although the sleeves had been rolled down. 'From my window.'

'You actually saw him fishing?' Myerson pushed his way eagerly towards her. 'And he was all right? You're sure?'

'He looked all right,' Edith said. Quietly she began to set out the cups and saucers, her roughened hands handling the delicate Worcester china with deliberate care. 'But he wasn't fishing. He was rowing away from the jetty. I don't know what happened after that, because I went downstairs to help Madame with the dinner.'

Myerson stared at her. He seemed to shrink in size. Then he went quietly from the room and shut the door behind him. David looked at Bessie, expecting her to follow her husband. But she stayed by the window, her face turned away from him so that he could not read her expression. His eyes went to the slender bare legs under the yellow dress, and he saw with surprise that she was wearing high-heeled shoes. She did not look comfortable in them.

'Harold may be abrupt, but he's got the

right idea,' Maurice said. 'Isn't all this rather a storm in a teacup? Does it matter how or where Jan lost his cigarette-case? In any case, it doesn't solve the problem of who found it and put it in the Baron's pocket.'

'And why,' Andrew added.

'Yes. And why. And frankly I couldn't care less.'

From the arguments that followed it was clear that they were divided on this. But two were silent. David, because he had no doubt that it did matter, that if it were allowed to be dismissed his story might be dismissed along with it; and Grevas, because if it were not dismissed, if it were allowed to remain open to discussion and argument, then suspicion would remain with it. And suspicion could ruin him.

Yet he could not insist that they forget it. To do so would be to arouse the suspicion he wished to kill. In this he could no longer play the leader. He could only hope and, where possible, suggest.

He was wondering what to suggest when the Baroness joined them. Ignoring the others, she went directly to her husband, the satin dress whispering softly.

'The police are here, Frederick,' she said, in her flat, toneless voice. 'They wish to see you.'

6

It was plain that the police wish was not reciprocated by the Baron. Confidence deserted him with the news. Licking his lips, he said nervously, 'I think it would be unwise to mention Jan's cigarette-case.' He slipped it into a side-pocket, and Susan felt that he was glad to have it out of his sight. 'It might complicate matters. There must be a perfectly simple and innocent explanation, but the police might decide otherwise.'

You bet they would, thought David. The police aren't as gullible as this lot.

'Fair enough,' Maurice said. He looked at the others. A few nodded; none of them disagreed. 'How about you and Susan, David? They'll want to see you, I expect. You found the body.'

'It's O.K. by us.' David took Susan's compliance for granted. And if Jan's cigarette-case contained a story he wanted it to be his story; he wasn't handing it to the police. 'I doubt if they would take action anyway unless Olive asked them to.'

Maurice and Andrew went with the Baron. After they had gone the conversation spread to more varied topics; the possibilities concerning the cigarette-case seemed to have been exhausted. Olive had recovered her former cheerfulness, and the Baroness sipped her coffee and talked quietly with Edith. Only Bessie seemed preoccupied. David tried to draw Susan apart, for he had things to say to her in confidence. But the others hemmed him in, and he realized he would have to wait.

The three men were not long gone. 'Just routine business,' Maurice said, as they crowded round him. 'They're taking the body back to the mainland.' He turned to David. 'They want to see you now.'

They were in the dining-room; two of them, a big dark sergeant and a big dark constable. But the similarity ended with their size and colouring. The constable was thin, with a long, thin face and hooded eyes, the sergeant round and plump and twinkling.

'I think we know all there is to know, sir,' the sergeant said. 'Bob Bissett, the lad as brought you across, has told us how you come to find the body. But we'd like to hear your version, if you wouldn't mind. Just to tidy things up, like.'

David gave it. When he had finished he said, 'Will you want to question Miss Long, the girl who was with me?'

'I don't think so, sir. We've got all we want. And the body's been identified by one of the gentlemen here.' He tapped his notebook. 'It's all quite straightforward.'

The constable spoke for the first time. He said darkly, 'Which is more than can be said for *this* place.'

'You can say that again.' The sergeant looked round the bare vastness of the dining-room, illuminated now by electricity. 'A proper queer set-up, and no mistake.' He gave an embarrassed cough. 'You on a visit here, Mr Wight? Or were you thinking of staying?'

'A visit,' David said. He wondered how much the men knew. 'What's queer about the set-up here, Sergeant?'

But the sergeant was not to be pumped. 'I dare say they've got the right idea, sir, but it isn't practicable. That's what I say. It's human nature to quarrel and to want to go one better than the next chap. And you can't change human nature.'

Privately David agreed with him. But he said, hoping to provoke further argument, 'You can try. And that's what they're doing here.'

The sergeant shrugged. The constable said, 'Is that all they're doing, sir? There's rumours they're not so high-minded as they make out to be.'

David knew what he meant. But the sergeant gave him no time to reply. He said briskly, 'We'll be getting along now, sir. Sounds as though the wind's freshening again; the crossing's no picnic at night with a sea running. If you're required to attend the inquest you'll be notified.' He picked up his cap from the table. 'Would you mind telling the Baron we're leaving, sir? We'll need help getting the body across the island.'

David did not offer to provide the help. He had no wish to act as bearer to a corpse, nor did he fancy a tramp across damp fields in the dark. And he still hoped for a private word with Susan. There were ideas forming in his mind that he wanted to put into words. Susan was his only confidante.

Andrew and Maurice went with the police, and with their going the Baron recovered his former assurance. He came into the library and apologized to David and Susan for what he termed 'this unfortunate incident.' 'After dinner we usually discuss plans and ideas for the future,' he told them, 'but it'll be too late for that by the time Maurice and Andrew return. And perhaps none of us is in quite the right frame of mind for it now. Well, there are other evenings.' He put a well-manicured hand on Susan's shoulder. 'You look tired, my dear; you should go to bed. Personally, I never retire before midnight, and more often than not it's after two o'clock before I turn in. I find my brain more nimble in the small hours.'

He went off to the study, and the

Baroness went with him. David wondered idly if the woman was always as silent and aloof, or whether the day's events were responsible. Her chill, unfriendly air repelled and yet fascinated him. He caught himself wondering what she thought about, how she viewed her husband's aims and the people he had collected around him. He was fairly certain, from the expression on her face as she watched him, that she disapproved.

Edith began to collect the empty coffee-cups and put them on the tray, her husband helping her; beside him she looked even smaller and dumpier than before. As she reached for a cup on the mantelshelf Susan saw that her dress was split under one armpit, and decided that Tom had not spent much of his winnings on his wife. She needs a hair-do and a facial and a manicure, she thought, and probably a new wardrobe. And he could do with a new suit himself. The one he's wearing looks as though it came out of the ark.

Edith picked up the tray and limped from the room without a word, her heavy ankles twisting as she walked. Tom fumbled in his pocket for a pipe, looked at it fondly, and then replaced it. He caught Susan watching him, and grinned. 'Better not,' he said. 'Time I was in bed. We're early risers, me and Edith. Always 'ave been. 'T'ain't necessary now, of course, but it's become an 'abit, like.' He waved a bony hand at the others. ' 'Night, all.'

As the door closed behind him a sudden flurry of rain rattled against the windows. David thought of the two policemen crossing that intemperate stretch of water, and shivered. Bessie Myerson shivered too. But not for the same reason, David suspected. She looked cold.

'I am,' she said, when he asked her. 'Sometimes at night I almost freeze.'

'When did you leave the West Indies?'

'About a year ago. A little less, perhaps.'

'And how do you like England?'

She smiled at him. It was a secret, almost a conspiratorial smile, although they had nothing to be conspiratorial about. It set up an intimacy between them that he welcomed half fearfully, half gladly. Did she intend that? Or was she unaware of it?

'I don't know,' she said. 'I haven't seen it. We come here after only a few days in London. And since then we stay here.'

There was a faint American twang to her rich, husky voice; he had noticed before her preference for the present tense. He wanted to ask about her life before she was married, but decided that this was not the time.

'How do you like it here, then? On the island?'

A tiny frown puckered her forehead. She said, 'It's nice when the sun shines. I don't like it when it rains, because then it's always cold. Not like in Jamaica.'

'And the people?'

She looked round the room. Beryl Hunt had left shortly after the Hampsons; Jutter and Susan were talking together in a far corner; Olive was reading, the book close to her eyes. And it was on Olive that Bessie's eyes lingered before turning back to David.

'You should ask them how they like

me,' she said, and giggled. 'The men do, I think, so I like them. But not some of the women. Not Olive or the Lady, for instance.'

'The Lady?'

'Yes.' She tried to contort her face into the thin, sharp features of the Baroness. It was not a successful caricature, but it was enough to make David laugh with her. He could imagine that a girl with Bessie's colour and background would not be to the Baroness's taste. Particularly if, as he suspected, Grevas liked to sun himself in her warmth. But why Olive?

Bessie raised her eyebrows in mock astonishment when he asked her. 'I'm black, aren't I? Good Southern women don't like niggers.'

'Bessie!'

They both turned sharply. Myerson stood there, his eyes angry. But the spoken reproof went no further than his wife's name. He said, 'Time you were in bed.' And to David, 'She's been rounding up the hens with Andrew for most of the day. She must be tired.'

It was a civil enough explanation for

the interruption, and David accepted it as such, despite the lack of friendliness in the man's voice and eyes. But the look Bessie gave him as she followed her husband from the room was warm and inviting, and again he wondered at it. Was it just the friendliness of a cheerful, ingenuous young woman, or did it promise more?

He was uncertain which way he wanted it.

Olive closed her book and scrambled up from her chair, exposing a generous length of plump, nylon-clad leg as she did so. Her eyes looked tired and watery.

'My, but I'm sleepy.' She stifled a yawn with a well-manicured hand, smoothing down the front of her dress with the other. 'Guess I'll say good night and finish this in bed. It's been a depressing day, hasn't it? Perhaps it'll be better tomorrow. I sure do hope so.'

Her parting smile was friendly if somewhat vacant. As the door closed behind her Jutter said sadly, 'Depressing, yes. But not only to-day. It has been raining and blowing ever since Jan was drowned. I wonder if that's an omen.'

Susan shuddered. 'Don't! You'll give me the willies.'

'I'm sorry. But it isn't only the weather.' She pronounced it 'vezzer,' then corrected herself. 'Suddenly everything is wrong.'

'Such as what?' asked David.

She laughed and stood up. Unlike Olive, she did it gracefully. She laughed with her eyes as well as her mouth, displaying white even teeth.

'Nothing. Andrew says I imagine things, and perhaps I do. But I'm not imagining the weather.' She got it right this time. 'Do you two know your rooms? Would you like me to show you?'

Her dark eyes were on David as she spoke, and he thought again how beautiful she was. He would have liked to go on looking at her; but while she was there he could not talk to Susan, and that was important. He said reluctantly, 'Don't bother about us. We'll find our way.'

'Good night, then.' She grimaced as another splutter of rain sounded on the window-panes. 'I hope this blows itself out by the morning. I haven't bathed for days. Not since — well, good night.'

When she had gone David said, 'I wonder what she meant by saying that everything is wrong.'

'I should have thought it was obvious. That poor man being drowned, and then this mystery over his cigarette-case. Not to mention the chickens.'

'I doubt if she's the type to care about chickens. Quite a looker, isn't she?'

'Quite.' Susan's voice was distant. 'Though her bust is too large and she hasn't any hips. Do you prefer her to your ebony friend?'

'Cut that out, Susan. Bessie's no more my friend than yours.' He sat down on the chair opposite her. 'But they're an odd crowd, aren't they? I wonder how many of them are phonies.'

'I'm sure the Baron isn't. He's a sweetie.'

'H'm! That's a point of view, certainly. A pity he doesn't instil some sweetness into that poisonous wife of his.'

'She probably suffers from acidity and

indigestion,' Susan said. 'Night starvation as well, I shouldn't wonder. She ought to read the advertisements. But the others — well, lots of people seem odd when you first meet them. It doesn't mean they're phonies.'

'I know. But they're not quite what the Baron led us to expect. Somehow I can't envisage them spreading peace and goodwill around the world. They're too fond of jumping on each other.'

Susan nodded. 'Like the Mackay woman snubbing Mr Myerson at dinner. He asked for it, of course. But she was so *rude*. And she didn't use his Christian name, either.'

'He wouldn't have one. He's a Jew.'

'Ha! Ha! Very funny.'

He told her what Bessie had said — that Olive disliked her because she was a Negress. 'They're incompatibles, I suppose, like Jutter and Myerson. Yet if this lot can't conquer incompatibility, or at least come to terms with it, a fat lot of use they'll be as future peace leaders. And Grevas is no fool; he must see that. That's why I think he's a phoney.'

'He's an idealist,' Susan objected. 'He's too engrossed in the future to see the present clearly.'

It was an argument he had not expected from one so worldly as Susan.

'Perhaps,' he agreed. 'Although at twenty smackers per head per week he's not exactly neglecting the present either. To say nothing of Olive's sixty thousand dollars.' He put his hands to his head and savaged his hair into greater disorder. 'I wish I could make out what happened to that damned cigarette-case. I'm sure it's important.'

'I don't see why. Because it's mysterious it doesn't have to be sinister.' Susan uncoiled herself from the armchair, stood up, and stretched luxuriously. 'Goodness, but I'm tired!' She smothered a yawn. 'I don't know about you, darling, but I'm for bed.'

'Not yet,' he objected. 'We have to thrash this out. Time is short; I'm supposed to be back in the office the day after to-morrow.' He scratched his chin, where the dark stubble showed clearly. 'I wonder if Snowball would stand for an extra day.'

'He might. I'm not sure that I would. The place isn't so bad, but I don't think I like the people. Apart from the Baron, of course. The difficulty is to get him alone. He's kind of hemmed in. Too much competition.'

'We're here on business,' he reminded her. 'Not to further your sex life.'

'I haven't got one, darling; too much time wasted on you.' She yawned again. 'Do we really have to talk now? Won't it keep till the morning?'

'Now,' he said firmly.

She sighed. 'All right. But give me ten minutes to undress, and then come along to my room. We can talk there. I think better in bed.'

'I didn't know you thought at all,' he told her. 'I understood you just had ready-made opinions.'

He left her on the first landing, and went up to his room and sat on the bed and made a few desultory notes. But his brain was not working clearly. He needed to put his thoughts into words, and before the ten minutes were up he had stuffed the notes impatiently into his pocket and was out in the passage again.

As he closed the door of his room Jutter came out of the far bathroom. Without make-up her face looked like ivory under the rich blackness of her hair. She smiled at him as she said goodnight, putting a hand up to her face to push back her hair. The thin négligé she wore fell slightly apart, and he saw that she wore nothing beneath it. Susan is right about the competition, he thought, scurrying down the stairs. It's pretty talented.

He had reached the first floor and was making for Susan's room when a scream, muffled but distinct, came from above. For a moment he paused, trying to locate the sound; then he turned and hurried back up the stairs. The scream came again, louder and nearer, and he ran along the passage to where a thin shaft of light showed vertically against the dim background. Without ceremony he thrust the door open and burst into the room, prepared to do battle.

There was no battle to do. Jutter stood

by the bed, her hands to her face; she had taken off her négligé and was nude. But she did not turn as David came in, nor give any indication that she knew he was there. For a moment he hesitated. His immediate impulse was to retreat; it was unpleasant to think on what Mackay might say and do were he to find him there. Yet Jutter would not have screamed without reason.

He stepped forward, trying to see her face without consciously observing her body. But her hands still hid her eyes, and he turned to the bed. The blankets had been drawn back, and on the sheet lay something furry and darkly brown, a spread of dull red fouling the expanse of white around it.

It was the dead and mutilated body of a large rat.

7

Only the moisture, glistening whitely on leaf and blade and petal in the thin morning sunlight, remained of the rainstorm. Gazing from his window at the now placid sea, David thought of Jutter. She had implied she was a keen swimmer; unless finding a dead rat in her bed had taken all the steam out of her, he suspected she would be down early for a bathe. And others might have the same idea.

The thought vaguely disturbed him. The mystery surrounding the dead man's cigarette-case had seemed to make a mystery of the death itself, and, without quite knowing why, he wanted to be first at the jetty that morning. According to Maurice, no one had been down there since Jan Muzyk had died. It was highly improbable that either the jetty or the beach could throw further light on the manner of his death, but if there was anything to discover David wanted to be the one to discover it.

He dressed quickly and went along to Susan's room. He knew Susan did not share his enthusiasm for detection, but he wanted her with him; she was a grindstone on which to sharpen his wits. But Susan was sleeping soundly; it was not yet seven, and for a moment he hesitated to wake her. She lay on her back with her elbows bent and her arms resting on the pillows, her auburn hair a flame, the long, pointed nails on the too stubby fingers curled into the palms of her hands. She looks much younger like that, he thought; almost the way she used to look when we were kids. Pretty, too. A pity I don't go for her the way I could go for Bessie or Jutter.

The girl's lips parted in a faint pouf, which was followed by a low whistle. David grinned. She might not like to be woken, but she'd like even less to know he was standing there listening to her snoring.

He bent and shook her gently.

'Go away,' she grumbled, stretching

lazily, her hands clasping and unclasping above her head. The grey-green eyes stared at him between half-closed lids. 'Go *away*. Only a bad conscience would be around this early.'

'Get up,' he said. 'I'm taking you down to the jetty for a swim.'

Susan squealed in horror. 'A swim? Me?' She clutched the bedclothes and drew them up tight under her chin. 'Are you crazy?'

'You don't have to get into the water, dammit!' he said impatiently. 'I just want you down there, that's all.'

'Why?'

He refused to give her the satisfaction of knowing why he wanted her with him, but he did try to tell her something of what was in his mind. 'And if we're to beat the others to it we'll have to be quick. So hop out of that bed before I drag you out.'

She started to protest again. But she knew her David, and as he caught hold of the blankets she said hastily, 'All right, all right! I'm coming, damn you! Wait outside while I dress.'

The house was quiet and still as they went downstairs and out through the big front door, but as they approached the jetty they saw that they were not the first. A dark head bobbed in the water; a glitter of spray followed the progress of the swimmer as she moved expertly through it.

It was Jutter. She put up an arm and waved to them, and then came surging in to the jetty. As she climbed the ladder and stood poking a finger into her ears to clear the water from them David was again struck by her beauty, both of face and figure. Maybe Susan had been right. Maybe her hips were a little too narrow, her breasts a little too full, for perfection. Nevertheless, he thought her terrific.

Her bikini was the briefest he had ever seen.

After the previous night's incident he had feared there would be embarrassment between them when next they met. But although he himself was at first embarrassed, Jutter gave no sign of it. Rubbing herself vigorously with the towel, she said cheerfully, 'Brrrh! It's cold. But the water's lovely. It always is after rain.'

Her body was warmly golden where the sun had found it, her hair, released from its coil, a glistening black cascade about her shoulders. Watching her in admiration, David said, 'Do you often bathe this early?'

'On mornings like this, yes.' She stooped to pick up her wrap. Still stooping, she glanced up at the dark band of trees that fringed the cliff.

'What about the others?'

She did not answer. Holding the wrap loosely against her, she stood up and pushed the hair away from her face, her eyes still fixed on the trees. David followed her gaze.

'Looking for some one?' he asked.

She turned and smiled at him. 'No. Are you two going to bathe?'

'I am. Susan isn't the type.'

Jutter nodded. Susan did not like her cool, appraising stare, and she said indignantly, 'I'm not a type, thank you. I just don't happen to enjoy heaving my body out of a warm bed and plunging it into a lot of cold water. I'm a sybarite, not a spartan.'

Jutter laughed. For a woman she had a deep laugh, in which all her body seemed to participate. But she made no comment. She said to David, 'I haven't yet thanked you for coming to my rescue last night. I was absolutely petrified.'

David blushed. 'It was a pleasure,' he said awkwardly. Then, remembering her nudity and realizing the possible construction she might put on that remark, his blush deepened. 'I — I don't blame you for being scared. It was a disgusting sight.'

Susan pulled her coat tighter about her, her indignation growing at his complete disregard of herself. If only he could see how silly he looks, she thought, gawping at all that over-done female flesh as though it were a revelation! She said tartly, 'Have you two nearly finished with the butter?'

Jutter laughed. David gave her a blank look, and turned again to Jutter. 'Any idea who put the rat there?' he asked. 'It seems so pointless. And damned crude.'

Jutter shrugged. 'Crude, yes. But I don't think it was pointless.' She draped the wrap over her shoulders. 'Did I shock you? I always sleep raw. I used to bathe raw too when we first came here. Alone, of course, or with Andrew. Not with the others.'

You weren't far off the raw this morning, Susan thought. She said, 'Don't let us stop you. David won't mind. And I'm going back to the house.'

David put out a hand, fingers spread, to detain her. Without turning he said urgently, 'Hang on a minute, Susan.'

He and Jutter were now both staring at the trees. Fascinated by their concentration, Susan stared too. A glint of light showed suddenly, winked again, and was gone.

'I thought so,' David said. 'We're being watched.'

'Not we, darling — Jutter. A Peeping Tom with binoculars,' Susan suggested indifferently. 'Some one forgot to tell him nude bathing was off.'

'That's why I stopped,' Jutter told them. 'I'm no prude, but I dislike the prurient.'

David was startled. He had attributed a different, more sinister motive to the watcher. 'Who is it?' he asked. 'Do you know?'

Jutter did not reply; but as if in answer to his question a figure emerged from the trees and began to walk briskly back towards the house. They could not see him clearly, but the sun shining on white hair caused David to whistle.

'Grevas!' he exclaimed. 'Well, I'm damned! The old so-and-so!'

Jutter shrugged, turning her back on the island. Her bathing-wrap was open at the front, and Susan looked at her, admiring her face and figure grudgingly. David's right, she thought; she *is* beautiful. I wish I could look the way she does in a bikini. But I don't; I know that. My legs are as good (she looked down at them and nodded to herself, reassured), but I'm too fat and too short. And if I let the sun get at my skin it goes all red and raw and blotchy, not a gorgeous colour like hers. It's a pity —

David said, 'How about your wonderful baron now, Susan? Do you still think he's an idealist?'

She said defensively, 'He's a man, anyway. And I didn't notice you turning your back, darling. If he's a kettle, aren't you being something of a pot?'

David frowned, but the allusion was lost on Jutter. Noting the way her eyebrows arched in bewilderment, Susan was reminded that she had not been given time to pencil in her own. Damn David and his early-morning capers, she thought. I must look positively bald.

After an awkward silence Jutter said, 'I must go. Don't tell Andrew about the Baron, will you? It isn't important, of course, but it might upset him.' Her dark eyes smiled at David. 'I hope you enjoy your swim.'

They watched her as she ran down the jetty to the beach, the wrap streaming behind her. Few women look graceful when they run, but Jutter did.

Susan said, 'I wonder why her husband wasn't with her.'

'Probably too busy with his agricultural chores,' David said. He was changing into his swimming-trunks.

'Um! He wasn't there last night either, when she did her striptease act for you. He didn't even come when she screamed, did he? So where was he?'

'I haven't the faintest idea. In the bathroom or the lavatory, perhaps, or stoking a boiler. He could have been anywhere. And it wasn't a striptease.' He pulled his shirt over his head, muffling the words. 'Nudity suits Jutter.'

'It doesn't suit you. Your pants are slipping.'

He clutched at them hastily. 'You're jealous,' he told her.

'Jutter looks a damned sight more modest in her birthday suit than you would in your step-ins, let me tell you.'

Susan sighed. 'That's a matter of opinion. But it wasn't modesty that inspired her when she staged her act last night.'

That shook him. 'What act? What are you getting at, Susan?'

'Isn't it obvious? She meets you in the passage, goes into her bedroom, takes off her négligé, pulls the door ajar so that you can't go wrong, and screams her head off.

And you fall for it.' She gave another, deeper sigh. 'You're still wet behind the ears, darling. It's time you grew up.'

'You must be crazy.' He threw his shirt on to the jetty in disgust. 'And the rat? She just happened to have that tucked away in a drawer, eh?' He kicked off his sandals; one of them landed perilously near the edge. 'I'm going for a swim. Signal when sanity returns, will you?'

She watched him swim away. He was a strong but an ungainly swimmer, and his progress through the water was marked by a certain amount of noise and considerable spray. Perhaps, because he was mad at her, he thrashed even more wildly than usual.

I suppose he's right, she decided. Jutter wasn't putting on an act; she really was scared. But I wish he didn't fall so easily for these damned women.

David swam out about fifty yards and started to dive down; according to Maurice, Jan had seldom ventured farther away from the jetty than that. He had the forlorn hope that the boat might still be where it had sunk, that the storm had not shifted it. But the water was deeper than he had anticipated. Time after time he filled his lungs with air and struck down towards the sea-bed; but he never reached it, and there was no sign of the boat or its wreckage. Eventually, tired out, he swam slowly back, and held on to the steps, recovering his breath preparatory to climbing out.

Susan leaned over him.

'I'm terribly sorry, darling, but one of your sandals accidentally fell into the water.' She pointed. 'Down there.'

'You mean you kicked it in, you crazy coot!' He glowered at her, but the effect was marred by the water trickling into his eyes. 'Why can't you keep your big feet under control?'

For answer she picked up the rest of his clothes and held them threateningly over the water. 'Any more rudery like that, my lamb, and you'll be fishing for a complete wardrobe, not just one miserable sandal.'

'Put them down, damn you!' He released his hold on the steps, swam to where she had pointed, and dived. Susan replaced the clothes on the jetty and leaned over to watch the blur of his body as it moved under the water.

It was some time before he surfaced. When he did it was to deposit his sandal on the jetty, take a deep breath, and disappear again. Surprised, Susan waited. What was he up to now?

He came up and swam slowly to the steps. As he climbed them she saw he had something in his hand. 'What have you found this time?' she asked.

It was a length of nylon rope, both ends of which led back to the water. 'Catch hold of that and haul it in,' he said, without explanation, and began to tug at the other end.

She did not haul for long. 'It's stuck,' she said, tugging hard.

'O.K. Drop it.'

The sun had disappeared behind a cloud, and Susan shivered and pulled her coat tighter about her. But David appeared not to notice the cold. She could see goose-pimples on his flesh, but he went on hauling, the rope falling into untidy coils at his feet. Presently the end came up out of the water, jerked over the edge of the jetty, and fell with a dull clatter on to the wet boards.

David picked it up. Attached to it was a piece of wood, painted green, and about three feet long and six inches wide. Through a hole in the centre was a metal bolt, with a wing-nut at one end and a tube, through which the rope had been threaded and knotted, at the other.

'What's that for?' Susan asked.

He did not answer at once; he was still examining his find. It was not completely rectangular, one edge being shorter than the other. There were screw-holes along the shorter edge and at both ends, with some of the screws still in the holes. The longer edge had been grooved, although now the groove was broken.

'Looks like part of the stern of a boat,' he said.

'Jan's boat?'

'I suppose so.'

Susan was excited, her previous irritation forgotten. 'Where's the other end?' she asked.

'It's attached to one of the jetty supports — presumably to stop the boat

131

from drifting out to sea while he was fishing.' David shivered. 'I'm cold. Throw me the towel, will you?'

She gave him the towel and took the piece of board from him. 'Is it important?' she asked. 'Will it help to explain what happened?'

'I shouldn't think so.' He rubbed vigorously to restore the circulation. 'The boat got a pounding and broke up; that's about all there is to it. We've recovered this bit because it happened to be attached to the rope. The rest could be anywhere.'

In his outsize bathing-trunks, reaching almost to his knees, he presented a comic spectacle. He was no weakling; but his body was lean and skinny and his joints knobbly, and his hair stood on end from the towelling. Susan smiled. Then the smile vanished, and she swore.

'What's the matter?' he asked.

'I pricked my finger on one of the nails,' she said, sucking it.

'Screws, not nails. Don't you women ever know the difference?'

Susan was indignant. 'Of course I know

the difference. Screws go round and round, nails don't. And these are nails.'

'But they — ' He stopped towelling. 'Here, give it to me.'

She watched him as he re-examined it. This time his examination was more thorough, and she knew that his interest was aroused. Then he gave a low whistle and stared at her, his eyes round.

'Well?' she demanded impatiently.

'We were way out.' Each word was uttered with extreme solemnity. 'The rope wasn't fixed to the boat to prevent drift, it was there to sink it.' Susan gasped. 'See for yourself. Look at those screws — they don't project the other side. But they didn't break off, they were sawn off; you can see the marks of the saw.' With a fingernail he scooped a small piece of putty from one of the screw-holes and rolled it between his fingers. 'And the putty's new. Some one unscrewed this plank from the stern, cut down the screws so that they were useless, and then banged it back into place with these brads. They'd hold for a while as long as there was no strain. The boat might leak a little. But then it probably leaked anyway.'

'But why the rope?'

'To supply the strain. When the boat reached the end of its tether it would jerk the board away. Or it would if Jan were rowing strongly enough.'

'And if he wasn't?'

'I don't know.' He considered this. 'If there was an ebbtide the boat would keep tugging at the rope, loosening the board with every tug, until eventually it would come away. And that would be that. She'd sink like a stone.'

Susan shuddered. 'How ghastly!'

'Yes.'

He did not sound aghast. His voice was exultant, his eyes bright. 'And it means that Jan's death was no accident. He was murdered.' He bent to pick up his shirt. 'Oh, boy! What a story this is going to be! Snowball will really go for this one!'

8

They hid the plank under the pebbles on the beach, marking the spot with a boulder; the rope and the bolt David wrapped in his towel and took back to the house. 'I hadn't reckoned on a murder hunt,' he said, solemnity replacing his previous exultation. 'We must keep this to ourselves until we've decided how to handle it. I'll come up to your room after breakfast.'

On the bottom terrace they met the Myersons, arrayed in gaudy bathrobes and carrying equally gaudy towels. Myerson's thin, skinny legs appeared challengingly white against his wife's barefooted brown ones. The sun was still obscured, and neither looked eager for the projected bathe. Bessie seemed disposed to stop and chat, but her husband, his prominent nose red-tipped, hurried her away. 'We'll have to be quick,' he said, teeth chattering.

'Breakfast is almost ready.'

As they started to climb up to the house Susan said, 'I shouldn't have thought he was the early-dipper type, would you?'

'No. And don't natter. I want to think.'

Susan was annoyed. 'You mean you have brains as well as brawn?' she said incredulously.

He stalked ahead without deigning to reply.

Breakfast was a reasonably cheerful meal; the early-morning sunshine and the prospect of a fine day seemed to have put them all in a good humour. All, that is, except the Baroness and the Myersons. As usual, the Baroness said little, but concentrated on the food; she ignored the bacon and sausages, nibbling away relentlessly at buttered toast and consuming several cups of coffee. The black satin had been discarded for skirt and blouse, and a long-sleeved cardigan buttoned up to the neck. The Myersons came in late without apology, and ate their meal in near silence. Myerson was a creature of moods, so that his silence was not surprising; but it was strange to see Bessie so preoccupied. Hunger was not responsible, for she ate little. When she sat down beside him David asked her if she had enjoyed the bathe. No, she said, she had not; but that was all she did say, either then or later. He was reminded of her preoccupation the previous evening, when the mystery of Jan Muzyk's cigarette-case had been under discussion. He had thought then that she was afraid, and that her fear was in some way connected with her husband. But how?

There was no mention of Jan or his cigarette-case during the meal; it was as though there had been tacit agreement to ignore the topic. But David was surprised that no one commented on Jutter's ordeal of the previous night. Her husband at least must know of it. Had they decided to keep it to themselves?

He looked down the table at her, remembering. For quite some seconds he had stood beside her, staring at the rat on the bed, deeply aware of her nakedness, but striving to conceal his awareness. Then both had moved; she to snatch her négligé from the chair and don it, he to pick up the rat and throw it out of the window. They had discussed it afterwards — a trifle breathlessly, avoiding each other's eyes — and wondered at the warped mind that could conceive such a disgusting trick. He had had the notion that she suspected a particular person, although she denied it vehemently when he said so. And then he had left, to go down and talk it over with Susan. Apparently no one, not even her husband, had heard Jutter's screams. Certainly no one had come to her room while he was there.

David's gaze shifted to Mackay. Mackay's beard was neatly trimmed, he had donned a well-cut tweed jacket and dark-grey flannels. As he discussed foodstuffs for the island cattle with Tom his small tufted eyebrows were working overtime; he did not look like a man consumed by anger or anxiety. But why not? wondered David. If my wife had been subjected to such a filthy trick I'd be hopping mad; I wouldn't rest until I'd got my hands on the wretch responsible. How can Andrew take it so calmly?

Or had Jutter decided to keep it a secret even from her husband?

Hoping to lead the conversation in the required direction, David said, 'I thought you'd all be down for a bathe this morning, taking advantage of the sunshine.'

'Some of us have work to do, Mr Wight.' He started at the unexpected sound of the Baroness's voice. 'You would not otherwise be eating breakfast now.'

He felt the warmth rising up his neck to his face. She made him feel small and young and foolish. And angry. Yet there was an impregnable air of aloofness about her that he knew he could never pierce. Did she affect Grevas in the same way? He tried unsuccessfully to visualize her as a young woman, a young wife. Could a man feel ardour for a creature so withdrawn?

Conversation had halted, as it invariably did when the Baroness spoke. Now it restarted. But David had lost his place in it. With the Baroness's cold eye upon him, and her rebuke still rankling, he no

139

longer felt equal to the task of directing it.

He turned his attention to the Baron.

Grevas and Maurice were discussing the necessity for a trip to the mainland and the purchase of fresh supplies. This was the fourth day since the storm had broken on the night Jan Muzyk had died, and stocks were running low. Choosing his moment, David said, 'Any chance of a lift, Maurice? Or do you have a full complement?'

'Thinking of leaving us?' the Baron asked pleasantly.

'No, sir. On the contrary, Susan and I were hoping you'd let us stay for a day or two. But I'd have to get my editor's permission. I thought I'd phone him this morning.'

'Stay by all means,' Grevas said. 'As for a lift — there'll be room in the boat, won't there, Maurice?' Maurice nodded. 'I presume you won't find it necessary to mention last night's unfortunate incident to your editor, eh?'

David had no intention of mentioning it to anyone, and said so. And he certainly wasn't feeding scraps of information to

Snowball over the telephone. Snowball must wait for the one magnificent exposure.

'Good!' The Baron beamed at him. 'Good! Shall we be permitted to see this article of yours when it's finished?'

'I don't see why not,' David told him. It seemed a safe, non-committal answer.

He went directly to Susan's room after breakfast; the launch would not be leaving for an hour, and he had work for Susan to do during his absence. But as usual Susan's fervour for detection did not match his own.

'We can't be *sure* Jan was murdered,' she objected. 'The police don't think he was, do they?'

'Of course they don't. No one does except us. But they would if they knew about the rope.'

'And you'll tell the police?'

'Not on your nelly! We're keeping this to ourselves until I'm good and ready.'

She doubted the wisdom of such a course, but she did not try to dissuade him. David could be stubborn. She said, 'It's incredible that anyone here could have murdered the poor man. And so deliberately, too.'

'It's incredible, all right. But it happened.'

'Ummm!' She still had her doubts. 'I wonder how he missed seeing that bolt thing. Would he have gone out in the boat, do you think, if he *had* seen it?'

'I wouldn't know.'

He had been wondering the same thing. It worried him slightly that he could not explain it. Even if Jan had not noticed the bolt before entering the boat, how could he have failed to see it while he was rowing? It would be slap in front of his eyes. Yet there must be an explanation. Jan Muzyk had most certainly been murdered.

'It may have been hidden by some of his gear,' he said. 'But quite obviously the board held while he was rowing. It must have come away later, when he was fishing. He wouldn't have his eye on it then. More likely he'd be facing out to sea.'

'Ummm!' Susan said again. She plumped herself down on the bed, and

142

smiled at him. 'Are you really putting to sea this morning, darling? Are you sure you'll be all right?'

'Of course I'll be all right. Or was that meant to be funny? And while I'm away you're going to be busy.'

'I know. I've promised to help in the kitchen. We can't both be drones.'

'I wasn't referring to your domestic chores. I want you to find out more about the boat — what it was like, who maintained it, did anyone use it other than Jan? When did he use it last before Friday? Who was bathing from the jetty that day? Things like that.'

'That all? You wouldn't like to know who killed him?' She got up from the bed and walked across to stand facing him. 'Has it occurred to you, darling, that if there *is* a murderer on the island inquisitiveness could be a very unhealthy occupation? Practically fatal, in fact.'

He brushed the objection aside.

'Not if you use tact. You don't have to snoop around like a female Sherlock Holmes. Inquisitiveness is natural in women; no one'll think anything of it. They might suspect me, but not you.'

'Meaning I look too dumb, eh? And on whom do I use the tact?'

'You could start with your fellow-domestics. A little below-stairs gossip. And there's always the Baron. The old lecher seems to fancy you.'

'Does that amaze you?'

'Not really. At his age one can't be choosy, I guess.' She aimed a slap at his face, but he caught her arm and held it. Laughing, he bent and kissed her. 'Now run along and get cracking. The spuds are waiting to be bashed.'

The door of his room was ajar when he reached it. He pushed it open, to see Tom standing by the window; he was gazing out to sea, his back to the door. Annoyed at the intrusion, David said, 'Is this a social call?'

The other man turned and grinned at him. He seemed quite unperturbed. 'Nice view you've got,' he said cheerfully.

'You came up to admire the view?'

'No. I came to tell you we're leaving in half an hour. But I've never been in this room before. Thought I'd have a look-see.'

When Tom had gone David sat down on the bed and considered what he should say to Snowball. Snowball could be tricky; he had no high opinion, David suspected, of David Wight's intelligence and ability, and if he thought there was a really big story about to break he might send down a more experienced reporter to handle it. The difficulty would be to wangle a few more days' absence out of the old devil without revealing just how big the story could be.

Before leaving he went down to see Susan. Because the kitchens had been built against the crest of the hill there was little natural light; the island had its own power-plant, recently installed, and electricity had replaced daylight. The walls were lined with an imposing array of cookers and mixers, of potato-peeler and dishwasher and refrigerator and deep-freeze. All part of the Olive Muzyk service, David suspected.

Susan was not there. Bessie was busy at the cooker, and Beryl was brushing a sports-jacket on the big table. She had turned out the pockets, and a pile of odds and ends bore testimony to her thoroughness.

To David the jacket looked familiar. 'Maurice's?' he hazarded.

'The Baron's,' Beryl said, still brushing. It was hot in the kitchen, and beads of perspiration glistened on her sallow skin and on the tiny hairs that shadowed her upper lip.

He eyed the odds and ends with casual disinterest. 'Looks like he uses the pockets as waste-baskets.'

Beryl shrugged. 'What man doesn't? Maurice is even worse. His pockets are more like dustbins. Everything goes into them.'

David wondered why Beryl, and not the Baroness, should act as Grevas's valet. 'Where's Susan?' he asked.

'In the scullery.'

Susan was peeling onions. Tears streamed from her eyes, and there were streaks in her make-up where she had rubbed her face with the back of her hand. 'They gave me this job on purpose,' she wailed. 'I know they did. They don't like me, so they're trying to humiliate me.'

'I've never seen you in an apron before,' David said. It was dirty, and far too big for her. 'Very fetching. It brings out the domestic appeal that was hitherto lacking. You should wear one more often.'

'Go away, damn you!' It was not only the onions that were responsible for her wretchedness. She was angry that she should have been allotted such an uncomfortable task, that David should see her so dishevelled. 'I hope the damned boat sinks.'

He knew better than to goad her further. Beryl and Bessie would be listening. 'It probably will,' he said. 'But make a good job of the lunch, just in case.' He lowered his voice. 'And go easy with the Baron. You don't know your own strength.'

The launch-party consisted of the Mackays and Tom Hampson. The sea was flat calm, and after the first few minutes, during which he kept anticipating the return of his former nausea, David began to enjoy the trip. The launch was modern and clean, and free of the smells which had added to his discomfort on the previous crossing. He sat in the stern with Jutter and watched Andrew steer the boat, with Tom crouched forward on the cabin roof, his bald head gleaming like an elderly billiard-ball.

Jutter looked particularly lovely, David thought. She wore a blue pleated skirt and a white figure-hugging woollen jersey, its low-cut circular neckline displaying the beauty of her neck and shoulders. Except when she spoke he did not think of her as German; he had had the impression that all true Teutons were blonde. Jutter, with her jet-black hair and her olive skin and expressive eyes, her flat little ears sporting long, hooped earrings, looked more like a beautiful gipsy than the daughter of a former Nazi.

He said, looking at the earrings, 'I thought jewellery was out.'

'It is.' She sat erect, her head thrown back to catch the faint breeze that the motion of the launch brought to them. 'These are just trinkets. They don't count.' She turned to look at him. 'Did you say you were going to telephone your editor?'

'Yes. I'm hoping he'll allow me a few more days down here.'

Her dark eyes narrowed. 'Is that because of what has happened since you arrived? Jan's cigarette-case, I mean, and that horrible dead rat. Are you trying to make something sensational out of us?'

'Of course not,' he assured her, knowing that he was. 'Although indirectly they're responsible, I suppose. You've all been so preoccupied that I haven't been able to get on with the job. Apart from what Maurice and the Baron told us when we arrived, I've learnt absolutely nothing. I'm getting to know you as people, that's all.'

'What more is there to know?'

'Plenty.' He spread his arms in an all-embracing gesture. To complete it he had to raise one arm above her head. He let it fall on the seat behind her. 'What made you join the Baron, what you believe in, what you expect to achieve. Not as a group, but as individuals. You, for instance. Why are you here?'

'To be with Andrew, of course. It's my wifely duty. And pleasure.'

'And is that the only reason? You've no personal beliefs?'

She considered this before replying, her eyes on her husband's broad back.

'I don't think so. Not in the sense you mean. But I believe in Andrew, and he believes in the Baron. That's good enough for me.'

It was also good enough for David.

When they reached the quay he walked up the steep hill with the others to the small modern shopping-centre. But the Mackays were not stopping in Littleport; the community kept a car there, and they were going on to Lingford in it to do the bulk of the shopping, leaving Tom to make the local purchases. 'The choice is too limited,' Andrew explained. 'Tom's about the only one who shops here. He seems to like the place. Can't think why; the lower town is picturesque enough, but there's nothing up here to attract anyone. How about you? Will you stay with Tom, or are you coming with us?'

David elected to go with them. He could telephone Snowball as easily from Lingford as from Littleport, and if the islanders shopped mainly in Lingford that was where he wanted to be. One of them had bought a length of nylon rope, possibly recently. It was not a strong lead, but it was the only lead he had.

It looked an even weaker lead when he saw the size of the town. Lingford was bigger than he had anticipated. To inquire at all the likely shops would take more time than he had at his disposal. Luck would have to be with him if he were to meet with success. And first he had to telephone Snowball.

'On to something?' Snowball bellowed, his voice almost bursting the diaphragm of the receiver. 'You should have been on to it and over it by now. I'm expecting you back this evening. To-morrow morning at the latest.'

'Impossible,' David said firmly. He heard the other clear his throat preparatory to blasting him off the wire, and added quickly, 'If I come back now you'll get only milk-and-water stuff. Give me another day or two and you'll really have something. Provided I get the breaks, of course.'

'You'd better,' Snowball growled. 'I don't pay you to gambol by the sea. What's the story?'

'Too tricky over the phone,' David said. 'But it's there. Just a matter of getting it. And don't worry about expense. We're staying on the island as the Baron's guests.'

'We? Who the hell have you got with you?'

'Just a friend.' David cursed himself for the slip. Now he would have to stand Susan's train fare himself. Snowball was tight on expenses. 'Good cover.'

'Good what?' David repeated it. 'Oh! Thought you said 'lover'.' There was a pause while Snowball considered. 'All right. I'll give you till Friday. And the Lord help you if you fail me. That all?'

'Not quite, sir. You mentioned a swindle in which Grevas was implicated some years back. Can you give me the names of any of the victims?'

'Hang on a minute.'

David hung on. It had occurred to him that some one on the island might have a grudge against the Baron, was trying to wreck his project by fomenting trouble and suspicion; although to murder an apparently innocent third party seemed to be overplaying the grudge to extremes. But one never knew. A fanatic . . .

'I can give you two,' Snowball told him. 'Jacob Steinberg, a Jew, and a fellow named Wall. Any help?'

'Could be.' At the word 'Jew' David's grip on the receiver had tightened. 'What happened to them?'

'Steinberg committed suicide. The other chap is probably dead too. He was over seventy at the time.'

David thanked him and replaced the receiver. Since he had had little faith in the theory he was not greatly disappointed at this abrupt end to it.

The callbox was on a corner of the carpark, near the centre of the High Street. David decided to work outward from there. The murderer could have had no reason to go far afield for his rope. He would try the first suitable shop he came to.

David did the same. He had brought a piece of the rope with him, but the assistant did not recognize it. 'We could order it for you, of course,' he said. 'Or we have the ordinary hemp rope in stock. What did you want it for, sir?'

David found that difficult to answer. He said, 'I don't know. It's not for me, you see. A friend of mine recently bought some in Lingford, and he asked me to get some more. Unfortunately, he couldn't remember the name of the shop.'

The assistant shook his head. 'He didn't buy it here, sir. We don't stock it.'

On his way down the High Street David passed the police-station, and a pang of doubt assailed him. By withholding evidence from the police he was playing a dangerous game; discovery could mean real trouble. Snowball couldn't help him; and even if he could he probably wouldn't. Yet to back out now was unthinkable. He had to go on. This was his big opportunity, the scoop he had dreamed about.

At the next shop he repeated his story. And this time his luck was in. The assistant recognized the rope at once, and produced a similar coil to prove it.

'You're sure it's the same?' David asked, fingering it. He was uncertain of the next step.

'Quite sure, sir.' The man looked at him. 'Is your friend from Shere Island? I remember selling them a similar coil to this about a week ago.'

This was better than he had dared to hope. He said eagerly, 'You don't remember the name, I suppose?'

'Of course. But — ' The man paused, looking over David's shoulder. 'Here's your friend now, sir.'

David turned. Behind him, staring at the rope with a puzzled frown on her beautiful face, stood Jutter Mackay.

9

They did not keep Susan long in the kitchen. And they were sympathetic about the onions. 'But some one had to do them,' Beryl said; 'and you did ask to help.'

Bessie watched her as she washed her face. As she handed Susan the towel she said, 'You've got nice hands.' She looked at her own, turning them over and over as though seeing them for the first time, and shook her head. 'Not like mine. Black hands never look nice, do they? Just dirty. I think it's the nails.'

Susan gave her back the towel. Privately she agreed with Bessie; there was something about the girl's pink palms and pink nails that gave her a faint twinge of nausea. But she said, 'Mine are too podgy,' and lifted them to her nose. 'Phew! What a pong! And after all that soap and water too. How long before I cease to smell like a drain?'

Bessie laughed, her teeth sparkling. Whatever had troubled her at breakfast was apparently forgotten. 'Come for a walk. The sea-air will blow it away.'

It was difficult to resist Bessie's charm. David had discovered that; now it was Susan's turn. They went down the terraces in front of the house, and then turned right and picked their way through the boulder-strewn gorse and fern to the western side of the island. They formed an ill-assorted pair. Bessie was back in the old grey jersey and orange skirt, her bare feet apparently impervious to stone and thorn. They were not pretty feet; the toes were spread and the nails ragged. Susan, her auburn head a good six inches lower than the dark curls of the young Negress, was less sensibly attired in the blue linen suit she had worn on the journey. In his desire for her company David had craftily misrepresented both the Baron and his island, and she had come prepared for a riviera-style holiday surrounded by luxury and with servants to wait on her. The linen suit was the most serviceable garb in her wardrobe. And at least she had thought to bring sandals.

Gradually Susan's resentment left her, and she began to respond to her companion's cheerful and often naïve chatter. They talked about themselves; they had so little in common, knew so little of the kind of life the other had led, that in both of them was an intense curiosity. But when they had reached the shore and had begun to plough their way back along the shingle, their feet sinking into the damp pebbles, Susan was reminded of the task David had given her. She could see the jetty, gradually lengthening in her sight as they rounded the south-west corner of the island. Less than a week ago there had been a boat riding alongside the jetty. But some one, David affirmed, had murdered Jan Muzyk. So now there was no boat, and no Jan Muzyk.

She stopped to remove a pebble from her sandal, and stood for a while staring at the jetty.

'People forget so quickly,' she said. 'It makes one feel terribly insignificant. I like to think that my own death will matter tremendously to a great many people, but I don't suppose it will. They'll forget it as quickly as everyone here seems to have forgotten Jan's.'

Bessie nodded. 'Like dropping a stone into water,' she said. 'It makes a big splash and a lot of ripples, but the water is soon still again. Only here I don't think Jan is forgotten.'

'Not forgotten, perhaps. But his absence doesn't seem to matter. Not even to Olive.' Bessie made no comment on this, and as they walked on Susan said, 'It seems particularly sad that he should have been drowned so close to the shore. He never ventured far, did he?' Bessie shook her head. 'Was it rough that evening?'

'No. When it was rough he didn't go fishing. He couldn't swim.'

'And on fine evenings?'

'Most fine evenings, yes.'

'Was he out the evening before?'

'Oh, yes. And the evening before that. Why?'

It was not a suspicious query, but Susan hastened to reassure her. 'If the boat had been lying idle for some time it might have sprung a leak or something. But obviously that didn't happen. Not if it was in daily use. So I suppose he just fell in. Is that the general opinion?'

'Perhaps. I don't know.'

Susan remembered that when the topic had been raised the previous evening only Myerson had advanced an opinion, which Maurice had immediately discredited. But surely they must have discussed it many times before? She said, 'The boat was rather a ramshackle affair, wasn't it? Home-made, Maurice said.'

'Yes.'

Was Bessie growing wary? Susan decided it was time to abandon that line of inquiry; use tact, David had cautioned her, and don't appear to be snooping. 'Probably no one will ever know exactly what did happen,' she said. 'And in a way it's not really important, is it? It can't alter the fact that he's dead. What sort of a man was he, Bessie?'

The black girl's former cheerfulness returned, and she flashed her white bright smile. It was as though a light had suddenly been switched on inside her.

'Tall, and a little fat. His face was red, and he had thick yellow hair. Sometimes he was gay, but often he sulked.'

'You didn't like him?'

'Oh, yes. I liked him very much.' She smiled to herself. 'So did most of the other women.'

'But not the men, eh?'

'Not much. Except Harold. He liked him — I think.'

Susan wondered at that final qualification. But how significant was it that Jan had been popular with the women and unpopular with the men? Could that be why he had been murdered? Had Andrew or Maurice or Myerson been the jealous husband, or Olive the jealous wife? No doubt David would also include Grevas; he would argue that Jan could have been the Baron's rival in his pursuit of one of the women. But then David was prejudiced; Snowball (was that really the man's name?) had seen to that. For herself, she would accept the Baron as she found him. And so far she had found him charming.

When Bessie left her, saying she had work to do in the house, Susan walked to the end of the jetty and sat gazing unseeing at the horizon, her mind pondering the problem that was Bessie. Bessie had youth and vitality and looks; clearly she was attractive to men, she would not have to search for a husband. Why, then, had she married that bad-tempered little Jew? For money? Because he was white? To get away from Jamaica? There was little evidence of love or affection. It was difficult, too, to understand why Myerson had married Bessie. Whatever was between them in private, in public he treated her with the same contempt he accorded the other women.

She was so lost in meditation that she did not hear the Baron's step behind her. When he laid a hand lightly on her shoulder she almost fell into the water.

'Peaceful, isn't it' he said. 'And to me somehow symbolic. How sad that there have to be storms!'

'Storms can be exciting.'

His hand was firm on her arm as he lifted her to her feet. 'So can wars, unfortunately.'

He was undeniably distinguished, she

thought; not only in looks, but in his bearing. Yesterday, it was true, a little of his composure, if not his dignity, had seemed to desert him. Yet that was understandable; he had had a trying evening. It was even welcome. It added humanity to nobility.

As they strolled back to the beach he said, 'I'm going across to the north jetty to meet the launch-party. They'll be well laden. Care to come with me?'

'As a porter?'

'As a companion. We'll leave the porterage to chance.'

She had no real wish to go. She was unused to exercise, and walking on the shingle with Bessie had tired her. But the Baron intrigued her; she had had no previous opportunity to be alone with him, to discover him as a man. And David had said to talk with him if she could.

'I'm flattered,' she said. 'But may we take it easy? I've walked a fair way already this morning.'

He nodded. 'I know. With Bessie, eh? I wonder what you two found in common.'

'Not much,' she admitted. 'That made

it the more interesting.'

They took it easy. They did not go up the hill past the house, but round by the east side of the island. Here the cliffs were high. As they walked Susan could see across the water to the mainland, with its pastel greens and blues and greys hazy behind a thin sea-mist. But presently the path led into the trees, and the far shore lost its identity and continuity, becoming a vague background to the sharp, clear lines of the firs.

'How do you like it here?' he asked.

'Heavenly. So peaceful.' And it is peaceful, she thought; Jan's death doesn't alter that. 'I'll hate the noise and bustle of London after this. For a while, anyway,' she added truthfully.

'H'm! I was referring to the fauna rather than the flora. I fancy your friend David regards us as cranks. Do you?'

It was a difficult question to answer tactfully and yet with honesty. Grevas himself she believed to be an idealist, no matter what David might say or think. But what of the others? And was an idealist akin to a crank?

164

'It depends on the ideal,' he said, when she put that to him. 'If it is completely unattainable, yes. Not otherwise.'

'Isn't that a matter of opinion? The attainability, I mean?'

'Perhaps. But here at least we have no doubts. We *must* succeed. The alternative is annihilation.'

After that they walked for a while in silence. It was cool among the trees, and although she found it difficult to keep up with him she did not protest when he quickened his pace. But presently she asked breathlessly, 'Have you no aims other than world peace?'

'Peace is the ultimate objective. The immediate is that we learn to love one another. It is the essential basis.'

'Love.' She repeated the word, savouring it. 'It has so many different forms, hasn't it? There's no end to them.'

'No end,' he agreed. 'But it's the beginning that's important. And the form doesn't matter, so long as it's sincere.'

Susan could see Harold Myerson in the rough ground above the chicken-run; he was gazing across the island, apparently lost in meditation. Suddenly he turned. Bessie came running down through the gardens; Susan could hear her shouting his name. For a brief moment they talked together. Then they went quickly back up the hill towards the house.

How long will that marriage last? she wondered. But she was not greatly interested in the Myersons, and summoning up her courage she said, 'I hope this doesn't sound frightfully inquisitive, but is it true that you're an advocate of free love?'

He did not seem annoyed.

'Free love, eh? An odd expression, that. As though love could be other than free. I suppose you got that from David?'

'It's just a rumour,' she answered weakly.

'And not the only one. No, I don't advocate it. But neither do I denounce it. I'm not a churchman, you see. I believe that genuine love should never be suppressed.'

'Not even if it cuts across marriage?'

'Not even then, provided no third person is harmed.' He took her arm to guide her round a muddy patch. 'Don't misunderstand me, my dear. I'm not opposing marriage. For the great majority it is right. But for a small minority it is wrong; it can destroy love rather than strengthen it. Don't you agree?'

'I don't know,' she said.

And it was true; she did not know. She supposed herself to be a Christian, although not an active one. I'm a modern, she had always told herself when the topic of free love had been raised. I don't indulge in it myself because I'm not attracted, but that doesn't mean I disapprove of it in others. I've no moral objections.

That was what she had told herself. Yet always there had been a nagging suspicion that she was deceiving herself, that her objections were not only moral, but prudish and Victorian.

She had that suspicion now.

They were back on the rude track, but the Baron still held her arm. 'It's my turn to be inquisitive,' he said. 'Are you in love with David?'

'I don't know that either,' she admitted.

'Ah!' He sighed. 'Then you're not.'

He held her arm more tightly, pressing it against his side. Gently she tried to free herself; but at the first slight tug she felt the pressure of his fingers increase, and at once she desisted. If he were growing suddenly amorous she had no wish to force an issue. But her heart beat more quickly, and she wished she had been more emphatic on David and free love.

They walked on slowly, and she stole a glance at his face. It had a set expression. His jaw looked aggressive, his lips were closed in a thin line; she guessed that his teeth were clenched. Drops of moisture had formed on his brow and on his upper lip; his nostrils flared as he breathed noisily through them, his cheeks were lined and grey. And suddenly Susan was frightened. Frightened and disgusted. The glamour that had hitherto surrounded him was gone. He no longer seemed handsome and distinguished; he was old and ugly and repulsive.

In a panic she tore her arm away and turned off the path to walk quickly out of the trees. In the open, she thought, he won't dare to touch me.

He did not try to stop her. She heard his footsteps behind her; but there was no urgent threat in them, and she did not look round. The long grass was wet, and the ground uneven. Of necessity she had to go slowly, picking her way, and in a few strides he was beside her.

Susan shivered involuntarily. 'Chilly?' he asked pleasantly.

He seemed completely at ease. His face was relaxed, no longer grey and sweating; there was a slight smile on his lips. Susan's panic left her. She even wondered if she could have been mistaken, if she had magnified the incident out of proportion. Then she saw his eyes, and knew there had been no mistake.

All right, she thought. If he wants to play it cool so will I.

'A little,' she said. 'But it's warmer out here. Only I wish the grass wasn't so wet; my feet are soaking already. Oh, look! There are the others. We'd better hurry.'

'Take it easy over this bit,' he warned. 'It's rough going.'

The launch-party were half-way across

169

the pasture by the time Susan reached them. Frightened and disgusted as she had been by the Baron's behaviour, she had been glad of his company as they made their way through the scattered cows. When one of the animals began to trot towards her with a look in its eyes of what seemed to Susan the acme of male-volence, she had even clutched the Baron's arm, terror predominant. He had smiled at her and patted her hand. But he had not attempted to take advantage of her panic.

'We've left some of the stuff on the jetty,' Andrew said. 'There was too much for us to carry.'

Grevas nodded. 'Susan and I will pick it up. That's why we're here.'

Jutter's eyes wandered from him to the girl. There was a quizzical smile on her face that annoyed Susan. 'You came a long way round,' she said.

David gave the Baron no time to reply. He said quickly, 'You take my load, sir, and I'll go back to the jetty with Susan.'

'Very well.' If Grevas was annoyed at this interference in his plans he did not show it. 'Did your editor agree to your staying?'

'He wasn't enthusiastic. But I think we can work it.'

As they entered the wood Susan gripped David's arm in gratitude. She knew it was not concern for her that had prompted him to take Grevas's place; he had done so simply because he wanted to talk to her away from the others. But for her the result was the same. It was unlikely that the Baron would have made a second attempt; had he been really determined he would not have let her break away from his grasp so easily. Nevertheless, it was good to be with David.

He looked at her in surprise as he felt the pressure of her fingers. 'Why the sudden surge of affection?' he asked. 'Have I been away that long?'

She rubbed her auburn head against the upper part of his arm; she could not reach his shoulder. The rough woollen jersey smelt of seawater and (strangely) decay, but she did not find it unpleasant. Rather the reverse. She was suddenly aware of what she had long suspected — that she was in love with David. And it was no longer the friendly, almost sisterly affection she had had for him ever since they were children together. This was a new kind of love; both tender and passionate, pain as well as pleasure. It did not matter (come to think of it, it never had mattered) that he was untidy and unkempt, that his nose was too pointed and his mouth too big and his teeth wickedly uneven, that he was flippant and stubborn and unpunctual and casual. She loved him, and that was that. It always would be that.

What a hell of a fix for a girl to be in, she thought ruefully. Here am I, willing and eager to marry money and wallow in luxury, and I have to fall for David.

'Don't get ideas,' she said, wondering if her voice sounded different. 'It's more relief than affection. I'm just glad that you're young and — and wholesome. I find I don't like old men.'

He stopped at that, a wide grin on his face.

'Oho! Made a pass at you, did he? How

172

did you make out? Still the innocent virgin?'

She drew away from him. 'I'm touched at your obvious concern,' she said coldly. But she could never be angry with David for long, and certainly not now. 'To be honest, I may have misjudged him. But I *thought* it was a pass.' She smiled. 'Not a very determined one, thank goodness! I didn't have to fight for my honour, if that interests you.'

'It does,' he said. 'Tell me the crude details.'

She knew his concern was that of the journalist, not of the man. An open break with the Baron would have forced them to leave the island before David was ready. But she did not care; she was too happy in his company. So she told him, and he listened, making occasional wisecracks. And afterwards, because she knew it would interest him most, she told him of her talk with Bessie.

He frowned. 'Didn't get much, did you?' he said, impatiently pushing the lank hair from his forehead, only for it to flop forward again. 'Obviously the boat sank too fast for Jan to get back to the jetty. Or he may have panicked and lost his oars. I wonder what happened to them. They should have been picked up.'

'It's a big ocean,' Susan said.

'And another thing.' His thoughts were running too fast to assimilate sarcasm. 'He must have almost busted himself shouting for help. Why didn't anyone hear him? He wasn't far out. Did Bessie say which way the wind was blowing?'

'I didn't ask.'

'H'm!' They had reached the beach, and crunched their way across the pebbles to the jetty, on which several packages were stacked. 'We ought to know that. It could be important.'

She held out her arms, and absent-mindedly he began to load them with packages. Staggering under their weight, she said weakly, 'Do you think you could manage one or two yourself? They're rather heavy.'

'Eh? Oh, sorry. I wasn't thinking.'

He removed the top two packages, and turned to make his way up the beach. Susan followed. She suspected that his load was lighter than her own, but she did not complain. Her delight in his company was still with her.

On the way back to the house he told her what Snowball had said, and of his visits to the ironmongers of Lingford. When she heard that it was Jutter who had bought the rope she nearly dropped her packages in astonishment.

'Jutter? You mean Jutter killed him?'

He shook his head. 'She didn't buy it for herself. Or so she said. Some one asked her to get it.'

She could not understand his gloom. If some one had asked Jutter to buy the rope, then that some one had killed Jan. The quest was over.

'Give, darling, give!' she pleaded. 'Who was it?'

He grunted. 'You can cut the excitement. It was Jan himself.'

10

The clouds started to bank up after lunch. The sun shone fitfully through the gaps, but Susan was glad of her cardigan as she waited on the terrace. With the exception of David the household was indoors. And it was for David she was waiting. Not for his presence, but for the sound of his voice.

For Susan the meal had at first been something of an ordeal. Should she sit at the Baron's end of the table, as she had hitherto done, or should she pointedly move to the other end? She had compromised by sitting in the middle, and had watched him surreptitiously for any sign of guilt. But she had seen none. He was quiet, certainly; but when he spoke to her, as he did once or twice, his manner had been normal and pleasantly friendly.

She wondered again if she had misinterpreted his behaviour.

The talk had been mostly of Beryl, who was absent. Beryl, it seemed, had had a narrow escape from what might have been a fatal accident. With the intention of cleaning some of the windows, Maurice had left a ladder propped against the house; and for some reason which none seemed able or willing to explain, Beryl had climbed it. Near the top a rung had snapped; as Beryl had clutched wildly at the rung above the ladder had slipped sideways, and she had clung there, unable to regain her footing. Had Bessie not heard her screams and summoned Maurice and Myerson to the rescue, she would have fallen the thirty feet or so to the terrace.

That was why Bessie had come running for her husband, thought Susan, remembering. But why didn't I hear Beryl cry out? The Baron hadn't started the funny business then.

She was still listening for the sound of David's voice when Maurice joined her on the terrace. He wore rugger shorts and a polo-necked sweater, with a towel slung over his shoulder.

'It doesn't look like bathing weather to me,' Susan said, glancing up at the darkening sky. 'And isn't it too soon after lunch? You'll get cramp.'

He laughed, showing dimples in his cheeks which she had not noticed before. How fascinating, she thought, in such a virile-looking man! As he stood gazing idly out to sea she admired him dreamily. His close-cropped brown hair was faintly tinged with grey at the temples; there was pride and assurance in the hooked nose and the firm, almost aggressive jaw. His bronzed legs, covered thickly with hair, looked strong and muscular; broad at the thighs, and bulging at the calves. Above all, he was tall. Well over six feet, she thought, craning her neck to look up at him.

'Come and keep an eye on me, then,' he suggested.

She shivered. 'No, thank you! I'd be no use, anyway. I can't swim.'

He stared at her quizzically, heavy eyebrows cocked.

'No? In that case I'll push off. I've a busy afternoon ahead of me. There are

178

still those damned windows to clean, and I have to mend the ladder first.'

She watched him go nimbly down the terraces, moving swiftly and agilely for such a big man. He had nearly reached the trees when she saw him stop. But he was not still for long. In another moment he was running towards the cliff, the towel streaming behind him.

Susan giggled. I suppose I should have tried to stop him, she thought. David's going to be absolutely livid.

*   *   *

David was more embarrassed than livid. As he watched Maurice come belting down the cliff path his main concern was how to convince the other that he was neither a fool nor a suspicious busybody.

At the foot of the path Maurice paused. He was too far off for David to see the expression on his face, but he could imagine it; there would be incredulity, swiftly followed by anger. As Maurice slung the towel over his shoulder and strode purposefully down the jetty towards him, David braced himself for the onslaught.

'What the hell are you playing at?' Maurice demanded. 'Have you gone stark loco, man, or did you think that was funny?'

David shook his head. 'I'm sorry. I thought you'd all be indoors, that if anyone heard me it would be Susan.'

'But what was the big idea? Why bawl for help when you don't need it?'

'It was an experiment.' This wasn't going to be easy. There was no way out but the truth, and the truth might not be palatable. It would need toning down. 'I realized that when Jan's boat started to sink and he knew he was for it he must have shouted for help. I couldn't understand why no one heard him; he wasn't far out. So I got Susan to stand up there on the terrace and listen. If she couldn't hear me — well, that explained it.' He shook his head. 'I'm surprised she didn't warn you.'

'She didn't hear you, that's why. Neither did I until I was half-way here.' He still looked angry. 'Are you suggesting that we might have heard Jan's call for help and ignored it?'

'Of course not.'

'Then what was the point of the experiment? I don't get it.'

'I don't blame you. It was just a damned silly idea that hit me, and I acted on it without thinking. I'm sorry.'

'It was silly, all right.'

David waited for more, but Maurice was frowning past him at the sea. A cross-wind had sprung up, whipping the crests of the waves, and as they slapped against the jetty the spray cascaded down on the two men. David wanted to be gone. But he also wanted to conciliate Maurice, so he said feebly, 'Yes. Yes, it was. How's Beryl?'

'Recovering. She wasn't hurt. Merely shocked.'

'I bet she was. It must have been a near thing. Have you managed to discover what prompted her to climb the ladder?'

'She says she got fed up waiting for me to clean the windows, and decided to make a start on them herself.' Maurice shrugged. 'Frankly, I think it was just an impulse. Like Everest, the ladder was there to be climbed. So she climbed it.'

'Could be,' David agreed. 'Did you know the ladder was dicky?'

'I don't think it is, apart from that one rung. It's always borne my weight. But I'll check up on it before using it again. We don't want any more accidents.'

'No. We seem to have brought you bad luck, Susan and I.'

'It started before you came,' Maurice said gloomily, and David knew he was referring to Jan. 'But I can't say you've improved it.'

David watched him peel off his clothes and dive in; he was an expert and powerful swimmer, and moved smoothly and fast through the water. A pity you weren't around when Jan Muzyk needed help, David thought, as he turned to walk back to the house.

Susan was in the library. To David's surprise, Beryl was there too. They were seated together on a settee.

'Quite recovered?' he asked Beryl.

'Yes, thank you.'

'Must have given you a nasty jolt. Did

the rung snap, or just come away?'

'I don't know,' she said. 'But I'd have been all right, I think, if the ladder hadn't slipped. I couldn't regain my footing.' She gave a fleeting smile. 'Anyway, it was entirely my own fault. In future I shall give stray ladders a miss.'

David smiled back. She had put on a green silk dress that clung to her body, and he was agreeably surprised to see that her figure was good. There was lipstick on her lips, and she had arranged her hair so that it partially concealed the squareness of her face. If only she could do something about her skin, he thought, she'd be quite attractive. And if falling off ladders peps her up like this she ought to do it more often.

'I should,' he agreed.

Susan said, 'We've been having a long natter about the Baron. Beryl thinks he's next door to a saint.'

'Oh? That must be nice for the saint.'

Neither girl smiled at this flippancy, and David mumbled an apology. A slight flush on her sallow cheeks, Beryl said quietly, 'Susan is exaggerating. But I'm sure he's a good man. Otherwise I wouldn't have stayed here.'

David sat down, wondering what hidden meaning lay in that last remark. He said, 'But isn't that the general opinion? Don't they all think he's a good man?'

She seemed distressed by the question. 'I hope they do,' she said, 'but sometimes I doubt it. There is too much bickering, too much argument; I've even heard them question his motives. It isn't right. If they don't believe in him and what he is trying to do they shouldn't be here. It upsets him, and it upsets those of us who trust him — as I do. And there can be no peace without trust.'

Spoken like the Baron's mouthpiece, David thought. And spoken so passionately that no one could doubt her sincerity.

'A desire for peace isn't the prerogative of the few,' he told her. 'It's almost universal, however little effort is made to achieve it. If your friends have doubts it must be on account of the Baron's methods, not his motives.'

She shook her head. 'They doubt both,' she asserted. 'Or it seems to me they do.'

'In what way?'

But she was not prepared to be specific. Nor was she prepared to say who 'they' were. 'You mustn't think there's a conspiracy against him,' she said, perhaps regretting her disclosures. 'There isn't. But none of them is as dedicated as he is, you see. They don't always understand him, and that makes them suspicious. And how can he succeed in that sort of atmosphere?'

All this equivocation, David thought irritably. He said, 'But what do they suspect him *of*? Fraud? Do they think he's in it for the lolly?'

She was shocked by his bluntness. 'Oh, no! No one has ever suggested *that*. At least, not since — '

The abruptness with which she cut short the sentence told David all he wanted to know. 'Not since Jan died' was what she would have said had not belated discretion stopped her. Jan had been suspicious, had been unwise enough to voice his suspicions too loudly. Was that why he had died? Had Grevas killed him because he was getting warm?

'You're on the wrong track, darling,' Susan said. 'Beryl wasn't referring to finance. It's sex that's troubling her, not cash.'

Before Beryl could protest a man's voice said crisply, 'You on your hobby horse again, Beryl? You might have spared our visitors that.'

David turned. 'Hallo, Maurice,' he said. 'That was quick. Water too chilly?'

'Water too damned wet.' Maurice waved a hand at the window. 'You may not have noticed it, but it's raining. I was all right, but my clothes were not.' He passed a hand over his damp hair and came farther into the room. 'What has my wife been telling you about the Baron's sex life, Susan? Nothing shocking, I hope.'

'Susan is impervious to shock,' David murmured, relieved that Maurice had recovered his good humour. Susan glared at him. But it was Beryl who rose to protest. She said, with true Welsh fire in her normally quiet voice, 'That's

186

despicable, Maurice. You make it sound crude and — and dirty. And it's not like that at all. You know it isn't.'

Her husband stared at her for a moment without replying, his strong fingers mechanically twisting the ring on his little finger. It was as though he were seeing her for the first time, for his eyes dwelt speculatively on her troubled face and then moved slowly away.

'Of course it isn't. I'm sorry.' All trace of sarcasm had vanished from his voice. He turned to Susan. 'That's a fair example of what my wife complains of. We all believe in the Baron and what he's trying to do, but we can't resist the occasional dig. I suppose it's a form of jealousy; jealousy of the imperfect for the perfect. Not that Grevas is perfect; merely less imperfect than the rest of us. With the possible exception of my wife.' He smiled fondly, almost proudly, at Beryl. 'If we all had her faith peace might be considerably nearer than it is.'

Beryl said nothing. She seemed to be in the grip of some deep emotion, and walked away to stand by the window, hiding her face from them. David, although he had a shrewd idea of what was in Maurice's mind, pretended to be puzzled.

'I don't get it. What's all this about the Baron's sex life?' Maurice shrugged his broad shoulders.

'Nothing sensational, I'm afraid. It's just that the Baron happens to be attractive to women, and my wife thinks that some of them give way to the attraction instead of resisting it. In other words, they run after him.'

How far do they run? wondered David. And how fast? Recalling Susan's account of her morning walk with the Baron, he looked at her quizzically. She gave him a slight ironic smile and a quick shake of the head, as if to say, 'I don't believe a word of it; it's the Baron who's doing the running. I should know. But don't let's be beastly about it. We'll keep it to ourselves.'

'Do you agree with her?' David asked.

'Not really. It was true at first, perhaps, although neither he nor they took it seriously, I fancy. But it didn't last. He's considerably older than most of them, and shy where women are concerned. It would take a determined woman to break down his reserve.' Susan stared at him, goggle-eyed. Did he really believe that? 'In a way it's a pity none of them has tried. It's what he needs, I think. He's a very lonely man.'

'He has his wife,' David said.

'Yes. But although the Baroness is a fine woman she's more of a Martha than a Mary. A good organizer, but lacking in the softer characteristics.' Maurice shrugged. 'I could be wrong, of course.'

I'd say you're dead right, David thought. But he kept the thought to himself. Beryl was less reticent. 'It's true,' she said eagerly, turning to face them with the faint trace of tears on her face. 'She's hard. I think she'd like to be softer, more — more feminine, but she doesn't know how.' She sighed. 'Poor man. You're right, Maurice. He must be very lonely.'

Maurice smiled at her. 'Most leaders are lonely men,' he said sententiously. 'Don't let's get sentimental about it.'

Tom Hampson came into the room,

yawning prodigiously. His upper dentures dropped with a faint clatter, and he snapped his mouth shut to prevent their complete escape. 'I overdone the kip,' he said, rubbing his eyes with the knuckles of his bony fingers. 'Anyone seen Andrew?'

'Probably still got his head down,' Maurice suggested. 'He was up bright and early this morning.' He picked up his towel and slung it round his neck. 'Well, I must away to the barn. That damned ladder still has to be repaired before I can get cracking on the windows.'

'I'll give you a hand,' David said.

The ladder lay on the floor of the barn, a long stone building to the south east of the house. Maurice lifted the narrow end, swivelling it round to rest on the bench. 'I'm not much of a carpenter,' he said, gazing blankly at the gap where the missing rung had been. 'How does one fit a new rung without taking the whole damned thing to pieces?'

David admitted that he didn't know; he was no carpenter himself. 'It must have snapped in the middle,' he said, poking a finger into the empty holes. 'Where are the pieces?'

'Probably still on the terrace.'

After some discussion they decided the only feasible plan was to drill a hole in one of the uprights and push the new rung through it into position, securing the exposed end with nail or screw. While Maurice wrestled with a spoke-shave, clumsily fashioning the new rung, David explored the barn. Its original use was obscure, but now it was both workshop and general storeroom. One end was lined with laden shelves, beneath which were stacked drums of oil and kerosene. At the other end stood the workbench, to one side of which was piled a varied assortment of junk. Two Lee-Enfield rifles, obviously well cared for, stood in a rack opposite the big doors.

'Who do the rifles belong to?' David asked.

'Harold,' Maurice said, without turning round. 'He's a crack shot. This wood's ruddy tough.'

David came over to have a look.

'Maybe the blade wants sharpening,' he suggested.

'Maybe.' Maurice sighed. 'I should have got Tom or Harold on to this. They're the experts.'

David commiserated with him in his struggle. But there was nothing he could do to help, and presently he wandered out into the open. The air was warm and heavy and still. The shower that had interrupted Maurice's bathe had ceased, but black clouds were banking up to the south-west, and he wondered if they were in for another storm. From the walled garden came the sound of a spade striking against stone. That'll be Andrew, he thought; no one but Andrew would engage in manual labour on such a sultry afternoon. Briefly he considered the idea of joining him, and quickly dismissed it. There might be a spare spade he would be expected to handle.

As he neared the western end of the house he paused. This was where the ladder had been. But there was no broken rung on the terrace, and idly he began to search the bushes beyond. It was not an easy search. The bushes were thick and the weeds plentiful, and the ground was heavy and moist. Briars tore at his clothes, and his hands became wet and muddy from scrabbling among the roots. But without quite knowing why he persisted.

When eventually his persistence was rewarded he found that his search had taken him some distance from the house; the rung must have been picked up and thrown away. He took it on to the terrace to examine it. From there, after careful deliberation, he went back to the barn.

Maurice was struggling with a brace and bit. 'Come and hold this blasted ladder for me,' he said. 'It keeps slipping.'

David slapped the old rung down on the bench. 'I found it in the bushes,' he said. 'Take a look at it.'

Maurice picked it up. 'Snapped off at the end, eh? I wonder why. The wood looks sound enough.'

'Not snapped off. Sawn off.'

David had been about to add that some one on Shere Island was obviously handy with a saw, but remembered in time that

193

Jan's murder was still his secret. His and Susan's.

Maurice stared at him in surprise. Then he inserted one end of the rung into its hole in the ladder and, while David watched, forced the other end into position. It looked to be safely secured; although it turned easily in its sockets when Maurice twisted it, there was no play. He gave it a sharp tug, and it came away in his hand.

'You see?' David said. 'Your wife's fall was no accident. It was deliberately planned.'

Maurice shook his head. He was still staring at the rung in his hand.

'No one — not even I — could have known Beryl would climb the ladder. It was pure chance. But every one knew *I* would.' His voice and face were grim. 'This little trap was set for me.'

11

Susan went to bed early that evening. It had been an exacting day; never had she walked so far or suffered so much nervous tension. But she was not allowed to sleep. For over an hour David sat on her bed and propounded innumerable hypotheses, to most of which neither could offer a solution.

'It beats me why they stay here,' he said eventually. 'Originally they may have been possessed of a burning desire to love their fellow-men, but they haven't got it now. The place is rife with suspicion and mistrust. Not to mention murder and dead rats and a stolen cigarette-case and attempted rape and a broken ladder.'

He rattled off the indictments and paused for breath.

'If you're referring to Grevas and me you can cut out the rape,' Susan said. 'I doubt if he'd have gone that far. What's Maurice doing about the ladder?'

'Nothing yet. He's sitting on it; swore me to secrecy. Grevas would do his nut, he said, if the police were brought in, and he doesn't want to upset the old boy unless he has to.'

'Taking a risk, isn't he?'

'He's tough. I guess he can take care of himself.'

Susan agreed that Maurice was tough. But she wondered how much of that decision to exclude the police had been due to David's persuasion. It wouldn't suit David to have them prying and questioning. She said, 'I hope you're right. I like Maurice. And at least it shows he's solidly behind the Baron. So's his wife.'

'Oh, she's just in love with the old boy — in a nice, holy sort of way, of course. He's her hero. But apart from that she's as bad as the rest of them. Didn't she accuse the other women of running after Grevas? And wrongly, according to Maurice.'

He pounded his thigh impatiently with his clenched fist, bouncing up and down on the bed. Susan bounced with it.

'Relax, darling,' she pleaded. 'It's too soon after dinner for violent exercise. You're ruining my digestion. It's not athletically minded.'

He stopped pounding. 'I just don't get it,' he said. 'If it hasn't turned out to be the happy family they expected, why the hell do they stay?'

'Habit,' she said. 'Or laziness. Or snobbery, perhaps.'

'Snobbery? How snobbery?'

'They're here to train as leaders, aren't they? To leave now would be to admit that they can't make it, that they're too petty for the job. So they stick it out regardless. Isn't that a form of snobbery?'

'I suppose it is,' he admitted. 'Sometimes, Susan, I begin to suspect that underneath your rather cretinous exterior there lies a brain. An intelligent, bluestocking kind of brain. You should watch it. One day it might get the upper hand.'

'Heaven forbid! I'd be ruined.'

He nodded absently, already back with his problems. 'I don't think it's habit,' he said. 'They haven't been here long enough for that. But it could be laziness.

This isn't a bad place to be; sea and solitude and damned good grub. They can even kid themselves they're doing something worth while. That could give 'em a kick they wouldn't get at Brighton or Blackpool.' He looked at her eagerly, his eyes bright. 'It makes sense, doesn't it? And in addition they've probably all got their personal reasons for staying. Maurice is a sort of second in command, which should satisfy his ego; and, with her crush on the Baron, Beryl is the last person to want to leave. The Hampsons must find this paradise after dockland; they're right in there with the upper crust, all nice and matey. Olive's the sort of silly woman who would be fascinated by the Baron's charm, whether she believes in him or not. I don't know what keeps the Myersons here, but at least there seems to be no antipathy to mixed marriages. As for Jutter, one place is probably as good as another to her, as long as she's with her old man. And he's got the farm to keep him happy.'

Susan gave a deep sigh and slid farther down the bed. 'Thank heaven that's settled. Now perhaps I can get some sleep. I need it.'

Through the blankets she prodded his behind vigorously with her toes, but he merely moved nearer the edge. 'I wonder how many of them know something of the old boy's past,' he said. 'You'd think they'd make a few inquiries before joining him, wouldn't you? Especially when he's playing around with their lolly.'

'Mugs,' she said sleepily. 'They're supposed to be plentiful, aren't they? A bright lad like the Baron shouldn't find it hard to rustle up a fair selection.'

'Maurice isn't a mug. Nor is Myerson. I bet he's as sharp as they come.'

For a few moments David was silent, staring unseeing at the floor. Susan closed her eyes, feeling sleep steal over her. She was drifting happily away when a hand descended heavily and suddenly on her thigh, and she awoke with a jerk.

'What we have to do, Susan,' he said, 'is to — '

She sat up sharply. The bedclothes fell away, pulling the nightdress from her shoulders. But she did not bother to adjust it. She was too angry.

'What you have to do, David Wight, is to get the hell out of here before I scream the place down. I will *not* be bullied and buffeted about like this. I want to sleep, damn you! And sleep I will.'

Her anger gave a sparkle to her eyes, her cheeks were flushed, her shoulders warm and rosy. Momentarily David saw the girl and not the childhood playmate, and he leaned forward and kissed her.

Susan was surprised. It was a most un-David-like action. He was affectionate so seldom, and usually only when he was tight. She wanted to throw her arms round his neck and hold him close, to run her fingers through his unruly hair and whisper that she loved him. But she knew that that was something she must never do; it would frighten him away, possibly for ever. One day, perhaps, he would discover that he loved her, and would tell her so. Until then she must be patient.

'Come to think of it, you're not a bad-looking wench.' He had a wide mouth, and the grin he gave her seemed to split his face. 'The nose is more or less missing, of course, and you're incredibly fat. But I suppose one can't have everything.'

'I suppose one can't.' She rubbed her cheek against his. 'Ouch! That hurts. Did you shave this morning, or have you gone native? It's like cuddling a porcupine.'

'Of course I shaved.' He drew away and stood up. 'And I'm not staying here to be insulted. It's a fine night; I think I'll take a stroll. Maybe the stars will give me inspiration. I'm certainly not getting it here.'

'More likely to give you pneumonia; the grass will be soaking.' Susan snuggled down again, drawing the blankets up to her chin. 'But if that's what you want, darling, you go ahead and do it.'

The upper landing was in darkness, but as David descended the stairs he saw the lights were still on in the hall and the library. He went quietly out of the house, hopeful that no one would hear him and engage him in conversation; he wanted to think. Once on the terrace he felt safe, and paused for a moment to light a cigarette and consider which way he should go.

Tom Hampson's voice boomed out of the darkness. 'Nice and peaceful, ain't it? Pity there's no moon. The sea looks real good with a moon.' He came closer, so that David saw him as a vague blur in the night, smelt the smoke of his tobacco. 'I often come out here for a pipe afore bed. Makes me sleep better.'

'Bad sleeper, eh?' asked David, accepting the inevitable.

'Used to be. Been getting better since we come here. Maybe it's the sea-air what does it.'

'You like it here?'

'I like it anywheres,' Tom said cheerfully. 'Leastways, anywheres as there's good grub and plenty of it. Edith says as how I lives for me stummick. Well, could be. Ain't much else to live for at my age.'

David tried to visualize what it would be like to live only for one's stomach. He could think of better reasons for living. Tom should have one too. Wasn't he supposed to be a man dedicated to the cause of peace? 'It's a pleasant spot,' he said. 'But I must say you don't all seem as contented as you should be. Would that be because of Jan Muzyk's death, perhaps?'

'It's made 'em more tetchy, if that's what you mean.'

'But not you?'

'Not me, mate. If a chap likes to kill hisself that's his worry, not mine.' Tom chuckled. 'It don't change the grub.'

'Kill himself?' David was startled. This was something new. 'Are you suggesting he committed suicide? That it wasn't an accident?'

'I ain't suggesting nothink.' Tom puffed noisily at his pipe, so that the bowl glowed in the darkness. 'But you got to look at it both ways, that's what I say. Maurice was right; the old tub was rotten, but she wouldn't 've upset. Not without a storm, and that didn't come up till later. And Jan being what he was — well, seems to me suicide's as likely as accident. Nor I ain't the only one what thinks so.'

'What sort of man was he, then?'

'Sort of moody. You never could tell how he'd be. Up in the clouds one minute, down in the ruddy depths the next. A chap like that ain't easy to live with. Nor he don't find it easy to live with hisself, neither.'

'How did he get on with his wife?'

Light streamed suddenly from the library windows at the far end of the terrace. Some one had drawn back the heavy curtains.

'Middling.' Silhouetted against the light, Tom made an indeterminate gesture with his hands. 'Olive's got a tongue, same as Jan had, when she's put to using it. Marriage didn't seem to come easy to neither of 'em. Perhaps her having all the lolly had somethink to do with it. That's a bad thing, that is. Makes a man feel real mean.'

'But apart from his temperament — was there any other reason for suspecting suicide?'

'Not as I knows on.' Tom started to knock out his pipe against the heel of his shoe, and a little shower of sparks fell to the ground. One by one they winked their way to obscurity. 'It was Harold what give me the idea, really. Like I said, there could be somethink in it. Harold knew him better than most on us.'

Myerson. Yet Myerson had not hinted at suicide the previous evening, when Jan's death had been discussed. Or had he? Was that what he had meant when he had said something about Jan tipping the boat up and drowning himself? If so, then Maurice, and presumably others, had misinterpreted him.

And Myerson had done nothing to disillusion them.

Tom gave his pipe a final tap, and blew down it noisily.

'Well, I'm for bed. Edith don't like it when I'm late; can't get to sleep, she says, till I come up.' He stretched and yawned. David heard the click as his upper set dropped. 'You coming?'

'I'll have one more cigarette first,' David said. 'Good night.'

Alone, he leant against a pillar and gazed out over the dark line of trees to the sea. A faint glow on the horizon illuminated the distance, and he could hear the waves breaking softly on the shingle. It was peaceful and soothing — and hopelessly incongruous. Yet Tom was right; there should be a moon. There should always be a moon on the sea. But Tom had been wrong about Jan Muzyk's death, thank goodness! Snowball wouldn't think much of suicide. To be news a suicide had to be famous.

He stuck a cigarette between his lips and flicked his lighter. Sparks came from it, but no flame. He put the cigarette back in the packet, and walked slowly along the terrace towards the open front door. As he reached it Olive came hurrying down the stairs. He saw her pause, and then go quickly into the library.

David himself was quicker. He was outside the open window before either occupant of the room had spoken.

'My, but thank goodness you're here!' he heard Olive say, her southern drawl sharpened by urgency. 'Maurice, I've been robbed! They've taken everything. Everything!'

'Who have?' But that was clearly a stupid question, and Maurice said, 'Sorry. Sit down and tell me about it. 'Everything' is a big word.'

'But it's true. All my lovely jewellery!'

'Jewellery!' Maurice sounded surprised. 'You mean you had valuable jewellery hidden in your room?' Presumably Olive nodded her head in assent, for he went on, 'Good Lord! It wasn't only stupid, Olive, it was downright indecent. You know how Grevas feels about that sort of thing.'

'But what else could I do? Leave it in the States? What good is jewellery if you can't even see it? And I've never worn it here. Never.'

'What was it worth?'

'I don't know exactly. But it was insured for over a hundred thousand dollars.'

'Phew!' Maurice's low whistle echoed David's thoughts. 'You're crazier than I thought, my dear. Any idea when it was pinched?'

'Well, it was there after dinner yesterday. I looked.'

'Why?'

'I thought — ' She paused. 'That cigarette-case, Maurice. It wasn't Jan's, you know, it was mine. It belonged to my first husband. Jan must have taken it.

So I thought — '

Maurice finished the sentence for her.

'You thought he'd pinched the rest of the stuff, eh?'

'Yes. But he hadn't. There were one or two pieces missing, but nothing important. And now it's all gone. All of it.'

She started to cry. Out in the darkness David waited. From where he stood he could not see into the room, but from the low murmur of the man's voice he guessed that Maurice was trying to console her.

'Did anyone but Jan know you had this jewellery in your room?' Maurice asked.

'Not unless he told them. And why should he?'

'Why, indeed!' There was a pause. 'Well, at least it must still be on the island. There's no call for panic. All we have to do is find it.'

'And if we don't?'

'Then at least you'll have the insurance money to console you.'

'But that's just it, Maurice. I shan't. The insurance company wanted such a high premium when I told them I was bringing it over here that I insured it only for the journey. On an island, I thought, with just the Baron and his friends — not even servants — well, it seemed so safe.'

There was no response from Maurice, but David could guess his thoughts. One hundred thousand dollars' worth of jewellery gone down the drain, and not a pennyworth of compensation for it! The woman was a fool, of course, but that didn't minimize the seriousness of her loss.

'What shall I do, Maurice?' Olive wailed. 'It's so — so embarrassing. What will the Baron say when I tell him?'

'Plenty, I imagine. But I could put up with a little embarrassment for a hundred thousand dollars,' Maurice said. Silently, David agreed with him. 'It beats me who'd be crazy enough to pull such a damn-fool trick. He hasn't a hope in hell of getting the stuff off the island. Not unless he swims for it.'

There was silence while they contemplated this. Then Olive said, her voice bleak, 'It couldn't be Bessie, could it? I guess she's about the most likely person.

And she and Jan — '

'It could be any of us,' Maurice cut in brusquely. 'Start accusing people on mere suspicion, Olive, and you'll make the mess worse than it is. Don't forget we've got a journalist in our midst. He seems a reasonable type, but — '

'My goodness!' Olive's voice shrilled out into the night. 'Those two young people! We don't *know* they're journalists, do we? And even if they are they're sure to be terribly underpaid. Can't you just imagine the temptation if they had gotten a peep at it? Wouldn't it be just too much for them?'

'H'm! You may have a point there. The girl isn't a journalist, she's an actress; but I suppose the reasoning still goes. Well, if they're guilty they won't get away with it; not even if it means searching them before they leave. Only don't let's jump to conclusions. We'll take a look round your room first. Maybe the thief didn't cover his tracks as carefully as he could have done.'

The light in the library went out, but David did not move. He was too dismayed. This was a development that could tear his high hopes to pieces. If the community as a whole shared Olive's suspicions — and despite his dismay he could appreciate that they might — then he and Susan would probably be hustled off the island at dawn, and handed over to the police. That the police could find no grounds for holding them was no consolation. What mattered was that they would be off the island, and with no hope of getting back.

And bang would go his story and his job.

Or would they? Might not the Baron hesitate before taking such drastic action? He had shown that he had no liking for the police, and Maurice, from what he had said, was unlikely to belittle the power of the Press. There was a meagre hope there.

Mechanically he took out a cigarette and put it between his lips, only to throw it away when he remembered the empty lighter. Then he turned towards the front door. It was time to go in; disaster or no disaster, Susan must be warned. It would be unfair to let her come down to breakfast the next morning unaware of the cloud that seemed likely to descend on them.

He found the front door closed. Not only closed, but bolted.

Cursing his luck, David sat down on the steps and considered his position. It was not an enviable one. Apart from the unpopularity that would be his were he to awaken the household by clamouring for admission, both Olive and Maurice would conclude that he had been out to bury the swag. And they were unlikely to keep their conclusion to themselves.

He got up from the steps and walked slowly along the terrace, seeking an open window. He had no luck at the front of the house. When he turned the east corner he had to feel his way carefully; although his eyes had become accustomed to the night, the shadows were darker here, and he was fearful of making a noise. He was nearing the kitchen-quarters. A metal dustbin (did they use dustbins on the island?) would make an unholy racket were he to bump into it.

The window, when he found it, was a high one. Grasping the sill with both hands, he began to work his way up the wall, knees and toes pressing and slipping against the rough stone. Progress was slow and painful. When eventually he sat astride the sill he paused for a moment, rubbing his knees gently to ease the pain in them.

It was then he heard Susan scream.

12

Susan never found sleep difficult to come by; the benefit, she boasted to her friends, of an easy conscience and clean living. 'But you haven't got a conscience,' David had objected. 'And I'm not so sure about the clean living. More likely it's a good digestion and lack of imagination.'

Whatever the cause, she was asleep within minutes of David leaving her that evening. But although she slept easily she slept lightly, and some time later she awoke to the unpleasant conviction that she was not alone in the room.

She did not immediately open her eyes. She lay on her back, her fingers clenched a little tighter on the pillow, and waited for whatever sound had woken her to recur. When it did not she opened her eyes.

At first it seemed that the darkness was complete. The door was closed, the curtains drawn, so that no light filtered in from outside. But gradually she grew accustomed to the dark, and the vague outlines of furniture became visible. Turning her head she surveyed them. It was not a familiar room, but nothing seemed out of place. There was no menacing figure lurking in the shadows.

She closed her eyes and relaxed. I must have been dreaming, she told herself; David's bedtime talk of murder has been giving me nightmares. She heaved a deep sigh, holding her breath for a few seconds; and it was then that she knew she had not been dreaming. Close beside her — so close that it seemed she had only to reach out her hand to touch the intruder — she could hear some one breathing.

Susan screamed.

Later, when she discussed it with David, she realized that it had been a stupid, even a dangerous, thing to do. The instinctive reaction of the intruder must have been to silence her; his proximity would have heightened that instinct. Luckily for Susan, he did not obey it. She heard the quick tread of feet, had a momentary glimpse of light and a figure silhouetted against it as the door opened and closed, and then he was gone. But the knowledge that she was safe took some time to crystallize in her mind, and she went on screaming until it did.

When the first of her would-be rescuers reached her she was sitting up in bed, grey-green eyes in a white frightened face staring fixedly at the door, both hands gripping the bedclothes. The Baron sat down on the bed, put one arm around her thinly-clad body, and with his free hand sought for one of hers and held it.

'What happened, my dear?' he asked, slightly out of breath.

'There was some one in the room,' she muttered, and shivered at the memory.

The encircling arm stretched and tightened. He said, without taking his eyes off her, 'In here? But that's impossible. I came as soon as I heard the scream, and there was no one on the stairs or the landing. You must have been dreaming.'

Through the flimsy nightdress she could feel the warmth of his hand on her breast, and was suddenly aware of him as a man. Into her mind flashed the recollection of that walk among the trees, and she shrank away from him. Reluctantly he let her go, his fingers lingering as they withdrew from her body.

'I wasn't dreaming,' she told him. 'I heard him breathing, and I got a vague glimpse of him as he ran out of the room. Or it may have been a she; I don't know. But I'm sure there was some one here.'

He stood up as others came crowding into the room; Olive and the Mackays, and Bessie and Maurice a few seconds later. They were all in dressing-gowns. They clustered round the bed excitedly, asking questions which Grevas at first took it on himself to answer.

'But what was the chap after?' Andrew looked worried as well as puzzled. Scratching a bearded cheek, he gazed round the room as though the intruder might still be there. 'Did he molest you in any way, Susan?'

'No,' Susan said. David and Tom had joined them now, and David fetched her dressing-gown and put it round her shoulders. She smiled her thanks at him, wondering whether he meant it for warmth or modesty. 'And I've nothing worth stealing. Though he wouldn't know that, of course.'

David saw the look that passed between Olive and Maurice. He was tempted to force their hands, but he knew that the consequences might be unfortunate. So he said mildly, 'Rule out assault and theft, and what have you? It must have been one of the two.'

Grevas shook his head. 'I find it impossible to believe that any one here would engage in either.'

'Which is as good as calling me a liar,' Susan said. She had regained her composure, was even able to feel annoyed with herself for the scream. Had she kept quiet she might have been able to identify the intruder. That would have dispelled the scepticism she could see now on their faces. Even David looked puzzled.

Grevas hastened to apologize. However impossible the incident might seem, he said, he did not doubt her word. 'Could he have mistaken the room, perhaps?' he suggested. 'That would explain his hasty retreat. It would be an embarrassing position in which to find oneself.'

'Less embarrassing than being taken for a thief or a — ' Andrew broke off. 'Besides, we all know this place like the back of our hands. Except David, of course.'

'It wasn't David,' Susan said. She gave David an intimate smile, and he felt himself blushing. He knew what the smile implied — that his intrusion would have embarrassed neither of them. Then the smile changed to a look of astonishment, and she said, 'Why, you're still fully dressed, David! Haven't you been to bed? And look at your trousers. They're filthy.'

He looked at his trousers. So did the others. There was a green stain on both knees, and for the first time David noticed that one of them was torn.

'Forcible entry,' he said, furious that the explanation was necessary. He knew what Olive and Maurice would be thinking. 'I went for a walk and found myself locked out. Had to climb in through a window.' To distract attention from himself he said. 'How about the rest of you? I suppose you were all in bed and asleep.'

Bessie, Tom, and the Mackays agreed that they had been. 'Although I don't remember hearing a scream,' Jutter said. 'Andrew had gone by the time I was fully conscious. I came up to see what the rumpus was about.' Olive and Maurice said they had been in bed, but not asleep. 'We'd been having a natter in the library,' Maurice explained. 'I was just dozing off when I heard the scream.' He grinned ruefully, and again Susan noticed the dimples. 'Like a damned fool, I dashed off in the wrong direction.'

David tried to calculate the time that had elapsed between the lights going out in the library and the sound of Susan's scream. Thirty minutes? Forty? He couldn't be sure. Surveying those who claimed to have been asleep, he had to admit that they looked as though they had; hair tousled, or flattened from being pressed against a pillow, cheeks flushed, and lined where a fold in sheet or pillow-case had marked them. All, with the exception of Jutter, wore pyjamas. And Jutter, as he had reason to know, slept nude.

But Grevas was not in pyjamas. Beneath his blue dressing-gown showed flannel trousers and sock-clad feet. A silk scarf was round his neck. 'How about you, sir?' David asked. 'I see you haven't been to bed.'

Grevas frowned. He was clearly annoyed that David should presume to question him. He said tersely, 'I was reading in my study.'

Andrew and Maurice nodded. They knew his habits. But Susan said at once, 'In your study? How on earth did you manage to get here so quickly?'

Grevas smiled at her. He was clearly more willing to be questioned by Susan than by David.

'The upstairs study, my dear.'

'Where's Harold, Bessie?' asked Andrew. 'Still in bed?'

Bessie's brown feet, encased in mules, shuffled beneath the crimson robe, her long brown fingers twined nervously together. She said softly, 'He may be. I don't know.'

To Susan the inference was plain; Bessie had been absent from the marital chamber. But with whom? Maurice? The Baron? They were the only men who did not share a bedroom with their wives. And David, thank goodness, had been out of the house.

Olive said curtly, 'That needs explaining, surely?'

'When I woke up — because Susan screamed, I suppose — Harold wasn't there.'

Her voice was firmer, almost defiant. Against her better judgment, Susan believed her. So did the others — and it put them in a quandary. The obvious course was to find Myerson and question him, but none was anxious to take it. They stood looking at Bessie and at one another, until Maurice said eventually, 'Where was he, then? Any idea?'

Only Susan saw the slight figure appear in the doorway; the others had their backs to the door. 'I was in the lavatory,' Myerson told them, and smiled his humourless smile as they turned on him. 'Do I need to explain why?'

'Not 'why,' but 'which',' Andrew said. 'The one next to your room is out of order.'

'I know that. I went up to the top floor.'

Neither David nor Susan joined in the discussion which followed. Nothing would come of it, thought David; it was talk for the sake of talk. They would all put forward apparently sound reasons for asserting their innocence; but one of them had to be lying, and all that turmoil of argument would not discover which. He doubted if any of them wanted to know the truth. It would necessitate action, and action of an unpleasant kind.

Tom said, 'I'd best go tell Edith. She'll be wondering. Where's Beryl, Maurice?'

'In her room, I imagine. She probably didn't hear the rumpus. But I'll make sure.'

They left together. Susan said wearily, 'Wouldn't you all like to go back to bed? It's late.'

She did not add that she wanted what was left of the night for sleep. That would be churlish; it was on her account they were there. But she hoped they would take the hint.

They did. One by one they murmured good-night and drifted from the room, until only David and the Baron were left. They stood one on either side of the bed, looking down at her. Susan wished they too would go. She did not want even David. Anything they had to say to each other could wait until the morning.

David was as tired as Susan, but he wasn't going to leave her alone with the Baron. Grevas was highly suspect; he was fully dressed under his dressing-gown, and he had made a pass at Susan only that morning. He was also, in David's opinion, the most likely person to have stolen Olive's jewellery.

Perhaps Grevas sensed the hostility. He said kindly, 'I hope you'll forgive us, Susan; I wouldn't have had this happen for the world. I still think there must be an innocent explanation, but we won't go into that now. Sleep well, my dear.'

Innocent, my foot! thought David. But he made no comment. He said, 'Lock the

224

door after us, Susan. I don't suppose there'll be a second attempt, but lock it nevertheless.'

'I'm afraid that's impossible,' said the Baron. 'None of the doors, other than bathrooms and lavatories, have locks. We have never considered them necessary.'

David frowned. Susan said lightly, 'Well, I'm not spending the rest of the night in a lavatory, so I'll take a chance.'

The two men left together. But when David reached his own room he did not at once prepare for bed; it had been an eventful day and, tired as he was, he wanted to straighten it out in his mind. The attempt to injure, if not to kill, Maurice by means of the rigged ladder, the theft of Olive's jewellery, the threat of assault on Susan. How did these fit into his discovery that Jan Muzyk had been murdered?

The bolt was in his pocket, the nylon rope he had left in his suitcase. He got out the suitcase now, hoping there might be something he had overlooked, something that might yet provide a lead. But as soon as he snapped open the lid he knew that some one had anticipated him. The rope was still there; but now it lay on top of the shirts and ties and underclothing, not concealed by them as he had left it.

He looked round the room, seeking further proof. The bed provided it. The pillows no longer fitted snugly under the covers, the covers themselves sagged loose instead of being tucked neatly under the mattress. Obviously his room had been searched, and searched in a hurry.

Maurice, he decided, had wasted no time in looking for the missing jewellery.

13

'I'm scared,' Susan said. 'Honest I am. It isn't healthy here, darling. Not for us.'

'Nonsense.' David spoke brusquely, hoping he was right. 'Maurice and Olive may think we pinched her precious jewellery, but we don't have to worry about that. It may be unpleasant, but not dangerous. And after last night they've probably had second thoughts about that too.'

'Because they found nothing in your room? But what about mine? They haven't searched that. Not properly, anyway.'

'They may be searching it now,' David said.

They were over on the west side of the island. It was a fine morning, with real warmth in the sun, and from where they sat they could see the mainland coast stretching into the hazy distance. Gulls wheeled and chattered overhead, and far out to sea a smudge of smoke marked the passage of an unseen steamer. It should have been peaceful and relaxing, but for David and Susan it was neither. They were too concerned with events to be aware of surroundings.

'You're quite sure it was Maurice who was in my room last night?' Susan asked.

'Him or Olive. And I can't see Olive cutting that sort of caper. Having drawn a blank in my room, I suppose he thought he'd try yours.'

'With me in it?'

'Why not? With a torch he could at least have a quick peep in the more likely places.' He grinned. 'If you woke up he could always plead passion; claim you'd given him the green light. You probably had, too.'

'I had not,' she said indignantly — a little too indignantly to be entirely convincing.

'All right, you hadn't. And when you told him so he'd apologize and depart. Nothing to it.' He scooped up a handful of pebbles and lobbed them into the sea. Most of them fell short. 'It beats me why nobody mentioned the theft at breakfast. Are Maurice and Olive keeping it to themselves? Or have they told the others, and are they all watching us to see which way we jump?'

'They're not watching us now.' Susan lifted herself up and peered over the bank of shingle. 'The island looks deserted. They must all be indoors.' She slid down beside him. 'Anyway, I'm glad it wasn't Maurice who murdered Jan. I like Maurice.'

'That's what I thought.' Then the smile vanished from his face. 'Here! Who says Maurice didn't murder Jan?'

'Of course he didn't. Some one tried to murder *him*, didn't they? Or are you suggesting there are two murderers on the island?'

'No. But Maurice could have fixed that ladder himself.'

'Why should he? To commit suicide? He couldn't know that some one else would use it. Beryl herself said she just climbed it on impulse. Besides, there's the rope.'

'What about the rope?'

'Well, he must have seen it when he searched your suitcase. If he'd killed Jan he'd have taken it away. But he didn't; he left it there. To him it was just an ordinary piece of rope, I suppose. He didn't appreciate its significance.'

David nodded glumly. He felt like saying that Maurice could have been bluffing, although he knew it wasn't true. The knowledge that at least one of the islanders could be erased from the list of suspects brought him no joy at that moment; it was depressing that that which Susan had spotted so easily should have completely escaped him. What chance had he of unmasking the killer if he was incapable of so obvious a piece of deduction?

Susan recognized his gloom and the reason for it. She tweaked his ear gently. 'Snap out of it, darling,' she said. 'You can't be on the ball all the time.'

'I don't seem to be anywhere near it, let alone on it.' Another handful of shingle was despatched seaward; with more venom this time, so that most of it reached the water. But David was essentially an optimist, and presently he said, 'You're right about Maurice, I suppose. And I've been thinking. Whoever used that rope would have wanted to recover it from the sea before anyone else found it.'

'Then why didn't he?'

'Because of the storm. It didn't let up until Monday, the day we arrived; even then it was pretty foul. But my guess is he wasn't unduly worried; if the weather was too rough for him it was too rough for anyone else. Besides, there was no great urgency. No one knew it was there, and no one was likely to stumble on it by accident. I wouldn't have found it myself if you hadn't kicked my sandal into the water.'

'Nudged, darling, not kicked. It was an accident.'

'All right, nudged. Anyway, yesterday morning was the first reasonable chance he had to recover it. Now, who went bathing? Jutter was already in the water when we got there, and we met the Myersons on our way back. Maurice had a bathe after lunch; but if he was after the rope he'd have gone in earlier. He'd had all the morning. Besides, we reckon he's in the clear. Who else?'

Susan shrugged. 'Don't ask me. You and I were closeted in my room for at least an hour after breakfast; for all we know, the whole boiling lot could have nipped in for a dip. But Jutter was the first. And don't forget it was Jutter who bought the rope. She *said* it was for Jan, but she could be lying.'

'She could. But she'd made no attempt to recover it by the time we got there; she was well out from the jetty. I don't think it was her.'

'You wouldn't,' Susan said. 'All right, then — if you don't like Jutter (speaking homicidally, of course), how about the Baron? He was skulking among the trees — remember? Jutter thought he was playing Peeping Tom, but he could have been waiting until the coast was clear.'

'Then why did he go back?'

'Because he saw we'd spotted him, I suppose, and decided to try again later.'

'Could be. Whoever it was, he must have had a shock when he found the rope gone. Unless he thought it had come adrift in the storm.' David rolled over to reach his trouser pocket, and pulled out the bolt. 'Not getting far with the rope, are we? It's a bum lead. So we're left with this.'

She took the bolt from him. 'It doesn't look any more helpful than the rope,' she said, examining it.

'It ought to tell us something. But what? It wasn't supplied with the rope. So where did it come from?'

'Bought separately, I suppose.'

'Was it?' Enthusiasm crept into David's voice. 'Jutter bought the rope on the last trip to the mainland prior to Jan's death. She said so. And presumably it was the rope that gave the murderer his idea. Jan must have shown it to him, may even have told him why he bought it — which no one else seems to know.'

'Not even Jutter?'

'She says not. But don't you see? It means the murderer didn't buy the bolt, he found it; here, on the island.' He almost snatched the bolt from her in his eagerness. 'And it isn't a type you'd find knocking around a workshop. More like a proprietary job, made specially.' He rubbed a thumb over one end of the tube, and gave a whoop of triumph. 'That's it! It's been sawn off. You can feel the rough edge.'

'Sawn off what?'

'That's what we have to find out.'

Susan did not share his enthusiasm. 'You'd have to search their rooms,' she said. 'Why not ask if anyone recognizes it?'

'Ask whom? It would be just my luck to pick on the murderer first go, and get myself rubbed out. No, thank you.'

Susan shuddered. 'Let the police handle it, darling. It would be safer.'

'And less lucrative.' He stood up, staggering in the loose shingle. 'Come on. Let's get back to the house and see what's cooking. There hasn't been a soul in sight all morning.'

'You could ask Maurice about the bolt,' she said, as he helped her up. 'He's safe enough.'

'That's true.' He waited while she adjusted her skirt and removed a pebble

234

from her shoe. 'But he'd probably insist on calling in the police. If he believed me, that is. I'd rather go it alone if I can.'

Andrew met them as they reached the steps. His face was grave. 'I was coming to look for you,' he said. 'I'm afraid there's more trouble afoot. Mind coming into the library? The Baron would like to see you.'

David looked at Susan. Despite her tremulous smile he knew she was scared. Her hand crept into his, and he gave it a reassuring squeeze. Then they followed Andrew into the library.

They were all there. They sat facing the door in a rough semicircle, so that the newcomers were immediately confronted by an arc of staring faces. David stared back, letting his eyes travel slowly along the line. The Baroness was back in the black satin, her arthritic-looking hands folded loosely in her lap, the habitual expression of disapproval on her long, thin face, beady eyes unwinking behind the spectacles. Edith sat next to her, hands hidden beneath her apron, her plump body spilling over the hard chair;

the indeterminate eyes in her grey pudding face sank as they met his. Maurice lolled back easily, one thigh bulging from his shorts as it lay across the other; an empty pipe was stuck in his mouth, a frown puckered his handsome face. Myerson too was frowning; he swallowed hard as David looked at him, his prominent Adam's apple moving jerkily. His right hand hung loose, the tips of the fingers beating a soundless tattoo on the ball of the thumb, as thought beating out the rhythm of a tune; David had seen him do it before, the full lips pursed in a soundless whistle. Beryl sat hunched forward, the brooding look back in her eyes, slim fingers intertwining nervously; Olive's gaze was guiltily unhappy, there was a high colour on her plump cheeks. Bessie gave him a nervous little smile, Jutter's dark eyes were coolly appraising but not unfriendly; he thought to see in them something of the sadness that had been there that first evening. And at the end of the line sat Tom, blue eyes almost hidden by bushy eyebrows, a sunbeam dancing on his marble-topped head.

Grevas alone was standing. And there was nothing menacing or inquisitorial in his manner as he smilingly greeted Susan and pushed forward a chair for her. Then he turned to David, the smile vanishing.

'Something extremely unpleasant has happened,' he said gravely. 'Some jewellery has been stolen from Olive's room. I'm told it was of purely intrinsic value, but that doesn't affect the moral issue. One of us — and I'm afraid I have to include you and Susan in this — is a thief. That is something we can't dismiss lightly.'

David glanced at Olive, but her expression was unchanged. Intrinsic value, my foot! he thought; so that's how she's putting it over! He wondered how Grevas felt; if he were sincere in his expressed aims this could deal them a shattering blow. Yet he looked pompously solemn rather than downcast. David fancied he might even be enjoying himself, that the issue was momentarily lost in the occasion; he was the leader again, asserting his authority, stressing the moral angle. Or was he laughing at them all, playing with them? Was this just part of the big bluff that Snowball had anticipated? Had he, in fact, stolen the jewellery himself?

David tried to look shocked. 'That's a hell of a thing to happen,' he said. 'I'm truly sorry. When did it happen?'

'Some time yesterday or the night before,' Maurice told him. His voice was curt.

'I didn't think you people went in for jewellery,' David said. 'But it looks like some one's going the rounds. First Olive's room, and then Susan's.' He decided not to mention that his own room had also been searched. Maurice had done that, and it was unlikely that Maurice was the thief. 'Well, at least that lets Susan out.'

The Baroness said frigidly, 'No one can be exonerated. We have only Miss Long's word that some one was in her room. Under the circumstances I'm afraid that isn't enough.'

Words sprang hotly to David's lips, but Susan forestalled him. She too was angry, her former nervousness forgotten. 'I'm neither a thief nor a liar, Baroness,' she said, 'but go right ahead and suspect me if it makes you feel better. I'm not begging for favours.'

And I'm not likely to get them, she thought. Not from her And her husband's favours aren't the kind I fancy.

The Baron was speaking again, his tone solemn and measured. Susan, more at ease now after having found the courage to hit back at the formidable Baroness, wanted to giggle. He's a pompous old hypocrite, she decided; one moment he's moralizing, the next he's womanizing. Why haven't they got wise to him?

She forgot that she had taken a little while to get wise to him herself.

'Olive was wrong to bring jewellery here, of course, but that's not the point at issue. Success in our aims depends on mutual trust and love, and a thief betrays both.' Grevas turned to David. 'You and Susan are strangers here; you may share our ideals, but you are not dedicated to them as we are. So I hope you will appreciate that we have less reason to trust you. I put it no more strongly than that.'

'Fair enough,' David agreed.

'Thank you. And although this is undoubtedly prejudice, if there has to be a thief I would prefer it to be you or Susan rather than one of us. Perhaps you can understand that?'

'I understand, all right. But I'm afraid you're on a loser there, Baron. Whoever pinched Olive's jewellery must have known it was there to be pinched. We certainly didn't.'

'Neither did anyone else,' Olive said.

There was a confused murmur of agreement. Maurice said curtly, 'Olive's right; none of us knew. She kept quiet about it because she knew jewellery was out. So we all start from scratch, you and Susan included.'

'Rubbish!' Myerson snapped. 'We've had months in which to ferret it out, they've had less than two days. I don't call that starting from scratch. Leave Susan and David out of it, I say. This is a domestic matter.'

David stared at him blankly, startled by

this support from such an unexpected quarter. Susan was startled too, but she managed a smile of gratitude.

Maurice shrugged. 'Domestic or not, how do we set about catching the thief? That's our main worry right now.'

'It isn't mine,' Grevas said sadly. 'Certainly the thief must be caught — but what then? If Harold is right it looks as if all our efforts here have been in vain. If we can't trust our friends, how can we expect trust elsewhere?'

Andrew said quietly, 'Don't let's be unnecessarily pessimistic. Personally, I don't go along with Harold in thinking our visitors must be blameless. Suppose we find the thief before indulging in lamentations? We can decide the future when we've settled the present.'

'A most sensible suggestion.' This from the Baroness. 'We might start by searching our visitors' rooms.'

Grevas hesitated, unwilling to accept the suggestion, and looked doubtfully from David to Susan and back to David. To his surprise, the latter nodded.

'We've no objection,' David said. 'But if

241

you're going to search ours you must search the others' too. You've no right to single us out.'

Maurice stood up, slapping his broad thigh. 'Right! Then let's get cracking. Not that we're likely to find anything; only a fool would hide the stuff in his room. But obviously we have to try.'

The others rose too; some reluctantly, but none protesting. David wondered if there might be other secrets they wished to hide. Jutter said, 'Do we all go? Aren't we rather a crowd?'

'Four should be enough,' Maurice said. 'Any volunteers?'

'I'll make one if there are no objections,' David said.

There were no spoken objections, but he sensed an under-current against him. 'Who else?' Maurice asked. 'Olive had better be one. How about you, Baron?'

Grevas shook his head. 'Let Tom and Andrew go. That makes the four.'

After his outburst in support of David, Myerson had been silent. He had listened to the argument with a sardonic smile on his lean face, as though the whole thing amused him. Now he said, 'I've no ambition to be one of the snoopers, but no one's searching my room unless I'm present.'

Jutter smiled. 'I see what you mean about a lack of trust, Baron,' she said. 'It seems to be spreading.'

Grevas frowned. 'Harold is right,' he said. 'We want no misunderstandings. We had all better go to our rooms and wait there.'

David's room was the first to be searched. He stood watching them from the doorway, apparently disinterested but alert to their every move. The two men tackled the task conscientiously, though with obvious distaste. Andrew was particularly thorough. Olive did little but wander aimlessly round the room, peering over the men's shoulders as they searched the bed and investigated drawers and cupboards.

It was Tom who brought out the suitcase. Mackay and Olive joined him as he opened it, and unfortunately for David all three had their backs to him. His impulse was to walk into the room so that he could see their faces; but to show a sudden interest would be to arouse suspicion, and he stayed where he was, waiting for their comments when they saw the rope.

The comments did not come. Tom rummaged quickly through the contents while the others watched, then closed the lid and replaced the suitcase in the cupboard.

'O.K.,' Andrew said. 'Let's get on to the next.'

Bewildered, David followed them down the passage. Fifty yards of nylon rope was surely an odd item to find in a visitor's luggage, yet all three had apparently accepted it without comment. What was to be inferred from that?

He wished he knew.

As Maurice had foretold, the search proved fruitless. Yet for David, in addition to the problem his own room had posed, it was not without interest. He felt he was getting to know the islanders better, not only from the contents of their rooms but from their behaviour. Olive protested loudly at their invasion of her privacy, contending that it was completely unnecessary, since it was her jewellery that had been stolen; when Andrew insisted she plumped herself down inelegantly in an armchair and sat glowering at them silently throughout the search.

Hers was a large room on the first floor, and even to David's uncritical eye it looked a mess. Clothing was draped over the backs of chairs, the dressing-table was an untidy jumble of a woman's aids to beauty; the ashtrays were spilling over, shoes were piled in a corner, there were suitcases and boxes stacked on the floor. It was as though she had unpacked in a hurry when she and Jan had first arrived, and had since found neither the time nor the will to bring order to the chaos. David wondered whether her pique was due to their discovery of the untidy state of the room or the extent of her wardrobe. And Jan's; his belongings were still much in evidence. If Grevas were sincere in his desire for equality he would undoubtedly have found much to criticize.

Andrew took no active part in the search of his own room. He stood in the doorway with Jutter, an arm about her waist, offering an occasional word of advice but for the most part silent. Jutter too said little; but theirs seemed the silence of sympathy, not of pique. The couple were of equal height; the woman's slim build accentuated her husband's breadth, her sleek dark hair was in sharp contrast to the silvery whiteness of his. Occasionally they looked at each other, smiling intimately, and David realized that they were much in love.

Unlike Olive's, their room was a model of orderliness; an example of Teutonic thoroughness, thought David. So too was the Hampsons'. But Edith was clearly embarrassed. She immediately excused herself on the pretext of 'seeing to the lunch,' and limped away with a mumbled apology for any untidiness they might find. Tom lolled on the bed while the search went on around him, reading a paperback Western. He wore a dirty beige pullover over a grey woollen shirt, the sleeves of which were unbuttoned so that they flapped untidily over his bony wrists. The grey flannel trousers were worn thin at the knees, the turn-ups were badly frayed. Susan is always telling me I look like a scarecrow, thought David, unconsciously hitching up his trousers. I must ask her what she thinks of old Tom.

Bessie was uneasy. As each drawer or cupboard or case was opened she peered anxiously over the shoulders of the searchers as though doubtful of what it might contain, while Myerson stood by the door making malicious comments on their clumsiness and ineptitude. The room was tidy, but it had an uninhabited look — like a hotel bedroom waiting for the arrival of an expected guest. The drawers were mostly empty, the glass-topped dressing-table devoid of the usual paraphernalia. It seemed to David that the Myersons were living out of suitcases. There were plenty of these, and most of them full.

Maurice went round his own room disclosing everything, as though in a hurry to be done, but in his wife's room he showed no interest whatever. Neither did Beryl. She seemed not so much indifferent as unaware, gazing moodily out of the window as the search went on behind her. She keeps her husband's room in better order than her own, thought David. Yet the untidiness here was different from Olive's; it gave the impression of being temporary rather than permanent, as though Beryl possessed the will but not the time.

Outside the Baron's room they paused. 'This is more than awkward,' Andrew said, pulling thoughtfully at his beard, his deep-set eyes troubled. 'Do we go in, or don't we?'

'Why not?' asked David. 'There's nothing sacred about it, is there?'

Tom grunted, twisting his scraggy neck in the open collar. 'Sort of,' he said. 'He won't like it, that's for sure. Even the flippin' cleaning has to be done by his missus. No one else ain't allowed in.'

'Well, we can't give him a miss now,' David objected. 'It wouldn't be fair. Neither to him nor to the rest of us.'

When eventually they knocked the Baron made no demur to the search, although he seemed ill at ease. David wondered whether that was because the room was more luxuriously appointed than the others. The mahogany furniture was Victorian and massive and well made; the drawers slid smoothly on their runners, the doors swung easily. The close-fitting carpet had a thick, rich pile, the deep mattress on the large double bed was of foam rubber, the well-padded armchairs looked inviting. It was a room planned for comfort rather than aesthetics.

The Grevases had a private suite on the first floor; two bedrooms with a study between them, and no communicating doors. The study was simply yet comfortably furnished, and they searched it quickly while the Baron waited silently at the door.

'Is that all?' he asked, when they had finished.

'All except the Baroness,' Andrew told him.

The Baroness kept them waiting. When eventually her door was opened she said acidly, clipping the words as though their utterance was painful, 'You will have to come in, I suppose.' With her cold eye upon them they made only a cursory search, but David for one was soon satisfied that the jewellery was not there. It was a spartan room, and possible places of concealment were few. It seemed odd that Grevas should do himself so well and his wife so poorly. Or did she prefer austerity? It was certainly in keeping with her countenance.

Disappointed, David went downstairs with the others. He did not care greatly about the jewellery; he had volunteered for the search in the hope that he might unearth some clue to the identity of Jan Muzyk's murderer, and in particular the article from which the bolt had been sawn off. He had seen nothing remotely resembling what he had in mind.

As they trooped into the library the others were waiting for them. Jutter said smoothly, 'Well? Which of us wears the handcuffs?'

Andrew shook his head. Maurice said, 'What did you expect? It'll be hidden well away from the house. Only way to find it would be to search the whole damned island.'

'That'd take a month of Sundays,' Tom objected.

'I suppose we could try,' Andrew said doubtfully. 'It's a long chance, but if we worked systematically we could at least make a rudimentary search. And it might come up.'

Myerson gave a mirthless laugh. 'Andrew wants the soil turned ready for autumn sowing. You can count me out. Agriculture isn't in my line.'

'I'll get my bucket and spade,' Jutter said, turning to the door. But Maurice stopped her. 'We don't dig, we look,' he said. 'If we go at all, that is. In any case we eat first. I'm starving.'

They discussed the problem over lunch. Only the Mackays seemed to be in favour of searching the island; Andrew because he liked to be thorough, and Jutter, David suspected, out of wifely loyalty. 'You won't get them jewels of yours back without the police, Olive,' Tom said, helping himself liberally to potato salad. He looked apologetically at Grevas. 'I know you don't hold with cops, Baron, but facks is flippin' facks.'

'Exactly,' Myerson agreed. 'To misquote the Scriptures, 'render unto Grevas the things that are Grevas's, and to cops the things that are cops'.''

This was received in silence, apart from a guffaw from Tom, instantly suppressed by a nudge in the ribs from his wife. Grevas frowned heavily. 'It would be an admission of failure,' he said. 'Not only to ourselves, but to the world. How can we appeal for universal peace, denigrate the use of force, if we employ force to keep the peace among ourselves?'

'The police don't use force,' Andrew said. 'Not in this country.'

Tom laughed. 'Not 'arf, they don't. Ever been down White-chapel way, mate, of a Friday night?'

Grevas shook his head. He looked sad, and Susan wondered again how big a humbug he was.

'You don't understand. Whether they use force or not, they represent it. Their existence is a tacit admission of crime and disorder; it denies all our ideals. If we resort to the police to resolve our problems we deny them too.'

'No good shutting your eyes to facks, Baron,' Tom said cheerfully. 'We got crime, and we got it bad.'

David wondered where he himself stood in the argument. Common sense demanded that the police be informed, yet with their arrival would go all hope of a successful conclusion to his quest. No doubt he could rake up enough dirt to satisfy Snowball; but he could not satisfy himself. To do that he had to make a personal exposure of Jan's murderer. And that dramatic moment seemed a long way off.

Andrew said gently, 'There's no question of denying ideals, Baron; just the recognition that Utopia isn't with us yet. We live in the world as it is, not as we would have it. And while it remains imperfect we need a police-force.'

'And we need to use it,' Myerson added.

But Grevas could be stubborn. Listening to his rhetoric, David wondered, as Susan had done, how much of it the man believed. Some, perhaps; he had built an edifice and put himself at the top, and now the edifice was crumbling. He must fight to save it. Or was he fighting for something else? Had he a more personal reason to fear the advent of the police?

They were not easily convinced. In desperation Grevas appealed to Maurice for support, but Maurice refused to commit himself. 'Ask Olive,' he suggested. 'It's her property that's missing.'

Olive flushed. 'My goodness!' she said unhappily, the squint more prominent as she peered round the table in an attempt to read their faces. She appeared to have recovered from her fit of pique. 'I certainly would hate to spoil things for you, Baron. It'd be real mean. And yet — well, if we can't figure it out for ourselves, don't we just have to send for the police? It doesn't matter about the jewellery — leastways, not so much — it's the nasty taste, isn't it? I mean — well — we'll never know, will we? And we can't just pretend it didn't happen.'

The Baron sighed.

'No, we can't do that. As you say, Olive, we have to know.' He sighed again. 'You had better fetch the police, Maurice.'

Unexpectedly, Tom came to his rescue.

'No 'arm in havin' a bash at the island first, I suppose,' he said grudgingly. 'It's a fine afternoon for a walk. If it'll make you any happier we can leave the cops till the morning. Nothing'll be lost except a little time, and we got plenty of that.'

Grevas snatched eagerly at the straw.

'Thank you, Tom. As you say, time is plentiful. And it may not be wasted; not even if the search proves fruitless. The thief's conscience must be troubling him; the longer we delay the greater the hope that he or she will suffer a change of heart and confess. That wouldn't resolve all our problems. But it would help.'

'Fair enough,' Maurice agreed. 'Tom's right; it's a fine day, and we've nothing to lose. Or does anyone object?'

No one did. Not, that is, to the delay. But Myerson refused to co-operate in the search. 'I don't mind wasting time; it's the waste of energy I object to.' He gave his high little giggle. 'If you want to play Hide-and-seek round the island, then good luck to you. But not me. I'm for an armchair.'

It was Maurice who organized the search and arranged them into pairs — the Mackays to take the southern quarter of the island, Tom and Susan the east, Olive and Beryl the west, and David and Bessie the north. He and the Baron would search the buildings and the gardens.

'Cunning bastard,' Tom said cheerfully.

Susan guessed that she and David had been separated because they were still under suspicion, but she disapproved of Bessie as a companion for David. 'You keep your mind on the job,' she warned him as they went upstairs together. 'There are enough complications without you adding to them.'

'I'll do my best,' he assured her, grinning. 'Don't blame me if it isn't enough.'

His walking-shoes were in the cupboard with the suitcase, and as he picked them up he was reminded of the morning's search. Just why had Tom and Andrew and Olive accepted the presence of the rope so calmly? They couldn't have failed to see it. Why had they made no comment?

He pulled out the case and opened it. The rope had gone.

14

David found Bessie a rather silent companion at first. As they went down the hill through the orchard he tried to discuss the theft with her, but she offered no comments and answered his questions briefly.

'You don't seem particularly concerned,' he said, irritated. 'Why? As the Baron said, this business could put the whole scheme in jeopardy. Doesn't that worry you?'

She shrugged her shoulders without speaking.

'Not interested in world peace, eh?' he persisted. 'Then why are you here? Because your husband brought you? The tame, obedient, slave-wife?'

That stung her. She flashed her eyes at him.

'No one makes me do what I don't want,' she said indignantly. 'Coloured folk aren't all slaves. Sure I want peace. But

258

the jewellery — that's different.'

'Because it's Olive's?'

'She's like all Virginians,' she said. 'She don't like coloured folk.' She made a hissing noise through her teeth. 'They talk about brotherly love, but they don't think of people like me when they say it. We're just niggers. We don't count.'

'I don't blame you for feeling sore,' he said. 'But we're not out here just to please Olive. It's for our own benefit.'

'How?'

'Until we know what happened to that jewellery of hers we're all under suspicion. Susan and me in particular.'

She smiled at that. 'And me,' she said. 'Olive would just love it to be me.'

He smiled back, knowing that to be true. 'Let's get down to business, then, shall we? We're backing a rank outsider, but it might come up.'

They searched the hen-run and the fields first, looking for signs of earth recently disturbed. When they drew a blank they went on into the woods, with David taking the area to the east of the path, and Bessie that to the west. It was difficult going in places, for the brambles had been allowed to spread undisturbed, and searching them resulted in torn and scratched hands. But David persevered, gradually making his way farther east, until a cry from Bessie stopped him.

He found her sitting at the foot of a tree, nursing an ankle. When she saw him she grimaced.

'I fell over,' she said. 'It hurts.'

He knelt down and gently touched her ankle. As usual she wore no stockings, but she had donned a pair of white plimsolls, which emphasized the dark richness of her skin. It was warm to the touch, sending a tingle through his veins that made him shiver with excitement. He wanted to run his hand up her firm brown leg, to caress its satin smoothness.

He said, examining it gently, recoiling at each exclamation of pain, 'You've sprained it, I expect. It's beginning to swell already. You won't be able to walk on that.'

She bent over to peer at it, holding his arm to steady herself. Gingerly she explored it with her free hand, wincing at the pain. 'I'll have to try,' she said. 'Help me up, please.'

It was a task that gave him pleasure. Her waist was slim and firm, her body supple as he held her close; she had a faint, musky scent that he found exciting. But when she put her foot to the ground and tried placing her weight on it she groaned in agony.

'I can't,' she said. 'I just can't.'

David tightened his grip. 'I'll have to carry you.'

She laughed. 'All that way? Impossible. I'm much too heavy.'

'I can try.'

'No. Not yet. Put me down, David. We'll wait a little. It may be better presently.'

Reluctantly he obeyed. He went through the woods to the beach, where he soaked his handkerchief in the sea, and then returned to wrap it round her ankle, hoping to reduce the swelling. Then he stretched himself out on the ground beside her. He did not think that waiting would help. But if that was what she wanted he was perfectly content to wait.

'Shouldn't you look for the jewellery?' she asked.

He grinned up at her. 'Professional etiquette. I can't abandon my patient.'

At first they talked idly, with intervals of silence between each burst of words. But as their interest in each other quickened the conversation became more intimate. David found her fascinating. Equally fascinating was her account of life on a West Indian sugar plantation, where her parents still worked; where she would be working herself, she supposed, had not the manager taken an interest in her. 'No, not that sort of interest,' she said, in answer to his unspoken query. 'Mr Stokes was a good man.'

It was Stokes who had had her trained as a secretary, Stokes who had found her employment. And it was in her new employer's office that she had met Harold Myerson.

'And fell in love, eh?' She shook her head. 'No? Then why did you marry him?'

'Why not? We were both lonely. I thought — ' She shrugged. 'Oh, never mind. Tell me about you.'

He told her. He was still telling her when he chanced to look at his watch. 'Hey! It's after five,' he exclaimed, scrambling to his feet. 'Let's try that ankle of yours.'

He helped her up, and she took a few painful steps. But it was clear that she would never make it back to the house. 'Carry you, it is,' he said. 'Nothing else for it.'

His right arm was about her waist; heedless of her protests, he put his left arm under her knees and lifted her. Her skirt was short, and as his hand gripped the warm flesh of her thigh his heart beat faster. She leaned against him, her left arm around his neck. He felt like a million dollars.

He wasn't feeling so good by the time they reached the path. He was breathing heavily and his heartbeat was still rapid, but now more from exertion than from excitement. Although young and healthy, he had never been athletically inclined.

And Bessie, as she had warned him, was no light weight.

'Put me down, David,' she pleaded, as she felt him stagger.

'Presently,' he panted. 'I'm not done yet.'

He stopped at the edge of the wood, letting her slide to the ground more roughly than he intended, his aching muscles responding only weakly to the task. But he kept one arm about her as she leaned against him for support, and gradually his breathing returned to normal.

She twisted her body towards him. 'You will have to go back to the house for help,' she said, smiling up at him. 'I'll wait here. You'd never be able to carry me up the hill.'

Regretfully he admitted the truth of that. 'The old muscles aren't what they were. They've gone soft on me.' He took a deep breath. 'A pity. The spirit is willing and eager. You make an attractive load.'

Her eyes sparkled. 'I do?'

'You do.'

Her face was close to his, and without

thought he bent and kissed her. It was a long kiss. Her full lips were soft and mobile, her arms were around his neck, her body fitted snugly to his. Then he felt her relax, and he lifted his head to look at her.

She was still smiling. It was a childish, gleeful smile, with no hint of sophistry or self-consciousness.

'Umm! That was nice.'

It was an unusual but pleasing compliment. 'Properly conducted, it usually is,' he said, smiling back at her. 'Would you care for an encore?'

She shook her head. 'I'm a married woman. It wouldn't be proper. Once, yes; that is just an experience. More might become a habit.'

He wondered if she had borrowed that piece of philosophy.

'You could fight it,' he suggested. 'Not too hard, of course, but — '

From across the island came a sharp report, and he heard something thud into a tree behind them. For a moment he stood rigid, paralysed by fear and uncertainty. Then, forgetful of her damaged ankle, he picked up the girl and almost threw her to the ground, hurling himself down beside her.

She cried out once and then was silent, the breath knocked out of her. David felt himself trembling. He wanted to burrow deep into the earth, but he forced himself to his knees and peered anxiously across the fields to the house.

Her hand gripped his ankle, startling him. He felt her move behind him, and turned quickly. 'Keep down!' he said urgently, and gulped. 'Keep *down*!'

'What is it? What happened?'

'A bullet.' He gulped again, gripping his thighs in an attempt to control his trembling body. 'Some bastard is using us for target practice.'

15

'Harold?' Maurice shook his head. 'If Harold had wanted to kill you, my lad, you wouldn't be talking to me now. Harold doesn't miss, not even at that distance. He's a crack shot.' Mechanically he pulled back the bolt of the Lee-Enfield he was holding and sniffed again at the breech. Then he closed it and squeezed the trigger. 'Why do you suppose it was Harold?'

'Because of Bessie. It might have looked to him as though I was embracing her.'

Maurice's heavy eyebrows lifted in surprise. 'And were you?'

'Of course not.' With heightened colour David recounted what had happened, omitting the kiss. 'It was a nasty shock to be greeted with a bullet.'

'So I can imagine.' Maurice placed the rifle beside its fellow in the rack, and walked across the barn to seat himself on the bench. He grinned at David. 'I bet you had butterflies in your stomach all the way back, wondering when the next shot was coming.'

David nodded. But he did not return the grin; the experience was too fresh in his memory. Bessie had tried to detain him. It would be wiser to stay under cover, she had said; sooner or later they would be missed, and then some one would come to look for them. Why take unnecessary risks? But despite his fear he had known he must go, if only to prove himself. He could not lie there indefinitely, waiting for others to rescue them. He must handle this himself.

Nevertheless he had waited some time before making a move, his eyes anxiously scanning the island for the unknown marksman. But he had seen no one. Presumably the searchers had already returned to the house; and the outbuildings and orchard to the east, and the walled garden to the west, would hide anyone lurking on the terrace. Once he had thought he'd seen movement among the trees over to his left, where Susan and

Tom had gone. But that was all.

When eventually he had forced himself to his feet and had ventured into the open his whole body was trembling; his legs were like jelly, and his stomach, as Maurice had surmised, was filled with butterflies. But he had gone on. Crouching low, half running and half walking, he was nearly across the lower pasture when he had heard a shout to his left and had looked up to see Tom coming to meet him.

Maurice was watching him, the grin still on his face. He said, 'You've let excitement colour your imaginaton, I shouldn't wonder. The rifles belong to Harold, but we all use them. Even some of the women. Jutter, for instance — she's quite a useful shot. So is Beryl, oddly enough. If you ask me, some one was indulging in a little target practice and happened to loose off a round in your direction. Andrew, most likely, or Tom. They're both keen.'

Not Tom. Tom had had no rifle. It was that knowledge which had emboldened David to stand up and wait for him.

'Looked like you'd taken an overdose of salts and was in a hurry,' Tom had said. Then, observing David more closely, 'What's up, mate? Bin took bad?' And David had told him of Bessie's accident, and between them they had carried her back to the house.

But neither he nor Bessie had mentioned the shooting to Tom.

'There was only the one shot,' David said. 'Does that sound like target practice to you?'

Maurice uttered something inaudible and slid off the bench.

'O.K. So some one tried to kill you. Who?' He sounded impatient. 'You can cut Myerson out. Unless he missed on purpose. Just wanted to scare you.'

'He scared me, all right. But if it wasn't Myerson — ' David shrugged. 'I'm damned if I know. What time did they all get back? Before five?'

'Well before. Except Tom and Susan. I doubt if anyone took the search seriously. Can't say I blame them, either. It was a lost cause from the start.'

There was no help there, then. Tom

could be eliminated, but no one else. Not even Maurice. And yet —

'Did you hear the shot?' he asked.

'Yes. I was in the study. As a matter of fact, I thought I heard two, but I could have been mistaken.'

'There was only one,' David said again.

'O.K., there was only one. And in case you're wondering why I didn't rush to your rescue, I might point out that shooting on the island is almost a daily occurrence — except that as far as possible we try to avoid using our friends as targets.' Maurice kicked impatiently at a piece of wood on the cobbled floor. 'Frankly, I think you've got it wrong. Why should anyone want to kill you? Not Harold; he wouldn't care two hoots if you and his missus had a bit of a cuddle. And even assuming you're right — what am I supposed to do? Round them all up and have a showdown? Is that what you want?'

It wasn't at all what he wanted. Maurice didn't believe him, and neither would they. Why, they would ask — as Maurice had asked — should anyone want to kill him? And he could not give them the answer. Not yet, anyway.

'I wasn't cuddling her,' he said absently. 'It just looked like it.'

All the way back to the house he had been telling himself that that was why the shot had been fired, and that it was Myerson who had fired it. He had told himself that in order to bolster his courage, believing that once Myerson knew the truth (or as much of the truth as he and Bessie would tell him), and with the sprained ankle as confirmation, the danger would be past. But now he was not so sure. Maurice was right; a cuddle was insufficient provocation for murder. There had to be a stronger, more urgent reason, and he thought he knew what it was. Some one had found the rope in his suitcase and had taken it; and that some one could only be Jan's murderer. But to repossess the rope would not be enough; the murderer would realize that only some one who had guessed the truth would bother to keep it. Therefore, he would argue, that some one must be eliminated.

'That doesn't answer my question,' Maurice said.

'No.'

He looked at Maurice, trying to see him afresh, noting his height and his broad shoulders, the firm jaw, the keen eyes under the bushy brows. Maurice would be a good man to have at one's back in time of trouble; he looked almost aggressively tough and reliable. Well, I'm in trouble, David thought unhappily; up to my neck in it. But can I trust him?

He had to trust some one. It was no longer only the unmasking of a killer that concerned him; now he had to fight and scheme to stay alive, and he doubted his ability to do that unaided. True, he had Susan. But Susan, capable as she might be as a schemer, was no fighter.

So there was only Maurice. Maurice had strength of character as well as physique, and he had not killed Jan. But how would he react to the information that Jan had been murdered — and by one of his friends?

David cleared his throat. He had made up his mind.

'Did you know Jan Muzyk's death wasn't an accident?' he asked abruptly. 'That he was deliberately murdered?'

Maurice's lower jaw dropped, his eyebrows shot up, his whole body seemed to go rigid. Then, slowly, he relaxed. But his eyes were hard and his face stern as he said flatly, 'Shot by some sportsman with a rifle, I suppose? You know, I don't find that funny.'

'It wasn't meant to be.'

Briefly — but not as briefly as he could have wished, for now he was too deeply, too personally involved to see the matter as concisely or as objectively as he had seen it before — David told him. And Maurice listened, his eyes following David as the latter wandered aimlessly up and down the barn, but his body tense and still except for the busily twisting ring. Once, as David paused, he took his pipe from his pocket and stuck it between his teeth, fumbling for matches. But David went on talking, and the pipe remained unlit.

'So that's how it is,' David said, coming to a stop by the door and staring unseeing across the island. 'I wanted to handle it myself. I saw it as an almighty scoop that would make me the envy of Fleet Street. But not any more. Not now the cold war's over and the shooting has started. My main concern now is to save my skin.'

'That so?' Maurice took the pipe from his mouth. 'I can put you ashore on the mainland within the hour.'

David flushed.

'I didn't mean that. I'm scared — like hell, I'm scared — but I'm not scared enough to quit. I still want that story. Only I don't want to be part of it, if you see what I mean. Not just another corpse.'

'Very reasonable.' Maurice joined him at the door. 'And you haven't a notion who the murderer is?'

'None whatever. Except that if it was the same person who tried to kill me this afternoon, then at least it wasn't Bessie. Nor Tom, I suppose. But it could be any of the others. That's what makes it so damned unnerving.'

Maurice looked at him curiously. 'Yet I

assume you have ruled me out. Why?'

It was a difficult question to answer without complete frankness. And frankness here could be double-edged. David said lamely, 'Well, there was the ladder. An odd way to commit suicide.'

'Not necessarily suicide. If I'd fixed that rung I could also avoid it. And I might have fixed it.'

'Why?'

'One doesn't look on the target to find the bow,' Maurice said. 'That's not original, but it's apt.'

'I hadn't looked at it like that,' David admitted. Nor had he. 'But again — why? A fire-raiser doesn't shout 'Fire' before others have even seen the smoke. And there was no sign of smoke here. Not to your knowledge.'

'True. All the same, if the ladder was your only reason for exonerating me I'd advise you to take to the boats. Or boat. With a war on you're too exposed.'

David's pride wouldn't stand for that. 'There was also the rope,' he snapped.

'What about it?'

'I was outside the library window when

Olive told you her jewellery had been stolen.'

Maurice was startled. 'Were you, indeed? Very unethical, eavesdropping.' He paused. 'Well, it bears out the old adage that eavesdroppers hear no good of themselves. But where does the rope come in? I don't get it.'

'It was in the suitcase when you searched my room later,' David told him bluntly. 'You must have seen it. And if you'd killed Jan you wouldn't have left it there. Not unless you were a fool as well as a murderer. I don't think you're either.'

There was a long pause. Then Maurice said slowly, 'What makes you think I searched your room?'

'Who else? Only you and Olive knew the jewellery was missing. And what other reason could there be for ransacking my things?'

'The rope?'

'Then why wasn't it taken? And it wasn't. Not then.'

'You mean it's been taken since?'

'Yes.'

'H'm! That's a pity. It could have

been useful evidence against some one.' Maurice shrugged. 'However, you're right about me searching your room. It was Olive's idea. I didn't fancy the task, but she insisted. And she was within her rights, I suppose. You looked a cinch as the thief.'

'I suppose I did.'

Maurice grinned. 'No hard feelings?'

'None.'

'Thanks. Well, now we're back where we started. What do you want me to do?'

'I don't know,' David confessed. 'I just had to tell some one, and you were the obvious person. It had suddenly got too big for me. Any suggestions?'

'This piece of wood from the boat,' Maurice said. 'Where is it?'

'Buried under the shingle. I can find it when I want to.'

'And the bolt?'

David produced it from his pocket and handed it over. He no longer felt scared. 'You can see where it's been sawn off,' he said. 'But sawn off what?'

Maurice handed it back. 'I wouldn't

know. But keep it. The police will want to see it.'

David stared at him in astonishment. 'The police? Are you calling them in on this?'

'Of course. We've no option, even if we wanted one. It was agreed that if the jewellery wasn't found this afternoon we'd fetch the police in the morning. Well, it wasn't found. And with a murderer loose on the island I'd say police intervention is all the more necessary. Which reminds me — ' he went over to the rifle-rack and abstracted the two bolts — 'I'll keep these. At least no one's going to get shot.'

David felt deflated. He had been frightened. Then the fear had gone, to be replaced by a sense of achievement at having conquered it. Now he saw no reason why, with Maurice's help, he should not complete the task he had begun. True, he was no nearer the identity of the murderer than when he had first discovered that murder had been committed. But sooner or later the break must come. With tension mounting on the island it could well be sooner.

'You want to make up your mind, lad,' Maurice said, noting his disappointment. 'A few minutes back you were scared stiff; now you're all set to do the Big Hero act and go it alone. But it just isn't on. It wouldn't be fair to the others to leave this to amateurs. It's a job for professionals.'

David nodded. Despite his disappointment he knew Maurice was right. And even if he were to be robbed of the crowning glory, at least he had glory enough to satisfy Snowball. He had found murder where the police had seen only an accident. And now that he too had become a target for murder his story would be doubly dramatic.

'I'm not beefing,' he said. 'Crying for the moon just happens to be one of my weaknesses. Do we tell the others about Jan?'

Maurice considered this. 'Better not,' he said. 'We don't want to start a panic. Jan was killed because — well, because he was Jan, I suppose. You were on the list because you were getting warm. But the rest of us should be safe enough.'

'I didn't feel warm. Bloody cold, in fact.'

'Well, something rattled him, and he reacted. To advertise our knowledge might give him ideas.'

'He's got those already,' David said. 'Nasty ones.'

From the terrace came Beryl's voice. It sounded urgent. 'Maurice!' she called. 'Maurice, where are you?'

Maurice looked his annoyance. He did not hurry to obey the summons. 'Sounds like I've got wife trouble,' he said, carefully tamping tobacco into the bowl of his pipe. 'Anything else before I obey the summons?'

'I don't think so. Except that I'll have to tell Susan, of course. We're in this together. And what about Grevas? After all, he's the boss.'

'No,' Maurice said firmly. 'Not Grevas.' Beryl called again, and he emitted a lungful of smoke in protest. 'Well, so long. And look after yourself.'

'I'll do that,' David promised.

When Maurice had gone he went back to the barn and sorted through the tools on the bench; he had remembered that there ought to be a hacksaw. It did not take him long to find it. It hung on a nail driven into the stone wall, and he was in the act of reaching for it when he stopped. The murderer had used that hacksaw twice; once to cut down the screws, and once to saw through the tube to which the bolt had been attached. It was unlikely that anyone had used it since; the murderer's fingerprints should be thick upon it, unless he had thought to rub them off. And why should he? There had been no whisper of foul play.

With a piece of cloth David unhooked the saw from the nail and hid it under some sacking; it had to be preserved, and if the murderer was getting jittery he might decide to dispose of it. It was odd, thought David, that there was no blade, either in the saw or on the bench. But it did not greatly matter. It was the saw itself that was important.

He turned his attention to the large pile of junk near the bench. While talking to Maurice it had occurred to him that the object from which the bolt had been sawn off would now be useless, and that this was the most likely place to find it. Maurice would not be going for the police until the morning. The more evidence he could collect in the meantime the greater the kudos — with the police, with Snowball, and with himself.

He scattered the pieces around him as he searched. They formed an odd and varied collection — an old bedspring, holed and battered pots and pans, broken coal-scuttles and hods and shovels, an enamelled chamber-pot (whose? he wondered, as he flung it aside), parts from a two-stroke engine, and numerous scraps of assorted metal and wooden objects. As he delved deeper the pieces seemed to grow smaller. His eye was caught by what appeared to be polished wood strapped with metal bands, and he yanked it out, causing part of the pile to collapse.

It was a trouser-press. The hinge consisted of a long chromium-plated sleeve turning on a rod, and to one end of the sleeve was attached a bolt fitted with a wing-nut. But the second bolt was missing, and that end of the sleeve had been cut away. David took the bolt from his pocket and placed it in position. It fitted exactly.

Kicking aside the scattered junk, he went over to the bench to examine his find. It was scratched and dusty, but less antiquated than he had expected. Turning it over, the initials J.R.S. caught his eye; but since there was no J.R.S. on the island he saw no help there, and he hid the press under the sacking with the hacksaw and went out on to the terrace.

Maurice and Beryl had disappeared. But Olive was there. Knees apart and showing plenty of leg, she lounged in a deck-chair, reading. David was surprised when she took off her dark glasses at his approach, and smiled a greeting. After what he had overheard in the library the previous evening he had expected scowls rather than smiles. Did she no longer regard him with suspicion?

'Sorry to hear your jewellery hasn't turned up,' he said. 'You haven't been lucky here, have you?'

'No,' she agreed, and sighed. David wondered whether the sigh was for the missing jewellery or the dead husband. 'I guess nothing's turned out the way I figured.'

Did that mean she was disillusioned as well as bereft? 'Was the jewellery insured?' he asked, knowing that it wasn't. And, when she shook her head, 'You didn't rate it as highly as your dreams, then?'

The pale blue eyes squinted at him in puzzled bewilderment. 'Dreams?'

'On my first evening here you told me you had put up sixty thousand dollars for this project. When I suggested that that was a lot of money to invest in something little more than an airy-fairy dream you said it sometimes did one good to dream. Particularly if the dream was insured.' He paused. 'I wondered what you meant by that. I'm still wondering.'

'Well, I've gotten a mortgage on the property. If the scheme fails this island's mine.'

'By Sycorax my mother,' David muttered.

'I beg your pardon?'

'Nothing. Do you think it's worth the sixty thousand?'

'My goodness, yes!' She sat up in the deckchair, showing her first sign of animation. 'I'd just love to have a place like this all to myself.' She waved a hand vaguely in the direction of the walled garden. 'It's all overgrown and untidy right now, but think how beautiful it could be if one spent money on it. I guess my friends in the States would be just crazy about it.'

He agreed that with money the island could be beautified. 'But how about the house? It's such a monstrosity. Would you pull it down?'

She shook her head. 'Certainly not. I think it's real cute.'

Well, that's one point on which you and Susan agree, he thought — and on which I differ. 'Wouldn't it hold unhappy memories for you?' he asked.

'The past is past,' she said sharply. 'I'm not a morbid person. Wives go on living in their homes after their husbands are dead, don't they? Why shouldn't I live here?'

'No reason at all,' he agreed.

He wondered if her liking for the island

was taking precedence over her interest in the Baron and his ideals. It did not sound as though she would be heartbroken were he to fail. But then, she had also been far from breaking her heart at her husband's demise. Perhaps it was immune to breaks.

He offered her a cigarette, which she refused. 'I always smoke Luckies,' she said, taking a pack from her bag. 'So did my first husband. He held a lot of their stock.'

'Jan preferred Senior Service, didn't he?'

'Yes.' She leaned forward to the match cupped in his hands, and puffed out a cloud of smoke. Then she sighed. 'Poor man. We quarrelled about that the day he was drowned. Such a silly thing to do.'

'How was that?' He presumed she meant the quarrel, not the drowning.

'I found he'd taken mine. It made me real mad — there wasn't a pack left. He didn't like them, but I guess a heavy smoker like Jan would smoke anything if he hadn't gotten his own brand. He'd clean forgot to buy them, he said.' She sighed again. 'I guess he was a very selfish man.'

'He doesn't sound like the Baron's ideal convert.'

'He wasn't. He was for ever begging me to leave. He wanted to travel and have fun.' She put the cigarettes back in her bag and looked at her watch. 'For goodness sake! It's a quarter after seven!'

Quite a profitable little chat, thought David, as he watched her gather up her belongings and depart.

16

At dinner that evening David regarded his companions with fresh eyes. Hitherto his interest in Jan Muzyk's death had been objective; he had sought the identity of the murderer more for his own advancement than out of any burning desire to see justice done. Now it was different. With the bullet that had missed him so narrowly that afternoon he had become personally involved, and as the conversation drifted up and down the table he watched each speaker with intense concentration, hoping that tone or phrase or gesture might more intimately reveal the person behind the façade, might betray a character hitherto unsuspected.

Susan and Maurice and Bessie he could safely ignore, and certainly it was not Tom who had tried to kill him that afternoon. Of the men, that left Myerson, Andrew, and the Baron. He could not see Andrew as the killer. Andrew might kill in sudden anger, but not in the cool, deliberate manner that had resulted in Jan Muzyk's death. Grevas was definitely a possibility. He was even a probability — a suave enigma with a shady past and a dubious present. And there were other, more pertinent reasons to suspect him — the cigarette-case, for example, and Beryl's unintentional revelation that Jan had voiced his doubts of the Baron's true aims. Yet some one had also tried to kill Maurice, and Maurice was the Baron's right-hand man. Could that, too, be the work of Grevas? Maurice had voiced no doubt of him. Or had he? Had that been in his mind when he had vetoed the suggestion that Grevas should be told of the shooting?

And Myerson? To David, Myerson was as great an enigma as was the Baron. Embittered, cruel, completely lacking in warmth and, David suspected, compassion, he seemed to possess all the essentials of a murderer. And what had brought him to the island? Could a man like Myerson share the lofty ideals proclaimed by Grevas? Or had he purported to embrace them solely to gain access to his intended victim? Had murder been his intention from the beginning?

The manner of the crime seemed to indicate a man rather than a woman, but the women must not be overlooked. Olive, David thought, was too stupid, although she might have had more reason than most to wish her husband dead. Beryl had a secret fire within her that, properly fed, could destroy; her passionate regard for the Baron could have provided the fuel. Jutter had bought the rope; she had been first at the jetty the previous morning. Yet what possible motive could she have had? As for the Baroness —

The Baroness, he decided, was capable of anything.

He had had no opportunity to confer with Maurice or Susan before the meal. Maurice had been busy, Susan had seemed deliberately to avoid him. She was still avoiding him. Occasionally Maurice gave him a conspiratorial glance across the table, but Susan neither spoke to him nor looked his way.

Something, he decided, had put Susan's nose out of joint.

As usual, the Baroness sat at one end of the table, intent on her food. Now and again she glanced at some speaker with the scornful look that seemed habitual to her, but for the most part she let the talk flow over and around her as though it were unworthy of her notice. Beryl, too, was silent; she sat next to Grevas, eyeing him avidly whenever she thought no one was looking, and only picking at her food. David wondered how the marital tussle had fared. Maurice looked thoughtful, but not downcast. But then he had more than domestic troubles to brood on.

Most of the talk centred on the anticipated arrival of the police the next morning, although no one, apart from Olive and the Baron, appeared to be in any way perturbed. Olive was uneasily apologetic for the fuss of which she was the unwilling cause. David suspected she was wondering how to reconcile the true worth of her jewellery, should the police recover it, with the 'intrinsic value' she had previously given it. And there was no need to seek a reason for the gloom that sat so heavily on the Baron's handsome face.

He made one final appeal as they rose from the table.

'There is still time for the thief to confess,' he said earnestly. 'I shall be in the lower study until I go to bed; if any of you should wish to confide in me you will know where to find me.' His grey eyes pleaded with each of them in turn. 'I beseech you all to consider most carefully what you should do. Apart from the unhappy consequences to the person concerned, unless we can settle this matter without the aid of the police it may be the end of everything we stand for. A rift can only widen or heal. Please help me to heal it.'

It was an impressive appeal, less for the oratory than for its apparently impassioned sincerity. Even David was impressed. The man might be a knave, he might even be a murderer; but could so much passion be based solely on fear of exposure? He must believe at least something of what he preached.

Beryl was in tears. As she dabbed at her eyes she glanced briefly at the Baroness, standing impassively by her chair, and then hurried from the room. Of the others, only Myerson showed indifference. He gave David a sardonic grin, tilted his eyes upward in a gesture of humourless despair, and sauntered away with hands dug deep into his trousers pockets.

Susan continued to avoid David after the meal. She sat talking to the Mackays in the library, and after a period of frustration he gave up trying to winkle her out. I'll catch her when she goes to bed, he told himself. She can't get away from me there.

Before going upstairs he had a word with Maurice. Maurice did not attach much significance to the trouser-press. 'There's no J.R.S. here. Never has been, to my knowledge. It's probably been lying on that scrap-heap for years. But it's as well you found it. There may be fingerprints.'

'Plenty, I should say. Including mine.'

Maurice shrugged. 'The police will sort them out. Did you tell Bessie not to mention the shooting?'

'Yes. But listen, Maurice. You know there were some Senior Service cigarettes in the cigarette-case Grevas found in his pocket? Well, they weren't Jan's. He hadn't got any; he was smoking Olive's. She told me so this evening.'

'Is that important?'

'Of course it's important! It means that they must have been put into the case by whoever pinched it. So — who else smokes Senior Service?'

'Harold does, I think. I seem to remember ordering them for him.' Maurice's face puckered into a puzzled frown, stretching the heavy eyebrows. 'But, damn it all — why?'

'To establish the case as Jan's, I suppose. I can't think of any other reason. You all knew what brand of cigarette he smoked. But would any of you have recognized the case?'

'Only Olive.' Maurice shook his head. 'But I still don't get it. Why should he *want* to establish that? I'd expect the reverse to be true.'

'So would I. But then it's no more odd than hiding the case in the Baron's pocket.' David pummelled his hair in perplexity. 'It's crazy, isn't it? But what do we do? Tackle Myerson?'

Maurice grinned. 'Still after that scoop, eh?' Then the grin faded. 'What if he admits it? Where do you go from there?'

'Lock him up and send for the police,' David said promptly.

'And if he denies it? As he probably will — innocent or guilty. You can't accuse a man of murder simply because he happens to smoke the same brand of cigarettes as the corpse. And you've nothing else against him. Or have you?'

'Nothing concrete,' David admitted.

'Then let the police handle it. They're better equipped.' Maurice consulted his watch. 'It's too late to fetch them now, but I'll be off first thing in the morning. And don't worry about that scoop. The glory shall be all yours.'

David flushed. 'I wasn't worrying.'

The other laughed. 'Like hell, you weren't! Not that I blame you. Bread and butter can be damned insipid after one's tasted jam. By the way, am I the only one you've taken into your confidence?'

'Yes.'

'Well, no one knows that, so I'm safe enough.' Maurice put a friendly hand on David's shoulder. 'But take my advice and shove the furniture against the door when you go to bed. You've had one narrow escape. Don't risk another.'

David went upstairs and lay on his bed with the door open and listened for Susan. Each time he heard footsteps on the stairs he went out to the landing. But Susan was one of the last to come up. He heard her say good-night to the Mackays on the first landing, and he went back into his room and closed the door. I'll give her ten minutes to get undressed, he thought, as he lay down again. That should be time enough.

Some time later he awoke. He sat up quickly and looked at his watch. Eleven fifteen; he had been asleep for nearly an hour. Susan wouldn't take kindly to being awakened now, but it had to be done. It was her own fault for giving him no opportunity to speak to her downstairs.

There was a light on the first landing. He went quietly down the stairs and along the passage to Susan's room. There he hesitated. But there was no point in knocking. He opened the door and went in.

He did not switch on the light. The curtains were partially drawn, and a thin gleam from an invisible moon penetrated to the centre of the room, leaving the corners in total darkness. He sat down on the bed, felt for the hump that was Susan, and shook it gently.

'Susan,' he whispered. 'Susan, wake up!'

He had feared that, with the memory of the previous night still strong in her, she might scream at being thus rudely awakened. But she did not scream. He felt a twitch shake her body. Then she turned on to her back, and he guessed that her eyes were open.

This was the critical moment. 'It's me, David,' he said quickly. She did not answer. His eyes were becoming accustomed to the dark, and he could see that she was looking at him. But he could not read her expression. 'Sorry about this,' he apologized. 'Hope I didn't startle you. But I had to talk to you, Susan.'

It was Susan who startled him. He felt and heard the deep breath she drew, but he was unprepared for the stream of abuse which followed. This, said Susan, was the absolute end. He had inveigled her to the island under false pretences, he had allowed her to be assaulted and humiliated, he had humiliated her himself. Some unknown person had entered her room by night; others, with his connivance, had searched it by day. She had been called a thief and a liar, there had been insinuations that she was a wanton; any moment now some one would decide she was also a murderess. 'And not one finger have you lifted to protect me,' she stormed. 'Yet now you have the nerve to burst into my room in the middle of the night, maul me about, and say you want to talk to me. Talk to me!' Her voice rose shrilly. 'Get out of my room at once, you — you Casanova, you! If you want a midnight chat try Black

Bess. From her performance this afternoon, I've no doubt she'll welcome you. But not me. I'm particular.'

So that was it. Susan must have seen them from the trees. And Tom? Had he also witnessed the embrace?

'Now you're just being childish,' he protested. 'And damned illogical. No one's persecuting you. As for this afternoon — '

'Childish, am I?' Impulsively she sat up. 'I'll show you how childish I am! If you're not out of this room by the time I count five I'll scream the place down. One . . . Two . . . '

He had to shock her into silence. He said quickly, 'They tried to kill me this afternoon.'

' . . . Four.' There was a brief silence. 'They *what*?' she gasped.

'They tried to kill me. That's what I've been trying to tell you all evening. Some one loosed off a rifle at me. Bessie and I had just come out of the wood, and I was about to — '

'You don't have to tell me. I saw you. Crude, I thought it.' Her voice was cool.

She slid down into the bed. 'It was probably Myerson, tired of turning the blind eye. I don't blame him, either. How do you know the shots were fired at you?'

'There was only one, luckily. The next might have got me. It hit a tree just behind us.'

'There were two. I heard them.' There was a pause. David remembered that Maurice had also heard two shots. 'Tom fired one,' Susan said.

'Tom? But that's impossible. It was Tom who helped me carry Bessie back to the house. He certainly didn't have a gun.'

'He left it in the wood,' she told him. 'He collected it from the barn as we went out; said he might put in a little target practice. But he didn't use it while I was with him.'

'Weren't you with him all the time?'

'No. Around five o'clock Tom said he'd had enough, he was through with looking for a needle in a haystack. So he sat himself down on a rock, and I wandered off. It was then I saw you and Bessie doing your wrestling act.'

'I was supporting her,' he protested. 'She'd sprained her ankle. You know that.'

'I didn't know it then. And I wasn't going to wait for what came next, so I went back into the wood. And it was after that I heard the shots. One from some distance away, and the other quite close.'

'Didn't that make you think?'

'Nothing makes me think when I'm mad. You know that. And right then I was mad as mad. Besides, I thought it was Tom. It was, too.'

He let the contradiction pass. 'Only the second shot, presumably. Who fired the first?'

'Don't ask me, darling. And Tom came up to me soon afterwards and said you were acting funny and he was going across to see what it was all about, and would I put the rifle back in the rack. So I did.'

'Was the other rifle there then?'

'Yes, it was.'

Two shots fired almost simultaneously from different parts of the island meant that both rifles had been used. So it did not follow that Tom was the killer. And

Susan, when he asked her, did not think that Tom's manner had been in any way strange. 'He was just the same as usual,' she said, and caught hold of his arm, all her former anger vanished at this new danger. 'What are you going to do, darling?'

He told her what he had already done. She was pleased that he had consulted Maurice, and even more pleased to learn that the police would arrive in the morning. 'About time too,' she declared. 'I'm scared.'

'You've got company,' he assured her.

But it wasn't true. He still had an uneasy sensation in his stomach when he recalled the sound of that bullet thudding into the tree, but he wasn't scared. Having Maurice as a partner had helped him to recover his nerve. He even hoped that something might happen before the morning to stop Maurice from going for the police. But of course it wouldn't. Not even a full confession from the thief, not all Grevas's pleading, could stop him now. Maurice was dealing with murder, not theft.

He kissed Susan good-night and went on tiptoe along the passage and up the stairs to the next landing. As he reached his room he heard a door shut softly below; looking over the balustrade, he saw a woman in a pale-blue dressing-gown disappear into the darkness of the passage that led to the back stairs. He had not seen her face, but he had no doubt at all that it was Beryl Hunt.

He went into his room and sat on the bed and wondered about Beryl. Anyone who moved stealthily about the house at night was of interest to him now. Where had she come from? In the few seconds that had elapsed between the sound of the door closing and his first glimpse of her she could have gone only a few yards. That seemed to indicate either a room in the Grevases' suite or the Myersons' bedroom. There was a lavatory on the corner; but that was the one Maurice had said was out of order.

Was Beryl the thief? Had she gone to the Baron's study to confess, forgetting in her emotional stress that he had said he would wait downstairs? No, that wouldn't do. Beryl wasn't the thief. She would do nothing that might embarrass her adored Grevas.

For the same reason she was unlikely to have killed Jan.

Stretching prodigiously, David got up from the bed. For the present Beryl's nocturnal mission must remain a mystery. Most probably it had been entirely innocent. He must not see crime and murder in every untoward incident.

He undressed and put on his pyjamas. Then, remembering Maurice's advice, he began to manœuvre the heavy chest of drawers towards the door, rocking it along on its stubby, uncastered feet. Once or twice it landed with a thud on the creaking floorboards, and he wondered if the sleeping Susan would wake to the noise. Her room must be almost directly underneath. She would think —

He let the chest drop on to its four feet and stood back, guiltily aware that he had been too concerned with his own safety to consider Susan's. Then he went over to the bed and began to strip it.

Susan awoke to the feel of a hand heavy

on her side and a voice whispering in her ear. 'Susan!' the voice said. She felt herself being rocked gently from side to side. 'Susan! It's me, David.'

'Oh, no!' Wearily she rolled over and regarded the shadowy form bending over her. 'Not again! Don't you ever go to bed, David?' She sighed. 'If they're going to kill you I wish they'd hurry up and get it over. Maybe I'll get some sleep then.'

'They'll kill you too,' he told her bluntly. After his concern, however belated, for her safety, he thought her attitude inconsiderate.

There was a moment of silence. Then Susan sat up with a jerk.

'Me?' The word was a high-pitched squeak. 'Why should anyone want to kill me?'

'Because the murderer will take it for granted that you know as much as I do. If he kills one he has to kill the other. That's logic, isn't it?'

'No, it isn't,' she said fiercely. 'It's murder.' She gripped his arm and held it. 'Oh, David, I'm scared. You won't leave me, will you?'

'I'll kip down here for the night,' he told her. 'I've brought my bedding. And you can take that look off your face.'

She relaxed at that, letting her head fall back on the pillow. But she kept a grip on his hand.

'What look?'

'You know. Like a coy vulture.'

Freeing his hand, he switched on the light and surveyed the room. There was nothing suitable for use as a mattress, and he collected the two cushions from the armchair and laid them on the floor by the door. 'No one'll catch me napping if I bed down there,' he declared.

Susan laughed. 'Too true, darling. If the floorboards don't keep you awake the draught will. Would you like another pillow?'

He put it alongside the cushions with one of his own. As he wound the blankets round him Susan said, 'I still don't see why anyone should want to kill us. Do you?'

'Of course. Only we know Jan was murdered.'

'But we don't know who did it? Or do we?'

'No. But it's logical to suppose we'll pass on what information we can to the police when they arrive. And they're likely to be a lot more nosey than us. More efficient too.'

He switched off the light and lay down on his makeshift bed. Provided he remained still, it was reasonably comfortable. But he made the mistake of turning on to his side. A pillow slid away, to leave his hip resting on the bare board.

'It's not only us,' Susan said. She sounded wide awake. 'There's Maurice as well. He knows.'

'The murderer doesn't know he knows.' Susan had been right about the draught; he could feel it even through the blankets. It was particularly savage on his exposed neck and feet. 'Maurice is safe enough.'

'And Bessie? Aren't you worried about her?'

'She doesn't know about the murder. Only the shooting, and that could have been accidental. I told her this evening I thought it was.'

His hip was sore. He lifted himself on one elbow and tried to slide the errant pillow back into position. The move was only partly successful. When he lay down again, on his back this time, he found that less than half the pillow was under him. And the cushion on which his elbow had rested had slid in the opposite direction.

He swore softly but savagely to himself. Susan said quickly, 'Are you all right, darling?'

'Snug as a bug.'

'Sure? You're very restless. Can't you sleep?'

'No,' he said angrily. 'Not with you nattering all the while. Go to sleep, damn you!'

Susan sighed. 'Oh, well! If you're going to be snooty — '

She was soon asleep; he could hear the faint burbling sound that came from her parted lips. After a while he dozed off himself. But not, as it seemed, for long. Something hard and sharp was butting him in the ribs, nudging him away from the door.

He rolled over and sat up. Swathed in blankets like a cocoon, it was difficult to move quickly; but he managed to fling himself against the door, slamming it shut.

Susan awoke with a start. 'What was that?' she called nervously.

The door was pushed ajar again. From outside a voice said urgently, 'Is that you, David? Open up. It's me, Maurice.'

David got awkwardly to his feet and kicked the pillows away. As he stepped back he tripped over a trailing blanket and fell with a resounding thud. Susan said querulously, 'What on earth are you doing, David? You'll wake the whole house.'

She switched on the bedside light. Maurice was already in the room; she uttered a little squeal as she saw him, and slid under the blankets. Maurice gave her a cursory glance and turned to the recumbent David. He said, 'I thought you might be here.'

David sat up. He did not feel equal to

standing. 'Well, I am,' he said unnecessarily. 'Susan was scared. What's up?'

'It's the Baroness,' Maurice told him. His tone was grim. 'She's dead.'

17

The household came drifting down to the library in night attire and dressing-gowns, looking cold and frightened and perplexed. Some one had switched on the electric-fire, and most of the women huddled round it, whispering to each other. David stood apart with Susan; his body was sore and his eyes heavy, and with only a light raincoat over his pyjamas he eyed the cluster of dressing-gowns enviously. Tom and Maurice and Andrew were together by the door, with Tom doing most of the talking. Momentarily forgetful of the new emergency, David watched him and wondered. Which of those two shots had been fired by Tom? The innocent or the guilty?

Maurice said, 'We're all here except the Myersons. Didn't anyone wake them?'

'I did,' Tom said. 'Maybe it took Bessie longer on account of her ankle. I'll go see.'

He was soon back, shepherding the limping Bessie and her husband into the room, and helping the girl to a chair. Myerson said, 'Well, we're here. But will some one please explain why? Tom says the Baroness is dead; if that's true, then I'm sorry. But was it necessary to get us all out of bed? There's nothing we can do about it.'

The silence, the accusing eyes, did not embarrass him. He draped himself on one leg and leant nonchalantly against Bessie's chair. Andrew's moustache seemed to quiver in a rare anger. He said, 'The Baroness was murdered.'

'Oh?' It was an exclamation of interest rather than surprise. 'How?'

'I'm not sure. Probably suffocated. The Baron found her when he came up. She was lying on his bed.'

The whispering started again. It was clear that this was news to the women, and that the news had startled them. David looked at Beryl. She was leaning against the mantelshelf, her head resting on her hands. Her body was tense.

'What time was that?' he asked.

'Around four o'clock, according to Grevas.'

Jutter said, 'That was late, even for him. What kept him? A late confession?'

Andrew shook his head. 'He fell asleep in his chair.'

His high-pitched voice sounding strangely like a querulous woman's, Myerson said, 'What evidence is there that she was murdered? How do you know she didn't die from natural causes? Couldn't she have had a heart attack?'

Maurice nodded. It was clear that he too doubted Andrew's diagnosis. But Andrew said, 'I saw her. So did Maurice and Tom. Her face was blue and her eyes were horribly congested.' His voice faltered. 'Death didn't come easily to her, poor thing. Her body was entangled with the bedclothes, as though she had been struggling to escape. But don't take my word for it. Go and look for yourself.'

Myerson raised a thin hand in protest at the suggestion. 'I think not, thank you.'

'Andrew is probably right,' Maurice said. 'I'm too inexperienced to judge. But she could have taken poison, I suppose.'

'Not taken it,' Andrew said firmly. 'There was no glass. But given it — yes, that's possible. And it still amounts to murder.'

Olive had turned from the fire and had been listening open-mouthed. Eyes almost popping out of her head, she said shrilly, 'My goodness, but how dreadful! I just can't imagine how anyone should want to murder the poor thing. I mean — well, *who*?'

She looked slowly round the room; not accusingly, but as if expecting a hand to be raised in guilty acknowledgment. No hand was. Yet she had voiced the question that was in all their minds. Who?

As if in context, Myerson asked, 'Where's Grevas? Shouldn't he be here? He's the person most concerned.'

What a nasty piece of work he is, David thought. He saw that Beryl's head had lifted sharply at the Jew's question. She did not turn round, but stared blankly at the wall, awaiting the answer.

'What do you use for blood, Harold?' Maurice asked roughly. 'Bile? Do you want the poor chap on view so that you can gloat over his misfortune?'

'All right, all right!' Myerson was taken aback by this attack, but he recovered quickly. 'But what now? Do we start pointing fingers and asking nasty questions? Or do we all go back to bed?'

Maurice looked across to the uncurtained windows and shook his head. Dawn was already breaking.

'I suggest you all get dressed and have an early breakfast. I'm going for the police. If they jump to it we should be back in just over the hour. And leave the questions to them.'

David went along to Susan's room after he had dressed. He walked in without knocking, and then hastily retreated as Susan, attired only in brassière and panties, squealed in alarm and snatched at a towel for cover.

'Since when have you had the right to barge into my room like that?' she demanded, when he was eventually permitted to enter.

'I got confused,' he said. 'I thought we were sharing the room. We were last night.'

'That was different.'

As she made up her face he told her about Beryl. 'I'm not saying it's significant, her wandering around the house at that hour. But I bet the police will be interested, all the same.'

'She's certainly a gone girl for the old man,' Susan said, carefully pencilling in her eyebrows. 'And did you see the look she gave the Baroness after dinner last night? But I don't think she killed her. It's more likely to have been the Baron.'

'Why?'

'Well, perhaps he wanted a change.'

'Rubbish. The Baroness may have been short on sex, but she was a damned good cook. At his age that's important. It's important at any age, come to that.'

'Don't be sacrilegious, darling. Sex is terribly important.' Carefully she adjusted an errant lock of hair. 'I'd like to know what she was doing in his room, though. I thought they didn't — well, you know. That's what Beryl told me.'

'Wishful thinking on Beryl's part, no doubt. The Baroness wasn't that senile.'

They went downstairs to find the

others assembled in the kitchen. 'We're eating here,' Jutter explained. 'It's warmer.' David wondered whether warmth was the true reason, or whether they had decided there would be greater safety in numbers. He looked round the room. Beryl was making toast and Edith was setting the table; both were still in their dressing-gowns. Bessie and the Baron were absent, and of the others only Myerson was busy. His obvious preoccupation with his task intrigued David.

He was cooking the breakfast. For a while David watched him as he dealt expertly with frying-pan and grill, with eggs and bacon and sausages and tomatoes. He said, 'You're quite a cook. Had much experience?'

Myerson smiled, and there was unusual warmth in the smile.

'Not as much as I'd like. I enjoy cooking. If I weren't such a gambler I'd have been a chef, I think. But one mustn't gamble with cooking. It's an exact science.'

'Isn't Bessie coming down?' David asked, fumbling for a cigarette.

'She's waiting for me to give her a hand on the stairs.' Myerson deftly turned an egg and lightly basted it with the hot fat. 'Forgotten your cigarettes? Have one of mine.'

Maurice had been right. Myerson *did* smoke Senior Service. But David made no comment as he handed back the packet with a brief word of thanks. He said, 'Can I collect Bessie for you? You look pretty busy.'

Susan had been listening. As David passed her on the way out she said sweetly, 'Don't be too long, darling, will you? You know how I worry when you're away.'

'It's the possessive instinct that comes with advancing years,' he told her. 'Watch it.'

He found Bessie sitting on the bed. 'I could have made it on my own, I think,' she said, smiling her thanks. 'But these slippers hurt. There's another pair at the bottom of the cupboard.'

'I thought you preferred to go barefoot.'

'Not in the house.'

He found the slippers. But also in the cupboard were several suitcases, and as he was closing the door he noticed one case in particular. It was old-fashioned and looked heavy, and was made of leather that was liberally bespattered with labels. He noticed it because on it were imprinted the initials J.R.S.

As he helped Bessie down the stairs he was only dimly aware of the supple softness of her body, of her arm around his waist. He was thinking of those initials. J.R.S. on the suitcase — and J.R.S. on the trouser-press. Who was J.R.S.?

They might, of course, have been Bessie's initials before her marriage. Yet what would she be doing with a trouser-press? Had Myerson acquired both suitcase and trouser-press from their previous owner? Or had he merely found the case on the island, and purloined it for his own use? Did the initials have no significance whatever?

There was only one way to the answer, and that was through Myerson himself. And if Myerson had guilt on his soul he was unlikely to supply it.

And then David's memory clicked, and he knew that he did not have to ask. He already knew the answer.

Breakfast had started when he and Bessie entered the kitchen. His elation at his own cleverness, the realization that he had, after all, beaten the police at their own game, was tinged with sadness at what he was about to do to Bessie. But he did not hesitate. He helped Bessie to a chair, and then walked firmly across to where Myerson still stood by the stove. In a voice unnaturally loud and vibrant he said, 'You're Jacob Steinberg's son, aren't you? Why the false colours? Could it be that you wanted to get some of your own back?'

The clatter of cutlery at the table, the subdued chatter, died away. There was a scraping of chairs as their occupants turned to stare at the couple by the stove, and then silence. Frying-pan in hand, Myerson looked up. The familiar lopsided grin was back, but there were deep lines on the thin face that David had not noticed before. They made him look old and tired.

But he wasn't looking at David. He was staring past him to the door, the fingers of his right hand once more playing their silent tune on his thumb. David turned to follow his gaze. So did the others.

Grevas stood there, as erect and well-groomed as ever. But the restless eyes, the slight twitching of one cheek, the nervous twiddling of his fingers, betrayed his agitation. His face was nearly as white as his hair.

'That was the general idea,' Myerson said, his eyes still on the Baron. 'But it seems to have got rather out of hand.'

18

Recalling that morning later — and it was to prove the most fantastic morning of his life — David was struck by the apparent calmness with which every one (and the women in particular) had greeted Myerson's announcement. Perhaps, he thought, they had not fully understood it. Certainly Olive had not. She said, in her fussy, plaintive voice, apparently completely unaware of any crisis, 'I sure would like you to know, Baron, how sorry I am to hear about the poor Baroness. Right now you won't want to talk about it, I guess. But if there's anything we can do — '

There was a general murmur of agreement and condolence, to which Grevas made no response. He seemed oblivious to every one in the room except Myerson, staring at him with narrowed eyes and a look of sad despair on his handsome face. Then Andrew said,

'What's all this about getting your own back, Harold? Seems to me that calls for an explanation.'

David looked at Myerson, who shrugged. David said, 'His real name is Steinberg. The Baron ruined his father, who committed suicide. He came here, not because he believed in the Baron's ideals, but to avenge his father.' He turned to the Jew. He had no doubts. He knew he was right — he *had* to be right. 'That's so, isn't it?'

'More or less. Except that my name isn't Steinberg. I changed it by deed poll.'

'It's not true,' Grevas said, as they all looked at him. It was like watching a tennis match, Susan thought, the way their heads kept turning first one way and then the other. She wished the two men would get together so that the heads could be still. 'Harold may believe that, but he's wrong. I had nothing to do with it.'

'You were on the board,' Myerson said. The savagery was creeping back into his voice. 'You knew what was going on, that my father and others like him would be ruined. You're guilty, all right. Perhaps the law couldn't touch you — but I could. I have, too. This is one racket that isn't going to pay off.'

'Racket?' Andrew was angry now, the Scot's accent more pronounced. 'There's no racket here, no matter what your warped mind may think. We believe in what we're trying to do. All of us.'

'Do you? Grevas doesn't. He's in it solely for the cash. Not the twenty quid a week we all pay him for the pleasure of living on this damned island and sitting at his table, but for the fat sums of money you and Olive and Tom have handed over for the furtherance of The Cause. Plus, of course, the money he hopes to wheedle out of you in the future.' Myerson laughed. It was not a pleasant sound. 'I'm sorry, Andrew, but you're a mug. You're all mugs.'

David was startled. He had known about Olive, but not about Tom and Andrew. And from the look on Jutter's face he suspected that it was news to her also.

'You got a big mouth, Harold,' Tom

said. 'Spills a lot o' dirt too, don't it? You say the Baron here is working a racket. Well, what *I* says is — can you prove it?'

'Of course I can't prove it.' Myerson snapped the words at him. 'Do you think I'd have waited all these years if I could have exposed him in the courts?'

'Then why expect us to believe you now?' Jutter asked coldly.

'I don't care a damn whether you believe me or not.' He was still holding the frying-pan, and he slammed it down angrily on the stove. 'Being mugs, you probably won't. But it makes no difference. After what's happened here during the past few days are you still going to carry on with this — this farce? Live in blissful, trusting harmony together, hand over your money like obedient disciples whenever he asks for it?' He snorted. 'Like hell, you won't! The Grevas peace movement is dead, and you know it.'

They did know it. David saw that in their faces. Whether they believed Myerson or not, there could be no going back to where they were before. His accusation, the things that had happened, had shaken their trust. No doubt they would retain their ideals, perhaps even continue to work for them. But not under the Baron's guidance. The foundations were now too insecure for successful building.

In silence their eyes ping-ponged back and forth from Myerson to the Baron, who still stood by the door. Some one had pushed forward a chair, but he ignored it. He seemed mesmerized into immobility and silence by the slight figure, the pinched, triumphant face of his accuser.

Tom Hampson scratched his bald head, the unbuttoned shirt-sleeve slipping down to expose a wrinkled brown forearm in which the veins were prominent. 'Seems to me, mate, you done us all a bit of no good,' he said. 'Messed things up proper, you have.'

Myerson shrugged. 'Sometimes the innocent must suffer for the guilty. I didn't plan it that way.'

'How did you plan it?' asked Andrew.

Breakfast was forgotten. Bacon and sausages congealed on the plates, the eggs had a glazed and solid look. Occasionally some one took a quick sip at a cup of rapidly cooling coffee; but, for all except Beryl, Myerson was the focus of their attention. Beryl was staring at the Baron, her sallow face a mask of misery. This must be a bigger blow to her than to any of them, thought Susan. She may not believe Myerson, but she must have doubts; and Grevas has said little to dispel them. Just that one, half-hearted denial — and then silence. Was Beryl reading guilt into his silence, or was she willing him to defend himself?

'You were all such mugs, you couldn't see Grevas was a phoney,' Myerson said disdainfully. 'If I'd told you what I knew you wouldn't have believed me, you'd have run me off the island. Some of you don't believe me now. So I made things happen. Things that would disrupt the harmony, upset your damned smugness. I knew Grevas and his love-peace façade wouldn't last long in that atmosphere.'

Jutter's dark eyes narrowed. She sat cross-legged, green corduroy trousers snug over narrow hips, the rolled neck of her loose yellow sweater nestling under the softly rounded chin. The harsh glare of the strip lighting did not deal kindly with some of the women, but Jutter's golden skin and sleek dark hair seemed to glow with vitality. 'Things such as putting a dead rat in my bed, I suppose,' she said in disgust.

Myerson nodded. 'And letting the chickens loose and pinching Olive's jewellery,' he added with some relish. 'They all helped to unsettle you.'

Olive had gasped out her usual 'My goodness' at the mention of her jewellery, and then was silent. Andrew said, 'How did you know there *was* any jewellery?'

'Jan told me.'

'And you repaid him by pinching his cigarette-case, eh?' David said. 'Only you made the mistake of filling it with Senior Service. You didn't know, did you, that Jan was smoking Olive's cigarettes? Very careless.'

Myerson shrugged. 'It achieved its purpose. And I didn't steal the case; Jan asked me to look after it for him while he went fishing. He'd forgotten he had it on him. When he didn't come back I decided the Baron's pocket would be an admirable place to put it.'

'Hoping to cause trouble, I suppose.'

'Exactly. It couldn't miss. Either he'd have a hell of a time explaining, or he'd decide to keep it quiet. And I'd see it didn't stay quiet for long.'

'Nice type, aren't you?' Andrew said. He sat next to his wife, his square frame erect, the deep-set eyes under the tufted brows fixed accusingly on the Jew. Susan thought he epitomized strength; not the trenchant, aggressive forcefulness of Maurice, but a quieter, more latent power. 'What have you done with Olive's jewellery?'

'I put it in the empty cistern in the lavatory next to my room. The one that's out of order. Unless it's been pinched a second time it's still there, I imagine.'

Andrew started to rise from his chair, and then sat down again. The jewellery could wait. There was something else that had to be explained, something far more dreadful than lost chickens or dead rats or stolen jewellery.

'Was the Baroness's death another of

the things you 'just made happen'?' he asked sternly.

Myerson stared at him. 'Good heavens, no!' All the triumph and malice had gone from his voice. Involuntarily he stepped back, put his hand on the cooker for support, and whipped it away with an oath as it touched the hot metal. 'You know damned well it wasn't!'

His indignation sounded genuine, David thought. Well, Andrew could be wrong about the Baroness. But there was no doubt about how Jan Muzyk had died. Myerson wasn't going to escape so easily from that.

Some one was coming down the stairs; he could hear the footsteps ringing in the silent emptiness of the stone corridor. That would be Maurice with the police, he thought. But they were not going to cheat him of his victory. There was still time for that. 'And Jan Muzyk?' he said. Again his voice was louder than he intended. 'He died too. Remember?'

'Of course I remember.' David saw the wariness in the other's face, and knew that again he had guessed right. 'Better than you, I remember. But that was an accident. Jan was drowned.'

'He was drowned, yes. But not by accident. Jan was murdered. And you killed him.'

There was a gasp of horror, perhaps of disbelief, from the others. Myerson heard it, and all the colour drained from his cheeks as he looked at them. Grevas reached for the near-by chair. Before he could sit down Maurice came in through the door and stood beside him.

David gave him a welcoming nod. 'You're right on cue, Maurice. Where are the police? Upstairs?'

'Still in their beds, for all I know.' Maurice's voice was grim. 'I couldn't get the damned boat to start. The engine fired readily enough, but it kept petering out. Some one's been mucking about with it.'

The announcement did not create the consternation he had anticipated. For a second or two they stared at him. Then their gaze drifted back to Myerson. Andrew said, 'Another of your tricks, I suppose.'

Myerson's shrug was a gesture of helplessness rather than of indifference. He said weakly, 'I just removed a small part.'

'So that we couldn't go for the police, eh?'

'No. No, it wasn't that. I did it on Tuesday, before there was any talk of the police.'

There was a puzzled look on Maurice's face. It was clear he had no idea of what lay behind Andrew's question. 'What's been going on here?' he asked. 'Anything I should know?'

David told him. As he talked the Baron pulled the chair up to the table, sat down, and poured himself a cup of coffee. The coffee was cold, but he sipped it delicately as though it were scalding hot. He seemed to have lost interest in the proceedings. Susan felt a twinge of pity for him. Myerson had been right; whatever the outcome, Grevas had no future in his present rôle. He might or might not be a fighter; but where was the sense in fighting if he had nothing to fight for?

She turned her attention to the others. Olive was obviously overcome by the turn of events. Edith too was lost. Her blue dressing-gown looked too small; buttoned up to the neck, it gaped over the ample bosom, the tight collar creasing her plump neck uncomfortably as she turned her head. Tom and the Mackays were completely absorbed. Susan suspected that Jutter was deriving pleasure from Myerson's agony; there was an eager, gloating look on her beautiful face as she watched him. But it was Bessie and Beryl who intrigued Susan most. Since David's first accusation neither had spoken. Bessie had not once looked in her husband's direction, had sought neither to accuse nor defend him; she sat at the table with downcast eyes, her strong brown fingers mechanically crumbling the piece of toast on her plate. Beryl still stood by the toaster; her buff-coloured dressing-gown seemed to merge with her skin, its masculine shapelessness concealing her figure. She wore no make-up, and the strong light emphasized the shadows under her eyes and the dark hairs along her upper lip. Occasionally she had glanced quickly at one or another of the speakers, but for most of the time she continued to stare at the Baron. She looked hurt and bewildered — like a dog who has been savagely kicked by its master, Susan thought.

'So Harold's the nigger in the wood-pile, is he?' Maurice put a hand on the Baron's shoulder, and Grevas winced at the touch. It must have felt like the arm of the Law already reaching out to grab him, thought David. 'Well, he's got the Baron all wrong. But right now that's unimportant. If he killed Jan — '

'I killed no one,' Myerson burst out. 'No one, I tell you.' His voice faltered. 'I — I may have been responsible for his death, but it was unintentional. I didn't *mean* to kill him.'

They received this in stony silence. Andrew said, 'We're wasting time, Maurice. I don't know about Jan — David sprung that on us as you came in — but I'm positive the Baroness was murdered. And the sooner the police are here the better.'

Maurice nodded agreement. 'I'll get them.' He turned to Myerson. 'What did you do with whatever it was you removed from the engine, damn you? What was it, anyway?'

'I don't know, damn *you*!' Myerson retorted, with a return of spirit. 'But I put it in the cabin locker.'

David followed Maurice into the passage. Maurice said, 'You're sure Myerson killed Jan?'

'He admitted it, didn't he? He's trying to make out it was an accident, but we know better.'

'And the Baroness?'

David was doubtful about the Baroness. 'What motive could he have had? It seems so senseless. And I can't believe he'd have killed her just to get even with the Baron. Even Myerson isn't as inhuman as that.'

'Did he have a motive for Jan's death?'

'He must have had. But that's different. We're on firm ground there.'

'So you say. It still has to be proved.' Maurice frowned. 'Have we one murderer or two? It's a sobering thought. You'll

336

have to keep them together, David. Don't let them disperse. I'll be as quick as I can.'

'Why pick on me?' David protested. 'Why not Andrew?'

'Because Andrew's one of us. You're not. You're outside all this.'

Remembering the bullet that had registered so close a miss, David was inclined to doubt that last statement. But he saw the force of Maurice's argument.

'I'll do my best,' he promised. 'But for the Lord's sake get a move on.'

He went back into the kitchen. Tom said, 'You and Maurice cooking something up?'

'He thinks we ought to stick together until the police arrive.' There was nothing else he could say. 'He thinks we'll be safer that way.'

'He does, does he?' Tom stood up, sleeves flapping. He hitched at his trousers pugnaciously. 'Well, here's one as ain't staying put. I got private business to attend to, if you see what I mean.'

David did see. And since there was nothing he could do to stop him he nodded agreement. 'But can you wait a few minutes? I wanted to explain about Jan. I said he was murdered, but I didn't say how.'

Tom sat down. Myerson said shrilly, 'All this talk of murder! It was an accident, I tell you. Pure accident.'

'Was it? Suppose you tell us, then.'

The Jew looked round for a vacant chair. He chose one away from the others and sat down, leaning forward with his knees apart and his hands clasped between them, his dark hair flopping untidily over his forehead. His Adam's apple bulged under the taut skin as he raised his head to face his accuser.

'Jan found he kept drifting out to sea while he was fishing,' he said tonelessly. 'And it was hard work pulling the old boat back afterwards. So he had the idea of anchoring it to the jetty with a long piece of rope. It would stop the drift, and he could haul himself in by it instead of rowing. Or that was the idea.'

'I bought some rope for him,' Jutter said, interested despite her antagonism. 'Nylon. Was that it?'

Myerson nodded. 'He asked me to fix it, and I did. He wasn't much good at that sort of thing.'

'It's how you fixed it that interests me,' David told him.

'It was nothing elaborate. I cut one of the thumbscrews off an old trouser-press and stuck it through a hole I'd made in the stern. It had a sort of metal sleeve attached, and I threaded the rope through that. The other end was tied to the jetty.' He lit a cigarette with nervous fingers, and threw the spent match on the floor. 'And that's all. Jan was satisfied and so was I; we both thought it would work. Neither of us had any idea it could end in tragedy. I still don't understand what happened. A rope that tough wouldn't break easily.' He gave a few quick puffs at the cigarette. 'I suppose the knot gave, although we both tested it.'

He looked at them in turn, hoping for sympathy. But he saw none. 'You can't call that murder,' he said hoarsely. 'I was only trying to help. He *asked* me to do it.'

That at least could be true, thought David. And it explained one thing that had puzzled him — why had Jan failed to see either the rope or the thumbscrew? The answer, of course, was that he *had* seen them. And they had caused him no concern because he had expected them to be there.

But if Myerson had told some of the truth he had not told it all. 'Granted the rope was Jan's idea,' David said. 'But you improved on it. You turned what was intended as a safety device into a death-trap.'

'I don't know what you're talking about.' Myerson was recovering his pugnacity. It was no new experience to have the world against him. 'You're back on this murder lark, I suppose. Why? Why should I want to murder him? Tell me that.'

It was one thing David could not tell him, and he admitted it. 'But I'm quite sure you had a motive,' he added.

Jutter said quietly, 'Perhaps Bessie could enlighten you on that.'

'My goodness, yes!' Olive had caught up with them at last. 'She could too.'

If she says 'My goodness!' again I'll

scream, thought Susan.

The sound of her name caused Bessie to look up from her crumbs. Her large, liquid eyes stared pensively across the table at Jutter. Olive she ignored.

'It isn't true,' she protested quietly. 'Harold knows that.'

'Of course it isn't true.' Myerson gave one of his high, giggly laughs. 'And it wouldn't have worried me if it were. Bessie knows *that*.' There was a gasp of outraged feminine pride at this insult to one of their sex. But not from Bessie; she seemed quite unmoved. 'Since this seems to be a time for plain speaking, you may as well know that Bessie and I married for convenience. She wanted to get away from Jamaica, I wanted a wife. Any wife. I'd heard that only married couples were being recruited for this particular enterprise, so I got myself married. It was as simple as that.'

Well, that disposes of that, thought David. But it didn't dispose of the murder. He said, 'Motive or no motive, you killed him; not accidentally, but deliberately. And I can prove it. You see, the rope wasn't carried away by the storm, as you thought. I found it. It's up in my room. Or it was until you took it.'

'I did what?' Myerson stared at him. 'I've never been in your room. What the hell are you talking about now?'

David let the protest pass. He had expected it.

'I not only found the rope; part of the stern of the boat was still attached to it. No doubt you thought that by the time it was recovered, if ever, the putty would have vanished and the screws with them. Well, most of them did. But not all. You were dead unlucky there, Myerson.'

Myerson was still staring. Andrew said, 'Myerson may know what you're talking about, David — though he claims he doesn't — but I'm damned if I do. Hadn't you better explain?'

'I'm sorry.' It had become so much a personal thing between him and the Jew that David had almost forgotten the others. 'I've no doubt he fixed the rope as he said. What he didn't mention was that later he went a stage farther. He removed the bottom board from the stern, to which the rope was affixed, and sawed off the ends of the screws so that they wouldn't hold. Then he nailed the board back into place with brads and filled the screwholes with putty — knowing full well that as soon as Jan reached the limit of the rope the resulting tug would pull the board away and the boat would sink. Which it did.'

With an effort Beryl turned her eyes from the Baron and focused them on David. She must have heard all that had been said, but clearly she had taken little of it in. She looked dazed. Bessie shook her head in disbelief, and there was a gasp of horror from Olive. Edith's eyes opened wider, and her fingers fluttered nervously in her lap. But of the men only Myerson showed any reaction. His voice higher than ever, he shouted, 'It isn't true. All I did was fix the rope. If you're right — if those screws were sawn off — '

'They were. The marks are clear.'

'Then some one else did it. Why the hell should I want to murder Jan? He and I had plenty in common. For one thing, we both hated Grevas.'

There was nothing in the Baron's demeanour to show that he had heard. Andrew said, 'Is that true, Olive? Did Jan hate the Baron?'

'Well, I guess he didn't always see things the same way,' Olive admitted. 'But he certainly didn't hate him'

'He hated Grevas and he hated the island. He wasn't far off hating you,' Myerson told her brutally. 'He didn't want to come here in the first place, and he only stuck it because he couldn't bear to be parted from all those lovely dollars of yours. Living on a dismal little island like this with a bunch of crazy idealists for company wasn't Jan's idea of how to be happy though rich. And you know it.'

Olive's homely face went a deep pink, swamping the freckles. Feeling sorry for her, David said quickly, 'If you didn't murder Jan, why steal the rope from my room?'

Myerson shook his head. It was a gesture of hopelessness rather than of denial. 'I've already told you I didn't. I didn't even know you had the damned rope.' He sat up, arching his back, and lit a cigarette. 'But nothing I say seems to cut any ice, so I may as well keep my denials for the police. They're probably less bigoted.'

It was a suggestion that met with some approval. Certainly no one objected. Tom said, 'Well, now that's settled, maybe I can take a walk. It's been a long few minutes. And while I'm up there I'll collect your ironmongery for you, Olive. If it's still in the lav, that is.'

'It'll be there,' Myerson told him.

With Tom's going there was a long, uneasy silence. Jutter sipped the cold liquid in her cup and wrinkled her nose in disgust. 'How about some more coffee, Edith?' she said.

David sat down at the table and looked covertly at Myerson, puzzled by the calm that seemed to have descended on the man with the cessation of verbal warfare. He was smoking his cigarette with an air of tranquillity, not as though it were a palliative to frayed nerves and the difficult passage of time. Had Myerson resigned himself to fate, or was he plotting some new devilry?

David yawned. He had had a night with no rest and little sleep, and it was warm in the kitchen. Excitement had invigorated his mind and his body, but now that excitement was temporarily at an end he became suddenly aware of his tiredness. He wanted to close his eyes and rest his head on the table and sleep. And there was nothing to stop him. Nobody seemed interested in him now.

'Coffee, David?' That was Susan's voice, a long way off. 'Hey, wake up, darling! You can't snooze now.'

'I wasn't snoozing.' He shook himself awake, nodded at the coffee-pot, and watched her pour. 'Just resting my eyes, that's all. Didn't get much sleep last night.'

As he picked up the cup he heard footsteps hurrying down the passage. There was an urgency in them that boded trouble, but he felt too lethargic to care. He took a quick sip at the coffee, blinked the heaviness from his eyes, and yawned.

The footsteps stopped behind him. They were all looking expectantly at the door. Then the expectancy faded from their faces, and he knew that something was wrong, that he would have to pick up the reins again.

'They ain't there,' Tom said, as David turned. 'I searched the whole flipping lav, but they ain't there.'

The eyes ping-ponged to Myerson. He looked helplessly at Tom. 'That's where I put them,' he said. 'Some one must have lifted them.'

'Did you tell anyone what you'd done?' Andrew asked.

'No.'

'Then that settles it. They're not there because you didn't put them there. It's just another of your damned lies.' Andrew spread his arms in a gesture of resignation. 'Well, you can save the rest of them for the police. I've had enough.'

There was a murmur of agreement, and then silence. If the thoughts that filled their minds were not to be argued or discussed, then conversation seemed pointless. The commonplace was not enough.

They passed the time in drinking coffee. Only Tom was hungry. The cooked food was beyond even his hearty appetite, but he munched steadily on toast and marmalade. The sound of his clicking teeth gradually got on Susan's nerves, and without thought she snapped out, 'Oh, for goodness sake!'

They looked at her in astonishment. Susan blushed, aware that involuntarily she had borrowed the words, if not the intonation, from Olive. And only a short time before she had thought to scream if ever she heard them again!

'What's biting you?' David asked.

'Nothing. I'm just edgy, that's all. Can't we talk about something? It may be ages before Maurice gets back. We can't just sit.'

'What is there to talk about?'

She looked at him scornfully. What a typically David-like question! But before she could answer Myerson said, 'Good idea. And seeing that this little venture has just about folded, perhaps the Baron would care to tell us what magnificent money-making scheme he has lined up for the future? Who knows — some of you may care to invest in it. You can't be broke yet. This one never really got going.'

The scorn in his voice brought a flush to the cheeks of some. Olive in particular looked embarrassed. But at first no one protested. David wondered how a man in Myerson's dangerous position could still be so wholehearted in his hate. Maurice was wrong, he thought. It's not bile that runs in his veins, it's venom.

Tom finished his mouthful, took a noisy draught of coffee, and wiped his lips with the back of his skinny hand. 'I've met some sportin' Jews in my time,' he said. 'Good boxers, some of 'em was. Clean fighters, too.' There was a pause while he ran his tongue under his lower dentures to remove a trouble-some crumb. 'But you ain't one of 'em, mate. You don't just hit a man when he's down; you ruddy well kick him to pieces.'

Myerson shrugged. Secure in his hate and his revenge, he seemed impervious to words. Andrew said sternly, 'You accuse the Baron of fraud, which he denies. But you can't deny your own fraud. You couldn't care less about world peace, could you? On your own admission you came here with the sole purpose of revenge. Well, you've got it. But you won't enjoy it for long. When it comes to murder — '

'You can cut that out.' Myerson spoke sharply. Apparently 'murder' was the one word that could shake him out of his indifference. 'I've done no murder. Nor has anyone else, to my mind. It's just a scare thought up by David to sell his damned paper. Jan's death was an accident.'

'And the Baroness?'

Here we go again, thought David. A few moments back they were leaving him to the police, now they're all set for a repeat performance. Yet it was only natural. With so much on their minds it was as difficult to be silent as to discuss trivialities. Even he, a relative outsider to the drama, found it difficult.

Grevas and Edith had seemed the most detached persons in the room. Even when Myerson had issued his last mocking challenge Grevas had continued to sip his coffee, apparently unmoved. Now the cup was empty. But it was still in his hand as he said quietly, 'I think I agree with Harold. No one had anything to gain by killing Jan. As for Laura — ' His voice faltered. 'No, it isn't possible. Me, perhaps. But not Laura.'

It was the first time David and Susan had heard the Baroness's Christian name. Susan thought it suited her; and then felt guilty, remembering that the woman was dead. David wondered at that 'Me, perhaps.' Surely only Myerson might want to harm the Baron? Then he smiled to himself, thinking that it was a pity he could not use the phrase 'Grevas bodily harm.' It was the sort of pun that appealed to readers of *Topical Truths*.

Myerson seemed astonished that anyone, and particularly the Baron, should agree with him. He did not attempt to answer Andrew, but sat staring moodily at the door. Andrew shook his head in disagreement, but he did not repeat the question. They would have lapsed once more into uneasy silence had not Susan, afraid of just that, said diffidently, 'For the sake of argument, why not assume that Mr Myerson is telling the truth, and see where that leads us? Or don't you think that's a good idea?'

'A very good idea,' Myerson said. 'So original.'

'Well, I think it's lousy,' David told her. 'What's the point?'

'To help pass the time, chiefly. And I like to hear both sides of an argument. Unless, of course, I'm convinced that one side is right. Then I just don't listen to the other.'

'H'm! Typically feminine.'

Jutter's pupils dilated, wide eyebrows arched. 'You mean you're not convinced now?'

'Not entirely. It's the rope being taken from David's room that puzzles me. If Mr Myerson took it he must have discovered it by chance. He couldn't have known it was there. But others did.'

'You mean Olive and Tom and Andrew?' David smiled indulgently. 'You've forgotten it was taken before they searched my room.'

She had forgotten, but she would not

admit it. 'How do you know that? You told me yourself that from where you were standing you couldn't see the suitcase. It could have been there. And one of them may have gone back later and taken it.'

David shrugged, and looked inquiringly at the three concerned. The two men shook their heads. More cautious, Olive said, 'I certainly didn't see any rope.'

'Satisfied, Susan? Or do we now have to assume that they too are lying?'

'No.' Susan was annoyed. It was not going as she had hoped. It had become a personal inquisition of herself. 'But there's still Maurice. He saw it when he searched your room Tuesday night, didn't he?'

'Maurice?' Andrew was startled. 'How come?'

Cursing Susan's interference, David explained. At the end he said, 'I don't blame him. I was the obvious suspect. With a hundred thousand dollars' worth of jewellery gone astray I'd say he was justified.'

At the gasp of astonishment that

greeted this piece of information he realized that he too had been indiscreet. But he did not greatly care. Tom whistled through his teeth, setting them rattling. He said, with awe in his voice. 'A hundred thousand dollars! Strewth! What's that in real money?'

No one enlightened him. Olive, her face a fiery red, muttered that the figure had been exaggerated, and glanced guiltily at Grevas. But Grevas, like David, did not appear to care. He contented himself with a gentle shake of the head.

David said, 'The point is, Maurice saw the rope and didn't take it. So don't try to pin it on him.'

'I'm not,' Susan retorted. 'I'm just assuming.'

'That's the trouble,' Myerson said. 'You're assuming, but you're not thinking. None of you are. You should try it some time. You're forgetting that the rope implicated no one but myself. I fixed it to the boat; murder or no murder, no one else had anything to do with it. It therefore follows that only I could have had any reason for taking it from David's room.' He sighed. 'But I didn't. Work that one out if you can.'

They couldn't. Nor did they try. Susan too gave up; she had tried and failed. All they could do now was to wait as patiently as they could for Maurice and the police.

All except David. Myerson had set him thinking. What he had said was true; the rope could be no danger to anyone but himself. But what he had not said — had not perhaps, even appreciated — was that the rope was no danger to him either. It was Jan, not Myerson, who had asked Jutter to buy it, and presumably for just the use that Myerson had described. And so it had been used; Myerson had readily admitted that. But its use did not prove that he or anyone else had committed murder. It was the manner of its use that mattered.

Yet if the rope constituted a danger to no one, why had it been taken? He could think of no answer to that. But one thing was perfectly clear; in this, at least, Myerson was no more suspect than the others.

David frowned. He found that knowledge disturbing. Myerson had admitted much and denied more, and in one denial at least he could be speaking the truth. What if he were speaking the truth in the others?

He tried to concentrate on the problem of the rope. He had put it in his suitcase before breakfast on the Tuesday, and Maurice had seen it there late that night when he was looking for Olive's jewellery. It must have been taken some time on the Wednesday morning, probably while he was out on the sand-dunes with Susan. And the thief must have expected to find it there. He must have known it had gone from the jetty and suspected that he, David, was responsible.

Without preamble he said, 'Who went bathing on Tuesday?'

They looked at him as though he had taken leave of his senses. Andrew said, 'What's biting you now, David? Aren't you slightly off target?' But Myerson understood. He said, 'He's bang on. He's taken my advice; he's started thinking.

And he's come to the logical conclusion that maybe the guilt isn't all mine. Right?' David nodded. 'Well, Bessie and I did. I wanted to see if the rope was still there. But it wasn't, and I assumed I'd been right in thinking that somehow it had come adrift.'

David said, 'Jutter was already in the water when Susan and I got down to the jetty. That was before breakfast. And Maurice had a swim after lunch. Anyone else?'

He happened to be looking at Olive as he spoke. 'My goodness, no!' she said, horrified. 'Not me. I can't swim.'

Andrew and Tom both said no. After a quick look at her husband, so did Edith. He had to repeat the question to Beryl before she shook her head. 'And you, Baron? I remember you were out on the cliffs early that morning.'

'Not for a bathe.' Grevas was more alert. He had lit a cigarette, and had begun to take an interest in the discussion. 'I dislike sea-water bathing.' He made it sound a vulgar pastime. 'But you did, Tom, surely? You were coming back to the house as I went out. Remember?'

'He must remember.' Jutter said. 'I met him too. And may I say that I went for a swim, not to look for a rope I didn't know was there?'

Tom's wrinkled face was too sun-burned to flush, but he was clearly embarrassed. He said, 'I went down to the jetty, but I didn't bathe. Put me big toe in, and that was enough. It was too flippin' cold.'

Edith opened her mouth, looked hard at Tom, and then shut it. Myerson said lightly, 'All men are liars. But damn me if I know why they're lying now.'

David nodded absently. Jutter, or Tom, or Grevas; if it wasn't Myerson it had to be one of those. But which? All three had been out early that morning. Jutter had bought the rope; she may not have been told why, but she could have found out later. There was no direct evidence against Grevas, but with the reputation both Snowball and Myerson had given him he must always be suspect. And Tom . . .

David frowned. He liked Tom. Yet Tom had been in his room on the Tuesday morning; he could not have taken the rope away with him then, but he could have seen it and returned for it later. It was Tom who had fired at least one of the two shots on the previous afternoon, and he had certainly lied just now. Edith's surprise at his denial had made that clear. What if he had also been lying when he said . . .

David felt the heat rise round his collar, felt his body go damp and sticky with sweat. He had suddenly realized, with a sense of shock that momentarily numbed his brain into inactivity, that most of his assumptions had been based on fallacies. The rope, for instance. He had thought it would lead him to the murderer, but it had led only to Myerson. And Myerson, he knew now, was not the murderer. There was Jan's cigarette-case, there was Olive's jewellery . . . there was . . .

He shook his head vigorously to clear it, lit a cigarette, and drew on it gratefully. Some of the people in the room had started to talk among themselves, but he heard their voices only vaguely, as a background to his thoughts. And as the thoughts crystallized he was appalled by what he saw.

'Myerson's right,' he said. Even to his own ears his voice sounded unnaturally shrill. 'We've based our assumptions on false premises. Even Myerson has.' He turned to the astonished Jew. 'You said you had told no one where you had hidden Olive's jewellery. That wasn't true. You did tell some one. So did I.'

'But I didn't,' Myerson protested. 'I'm not that crazy. It wasn't until — ' He paused. 'Good Lord!'

'Until just now,' David finished for him. 'That's what I mean. You told us.'

'Don't be absurd, David,' Jutter said. 'What difference does that make? Since we came down here none of us except Tom has left the room. And it was he who discovered that it wasn't where Mr Myerson said he'd put it.'

This was greeted in silence. Jutter looked round in surprise, wondering what had happened to her expected support. Andrew said quietly, 'I see what David means. We've only Tom's word that it wasn't in the lavatory. But suppose it was?'

Tom stared at him, his eyes narrowed. Jutter said sharply, 'Why should he say it wasn't if it was?'

'Because that was what we expected to hear. None of us believed Harold.' He turned to face Tom. 'How about it, Tom?'

'How about what?'

'The jewellery. David is suggesting that it *was* in the lavatory, and that you found it and have hidden it elsewhere.' He paused. 'Is that true?'

Edith gave a whimper of protest. But there was no whimper from her husband. He bounced out of his chair, pushed Andrew roughly aside, and advanced threateningly on David.

'You take that back,' he bellowed. 'I'll have no whipper-snapper like you calling me a thief and a liar and Gawd knows what else.'

David shook his head.

'You've got it wrong, Tom,' he said quietly. 'So has Andrew. I wasn't thinking of you, I was thinking of Maurice.'

19

They were less surprised than David had expected; Maurice had not occupied the unique position in their minds that he had in his. They had thought of Maurice as being in the same position as themselves, but to David he had become a rock on which to depend. Now Maurice was no longer rock. He had crumbled into sand.

Susan showed the most surprise. 'Only yesterday you were saying that Maurice was the one person you could rely on,' she protested.

'You said it. I agreed with you because he had shown no interest in the rope. That means nothing now.'

'But there was the ladder.'

Yes, David admitted, there was the ladder; and because the others were curious he told them about it. 'Don't ask me to explain,' he said. 'I can't. On the face of it one would assume, as I did, that it puts Maurice in the clear. But then we don't know all the facts.'

Andrew was sceptical. 'You're too free with your accusations, David. First Harold, now Maurice. Why?'

Beryl no longer had eyes for the Baron. She was watching David, and her expression told him he was right. She knew, he thought, Or if she didn't know before she knows now.

He said, 'Only Tom and Maurice have left this room since Myerson told us where the jewellery was hidden. If you believe Tom and Myerson, then it has to be Maurice.'

'That's asking a lot, isn't it? Personally, I'd trust Maurice rather than Myerson. I'm leaving Tom out of it.'

'Ta,' Tom said. He sat down on the table, still looking slightly belligerent.

'So would most of us, I imagine, after what we've heard this morning,' David agreed. 'But there's more to it than that. Jan's cigarette-case, for a start. Maurice told us it contained cigarettes when Jan last had it. Well, we know it didn't. They were put in later by Myerson.' He looked at the Jew. 'That's right, isn't it?'

Myerson nodded. Andrew said, 'So what? It's hardly sufficient evidence on which to accuse a man of murder.'

'I'm not saying it is. I'm saying it makes him a liar. He lied about the cigarette-case, and just now he lied about the launch.'

'How?'

'I don't believe he'd been anywhere near it. Didn't you notice his surprised look when Myerson admitted he'd tampered with it?' David hesitated. 'He was absent too long; if he'd found part of the engine missing he'd have come straight back. He knew that, and he suspected we might know it too. Hence the engine that kept starting and stopping. It was too late to rectify his mistake when Myerson spoke up; he just had to trust we wouldn't notice it. Or perhaps he didn't notice it himself.'

'If he did he's a sight cleverer than what I am,' Tom said. 'I'm not with you, mate. What mistake?'

David's smile had in it something of condescension. Despite the seriousness of their position the obvious perplexity of his audience was gratifying. It imbued him with a comfortable feeling of superiority.

'If you remove part of an engine it won't even fire.' He looked at Myerson. 'What was it, by the way? You said you didn't know. But can you describe it?'

'I can do better than that.' Myerson reached into his jacket pocket. 'I can show it to you.'

He threw a small object on to the table.

The men craned forward. Andrew said, 'The rotor arm. Why did you tell Maurice you'd put it in the cabin locker?'

'I didn't like his attitude. I thought it would do him good to have a second wasted journey.'

Andrew picked up the rotor arm and put it in his trouser pocket.

'O.K. So David's right; Maurice lied to us about the launch. It doesn't necessarily make him a murderer, of course, but — well, why? What's he up to?'

David shrugged. 'Your guess is as good as mine.'

Tom slid off the table. 'He'll be back

soon,' he said. 'In a flamin' temper, too. What happens then?'

That was something David did not care to contemplate. He said gravely, 'It could be unpleasant. When I told him yesterday that some one had been shooting at me he took the bolts out of the two rifles and pocketed them. So he's armed and we're not. And if he's what I think he is . . . if he murdered Jan . . . '

Beryl said quietly, 'He did.'

They all looked at her. Even Grevas. Andrew said sharply, 'You knew?'

'No. But I know now. David said some one cut the screws off with a hacksaw and filled the holes with putty.' Her voice did not falter. 'I'm not sure I know what a hacksaw is. But the day after Jan was drowned I was mending a tear in Maurice's jacket, and in the pocket there was a lump of putty and some pieces of a broken saw-blade.'

They greeted this news in silence, but fear crept into the eyes of the women. It had been sufficiently unnerving to have a supposed murderer among them, even though he protested his innocence and

366

was weak and unarmed. But to know that a murderer was stalking the island, angry at having been tricked and possibly with a rifle he would not hesitate to use — that was too alarming to think on.

Olive pushed back her chair and stood up. The sudden noise startled them.

'For goodness sake! What are we going to *do*? We can't just sit here and wait to be murdered!'

'What do you suggest we do?' Jutter's tone was scornful. 'Run around like a lot of frightened rabbits? I'd rather stay here, thank you. Why should Maurice want to kill us?'

'Why, indeed?' Maurice echoed from the doorway.

He stood surveying them, a slight smile on his bronzed, handsome face, the dimples in his cheeks coming and going. Rubber-soled suede shoes had replaced the boots he had previously worn, he had donned a check suit, smartly cut, in place of flannels and a sweater. In his hands he held a rifle, one finger on the trigger.

They looked at him, not knowing what to say and fearful of saying the wrong thing. David stood as though petrified. He was only a yard from the door, and any movement might irritate that finger.

The smile faded from Maurice's lips as he swung the muzzle towards him. 'Over there,' he said curtly, nodding at the far wall. 'All of you.' He prodded the Baron in the back with the rifle. 'You too, Grevas.'

He sat down in the vacated chair and rested the rifle on the table, its muzzle towards them. Momentarily he let go of it to reach for the coffee-pot, but they were too stunned to take advantage of the moment. They stood in line against the wall, watching him. Olive's mouth was agape, her fingers played nervously with her frock; Bessie shuffled uneasily from one foot to another, her dark skin glistening. The others were still.

'David eventually got his ideas right, did he?' Maurice poured himself a cup of coffee and looked at his wife. 'Or was it you? When I heard him prattling about putty and hacksaws I thought you might tumble to it. So I came prepared.' He patted the rifle. 'Well, it doesn't matter.

Has the Baron made a full confession? No?' He glanced at his wristwatch. 'Then I'll do it for him. There's time enough before I leave.'

He sipped at the coffee and grimaced. A glimmer of hope stirred in David's brain. Maurice was too genial, too sure of himself; clearly he had not yet discovered that Myerson had lied about the rotor arm. Instead of making for the launch he must have been changing and packing.

'We fixed it up between us,' Maurice said. 'He was the front, I was the brains. And you, as Harold has already told you, were the mugs. And that's all there is to it.'

'Except for a couple of murders,' Andrew said. His voice was taut. David wondered whether it was from fear or anger. He suspected anger, and was worried. Maurice did not look like a man intent on murder. But if his mind were unbalanced . . . if Andrew were to rile him . . .

Maurice smiled. 'Jan was no mug,' he said. 'Like us, he believed that fools should be parted from their money. Given time, he'd have parted you from yours, Olive. Unfortunately for him, he tangled with me first. He overheard a private argument between Grevas and myself, and promptly tried blackmail. While his demands were reasonable I let him be; when they got too big he had to go. And Harold supplied the means.'

Myerson said, 'Did Jan tell you about the rope?' He sounded neither frightened nor angry. Merely curious.

'No one told me. I saw you at work on the boat one evening and investigated later. Most ingenious, Harold; all I had to do was add the finishing touches. And it worked admirably. Even the elements approved. The storm disposed of the evidence, such as it was.'

'Except the rope,' David said.

'That's true. It gave me quite a turn when I saw it in your suitcase. It showed you were curious, if nothing else. But I left it; it could incriminate Harold, perhaps, but not me. I removed it later because I decided there must be no evidence of murder by anyone, let alone by me. The police had accepted Jan's death as an accident; no point in letting you rouse their curiosity. I didn't think they could pin it on me, but one can never be sure. There was always Beryl.' He smiled cheerfully at David. 'For the same reason I decided to dispose of you and Susan. Unfortunately, good shot as I am, I missed you. I never got around to Susan.'

Susan shuddered. Somehow his calm cheerfulness made him seem the more dangerous. His brain, not his instincts, would govern all his moves; even if it were deranged she had the feeling that it would still plan logically and, if need be, callously. And if reason told him that their deaths were essential, or merely even contributory, to his safety, then he would kill.

Maurice saw the shudder. 'Thinking of Tuesday night, Susan? But you're wrong; it was Olive's jewellery I was after, not you. When I learned its value I couldn't wait to get my hands on it.' He looked quizzically at Olive. 'This may surprise you, Olive; but having made you a widow it seemed logical to make you a wife again. With all your money I'd have proved an excellent husband. Besides, life here was boring. I can put up with boredom if it promises a profit, but this looked like fizzling out. Grevas had gone soft; the peace bug had got him, to the detriment of our pockets.' Bessie shifted her feet again, and he nodded at a chair. 'Sit down, Bessie, if your ankle's bad. No need to be uncomfortable.'

There was a telltale flush on Olive's cheeks that suggested Maurice's proposal might not have been unwelcome. Beryl showed neither disgust nor sorrow nor alarm. It was Jutter who said quietly, 'And Beryl? What did you propose to do about her?'

Maurice shrugged. 'What could I do? She doesn't hold with divorce. I hoped her passion for Grevas might offer a solution; believe me, it isn't based solely on his supposed moral virtues, although she likes to think it is. I kept stressing how much the poor man needed a good woman in his life, hoping she would eventually take the hint. I knew Grevas would play; women are one of his weaknesses.' He sighed. 'But it didn't seem to be working. Hence the ladder.'

Beryl echoed the sigh. It was as if she had been waiting for that. Myerson, still curious, said, 'But you couldn't know she would climb it.'

Maurice grinned. 'It was a fair bet. I'd put it against the Baron's bedroom window. She had never seen inside that Holy of Holies, and I guessed she wouldn't pass up the opportunity.' He shook his head. 'But it didn't come off. She survived.'

He had not once looked at Beryl; he spoke of her as though she were not there, exhibiting neither shame nor remorse. Susan found his callousness almost unbearable. To her, this murder that had failed was even more horrible than those that had succeeded.

David said, 'You were messing up the marriages a bit, weren't you? Was that why you killed the Baroness? To provide a husband for Beryl?'

'Good heavens, no!' He looked across at Grevas. 'I apologize for that. It was something of a mistake.' The Baron shuddered, but said nothing. 'I happened to see Beryl go into your bedroom, and I thought my original plan was at last bearing fruit. I waited until I heard you come upstairs, allowed you time to get going, and then walked in, prepared to do the wronged husband act. But again it went sour. You had gone to your study instead of the bedroom, and Beryl had got cold feet and opted out. The only person in the room was the Baroness, who had chosen that night of all nights to demonstrate her wifely affection.'

He paused. He seemed to appreciate their interest in his recital, and David said hastily, 'I don't see why you had to kill her.'

'You wouldn't. But as I started to ease out of the room with a graceful apology she told me she had seen me fire at you that afternoon. Not that she was alarmed for your safety; it was Grevas she was afraid for. She was in on our little scheme, of course, and she didn't like the way things were shaping. She thought it was time I dissolved the partnership and left.' He shook his head. 'I'm afraid I acted on impulse. If I'd given myself time to reflect I'd have realized that her threat to expose me was an empty one; she couldn't do that without ruining her husband. But there it is. I'm sorry.'

He's mad, thought David. He may have been sane when this dreadful business started, but he's mad now. No sane man could talk so dispassionately of the things Maurice has done.

'And now?' Andrew said. His anger seemed to have evaporated. Perhaps he too had decided that Maurice was mad, and that madness did not call for anger. 'I take it you're leaving us?'

'Very shortly.' Maurice drew the rifle towards him and stood up. 'I'm taking the launch to Pockling; it's not known there, so no one will start making inquiries if it's left for a while.' He backed towards the door. 'Sorry to leave you stranded, but it's unlikely to be for long. After a few days some one from Littleport will be out to look you up. You'll remember that happened when the launch packed up last month. And by then I shall be out of the country. Well out. Oh — one word of warning, Baron. Don't write any cheques on our account. They'll bounce. I shall be withdrawing the balance this afternoon. It should be quite a tidy sum. With that and Olive's jewellery I'm not likely to starve.'

In turn he surveyed them, a slight smile on his lips. David said quickly, 'Would you answer a couple of questions before you go?'

'There speaks the journalist. What are they?'

'The first evening I was here Myerson suggested Jan's boat had tipped up. I should have thought it would have suited your book to agree with him. But you didn't. Why?'

'Stupid of me, wasn't it? But I guessed Harold had a guilt complex about that rope, and was trying to convince himself it had nothing to do with Jan's death. I wasn't going to let him wriggle off the hook as easily as that.'

There was nothing evil or cruel in the smile he gave them. It was warm and friendly. I'll never trust a smile again, thought Susan. Nor a man with dimples in his cheeks.

'What else?' Maurice asked.

'Why did you say there were cigarettes in Jan's case when you knew there weren't? It seems such an unnecessary lie.'

Maurice nodded. 'A subconscious attempt to bolster another lie, perhaps. I said Jan produced the case to light a cigarette, and therefore there ought to have been cigarettes in it. What actually happened was that he wanted me to flog it for him; there were, I gathered, other items of value to follow.' He shook his head. 'A bad lot, Jan. Anything else?'

'I don't think so.'

'Then I'll get cracking.' He looked hard at David. 'You and Susan are lucky to be alive. Don't press your luck. After I've collected my gear from the hall I shall go straight to the launch, and I advise you not to follow. I shan't hesitate to shoot, believe me. And next time I may not miss.'

He jerked the rifle menacingly, gave a jaunty wave of the hand, and was gone.

David did believe him. His legs felt weak, and he was glad to sit down. So were most of the others. Bessie and Edith were in tears, but Beryl still stared glassily at the empty doorway. She alone had made no move to a chair.

The Baron's voice broke falteringly into the near silence.

'Before anyone says anything, I want you all to know that Maurice was right. Neither he nor I was interested in promoting peace; all we wanted was your money. But that was at the beginning. After a while I began to believe in what we were supposedly trying to achieve; it seemed to me that we might really succeed. Partially succeed, anyway. It came to mean more to me than anything else.' He passed a hand wearily across his forehead. 'That was where the trouble started. I wanted to put things right with you, to return as much of your money as I could, and then hope that we could go on from there. But Maurice wouldn't agree, and I suppose I hadn't the courage to break with him openly.' Grevas sighed. 'Well, I've paid for my sins. So, unfortunately, have others.'

The silence continued. One or two

glanced uncomfortably at each other, and then at Grevas; but there were no comments. David doubted if even now the Baron had given them the whole truth. Was it really the ideal of world peace that had converted him, or had he become obsessed with the promise of power that the leader of such a movement would enjoy?

Andrew cleared his throat. He said, 'Explanations and recriminations must wait. Maurice won't. In a little while he'll be back, and this time his madness may take a less genial form. What do we do about the rotor arm?'

'Give it to him,' Myerson said promptly. 'I'm not arguing with a gun. What's the alternative? If we don't give it he'll take it. And he may not be gentle in the taking.'

'There's another alternative,' Andrew said. 'But we'd have to act quickly. There's not much time.'

'What's that?' David asked. He did not fancy either of Myerson's alternatives.

'We can try to outsmart him. Without the rotor arm he's stuck. We're not. If we go round by the eastern shore, under cover of the trees, we should be able to reach the launch unseen. Given a little luck, we could be clear of the island before he catches on.' He paused for their comments, but none came. Reading assent into their silence, he said briskly, 'Edith, go up and dress. You too, Beryl. And hurry.'

Edith limped quietly from the room, but Beryl did not move. Andrew said, 'Jutter, take her up and dress her. And remember that every second could be precious.'

Jutter took Beryl's arm and led her away. She went unprotesting, but it was clear that she did not appreciate what was happening. Susan suspected that her shocked mind had been unable to bear the strain Maurice had imposed on it.

Myerson said, 'You're taking it for granted we agree. Well, I don't. I say it's too dangerous.'

'Of course it's dangerous. But it's dangerous to stay here. An angry Maurice, armed with a rifle he's probably itching to use, is some one I'm not

380

anxious to meet.' There was a gasp from Olive as the implication struck home. 'It'll take him fifteen minutes to reach the launch, and he can get back here in twelve if he hurries. He'll waste time searching the cabin for the rotor arm, more time searching the house for us; he can't leave without that arm. There's no telling how long it will be before he realizes what we're up to, but I reckon we have roughly three-quarters of an hour before he's back at the jetty for the second time. That should be enough.'

There was no further argument. The way Andrew put it, it seemed safer to go than to stay; and the knowledge that by going they would foil Maurice appealed to most of them. Only Grevas treated the decision with indifference. He got up wearily from his chair and shuffled out after the others without a word.

They took nothing with them. There was no time to pack, and if they were successful they would be coming back. They straggled hurriedly down to the shelter of the trees, with Andrew leading and Myerson and Grevas immediately behind him. For the first part of the journey the cover was thin, and they ran in little flurries of speed from tree to tree, like participants in an elongated game of musical chairs. But some could not run. Despite her fears, Olive was soon out of breath, and so was Edith. Jutter found Beryl a reluctant escapist. She had no will to hurry; and although she made no verbal protest she had almost to be dragged along by force. Susan and Bessie brought up the rear with David; Bessie because she could only hobble and had to use David as a human crutch, and Susan because, even under those dramatic circumstances, she disliked leaving David and Bessie together. That would have surprised David had he suspected it. Though he had an arm around Bessie's waist, the excitement which he had experienced the previous afternoon was lacking now. He thought of Bessie only as an encumbrance who had to be supported. As he went he kept casting an anxious eye over his left shoulder, and brooded darkly on the kind of man who could leave his crippled wife, however unloved, to the care and protection of another.

They were half-way to the launch when they saw Maurice. He came out from the little wood south of the jetty and strode purposefully along the path to the house, the rifle still clutched in his hands. He looked a menacing figure, and Susan was glad they had taken Andrew's advice. I wouldn't care to be waiting for him back at the house now, she thought.

Andrew looked round anxiously at his flock, wondering how visible they would be should Maurice chance to glance their way. But Maurice looked neither to right nor to left. Head bent, body leaning forward, he marched on up the hill, leaving behind him open gates and a scatter of squawking hens.

Andrew sighed with relief and waited for the others to come up to him. He said, 'I'm going ahead now to start the engine. Make straight for the jetty, and put on all the steam you can.' He looked at his wife, who still held Beryl's arm. 'How's she making, Jutter?'

Jutter shook her head. 'She's still in a

daze, poor thing. It's been too much for her, I'm afraid.'

'We'll get her to a doctor as soon as we can.'

'Is it wise to start the engine until we're all there?' Myerson objected. 'She's noisy. Maurice might hear.'

'Not unless he's on the way back. In that case it makes no odds whether he hears or not. He'll have guessed what we're up to.'

He turned to leave, but David caught his arm. 'There are eleven of us,' he said. 'Can you pack that lot into the launch?'

Andrew frowned. 'That's what worries me. Even if we get them aboard she'll be low in the water and damned sluggish. Some of us may have to stay behind. But I hope not.'

He ran off through the trees, his short, thick-set legs working overtime. David wanted to go with him, but he knew that he must stay with the others. Myerson said, 'Packed tight on the launch, there'd be no cover for most of us. What if Maurice gets back to the jetty before

384

we're out of range? It'd be sheer slaughter.'

That thought had been in David's mind too. 'Can we get all the women into the cabin?' he asked.

Myerson shrugged, but did not answer.

There was no longer a defined track; the undergrowth and brambles had run riot between the trees, and the women in particular found the going difficult and even painful. Yet they dared not venture into the open. Because progress was slower the party was less strung out; David was relieved to see that Bessie, helped now by Tom, was managing to keep up with the others. So too was Edith. The limp was more pronounced, and it was clear that her ankles were paining her; her round pudding face was greyer than ever, her tiny mouth gaped as she breathed through it noisily. But she struggled on, unaided and uncomplaining.

As he pulled aside a branch for Olive to pass, Grevas said, to no one in particular, 'If any have to stay I must be one. It's my right.'

'You'll be a dead duck if you do,' Myerson told him. 'Right or no right.'

'I don't think so.' The branch swished back into place. 'If the launch can get well clear of the jetty before Maurice reaches it he'll think he's alone on the island. I'll probably be safer in the wood than on the launch.'

He's right, David thought. But it's vital that when Maurice first sees the launch it should be too far out for him to count the numbers aboard. It doesn't matter then how many stay behind. The more the better; it'll give the launch maximum speed.

'I'll stay with you,' he said impetuously.

'Me too,' Myerson said. It seemed that expediency was turning them into heroes. Maybe into corpses. There was the possibility that Maurice might not be so easily fooled, that he might stalk the woods for them like a hunter after prey. 'Three of us might even be able to collar the brute if we can jump him from behind. That could save the police a load of trouble.'

'A load of damage too,' David said.

'Maurice isn't carrying that rifle for fun.'

It was a relief to hear the engine purring sweetly as they came out of the wood. They hurried down the jetty, casting anxious glances behind them; should Maurice come on them now they were lost. But Maurice did not come. Andrew began handing the women into the launch, and hastily David explained to him what he and Myerson and the Baron had agreed. 'You must go, of course,' he said. 'And the women. The rest of us should stay. The lighter the load the quicker you'll be out of range.'

Andrew nodded. 'But not Tom. We may need a spare helmsman if Maurice's eye is in.'

Tom was already in the launch. Protesting, he started to clamber out, but Andrew pushed him back and jumped aboard after him. David saw Susan's pert face peering up at him from the cabin porthole. He grinned at her and she put out her tongue, and then the launch was moving away from the jetty, its exhaust burbling merrily and a small fountain of spray marking its progress.

The three men did not stay to watch it go, but ran for the shelter of the wood. Once there they felt comparatively safe. Myerson, crouched behind a tree, said breathlessly, 'How about collecting a few fat stones? If Maurice lets fly at the launch we could sling them at him. We'd probably miss, but at least we'd disturb his aim. It would give them a sporting chance.'

'It wouldn't give us one,' David said, wondering at the change in the man. The threat of danger seemed to have blown away his former bitterness; he was eager and alert. 'Maurice has got to believe we're all on the launch.'

They heard Maurice before they saw him. He came pounding down the path, and at the sound of his hurrying feet they instinctively crouched lower. As he passed their place of concealment they could see the beads of sweat on his brow, the look of anger on his face. He paused at the edge of the shingle, rifle at the ready. Then he started forward again. The tide was in, and he ran across the narrow strip of shingle and down the jetty, bellowing as he went.

'Come back, you fools!' he shouted.

The launch was about a hundred and fifty yards out now, heading in a north-easterly direction. Andrew heard the shout and looked quickly over his shoulder, his white hair gleaming in the sunshine, and swung away to the north to narrow the target; but as Maurice raised the rifle to his shoulder and took careful aim it did not look narrow enough to the watchers in the wood. Then came the crack of the rifle. They saw Andrew stagger and slide out of sight, and the boat veered suddenly westward. Now it was broadside on. Maurice watched it for a moment. Then he ejected the spent casing, slammed back the bolt, and fired again.

David thought he heard the splintering of shattered glass, but there was no visible effect on the launch. Imagining the terror in the cabin, he jumped up with an oath. The others were also on their feet. Grevas said unsteadily, 'I can't stand this. We've got to do something,' and began to make his way through the trees.

David caught his arm. 'I'm coming with you. But take it easy. Don't try to rush him from here; we'll have to creep up on him first. And watch your step on the shingle.'

Myerson followed them. It was at his whispered suggestion that before crossing the shingle they paused to remove their shoes. Maurice still stood near the end of the jetty, his attention apparently concentrated on the launch. Twice more he fired, but they were too intent on ensuring the silence of their own progress to watch the effect of the shots.

Now they were half-way down the jetty, and still Maurice had not turned. They crept forward in single file, treading softly on their stockinged feet, with Grevas in the lead. David was close behind him; he was sweating freely and could hear his heart thumping. He felt horribly exposed. He knew he must watch Grevas closely to avoid bumping into him; to pause when he paused, go forward when he went forward. But Maurice's broad back had a terrible fascination for him, and he could not resist the occasional glance ahead.

Beyond Maurice he could see the launch. No helmsman was visible, but some one — Tom presumably — had taken control, for it had turned on to its original course and was going rapidly away.

Maurice raised his rifle, and Grevas turned to David and nodded. As the shot rang out they got to their feet and ran. Maurice heard them coming, and turned quickly. Using the rifle as a club, he swung at Grevas, catching him on his upraised arm as he tried to ward off the blow. As David sprang forward he saw the Baron teeter on the edge of the jetty and then go over. He heard the splash as Grevas hit the water, but he did not pause. Head down, he rammed straight into Maurice's stomach, and Maurice, caught off balance, went down as though pole-axed. David fell on top of him, unable to stop himself. He expected to feel Maurice's hands at his throat, was prepared to fight desperately for his life. But Maurice did not move. He lay on his back, his eyes closed, and a thin trickle of blood spread slowly over the rough stone.

From behind David, Myerson said,

'Nice work, David.' There was the sound of thrashing in the sea below, and Myerson said sharply, 'Grevas! He can't swim!'

As he leapt into the water after the Jew, David thought how ironical it was that Myerson should have devoted so much time and purpose to destroying his enemy, only to end by saving him.

Between them they hauled the Baron out and laid him on the jetty. He coughed and spluttered for a few seconds, but there was no need for artificial respiration. After a while he stopped coughing, and thanked them in his grave, quiet voice.

'Is Maurice dead?' he asked, peering at the still form.

Myerson put a hand inside Maurice's jacket and felt for his heart. The beat was still strong. 'Not yet,' he said, and shrugged. 'A pity for him, perhaps, that he isn't.'

Wet and uncomfortable, they settled down to await the return of the launch.

20

'I'm glad Andrew's going to be all right,' Susan said. She slid farther down into the corner seat so that her feet could just reach the opposite cushion, and sighed in blissful relaxation. 'Darling, can you really afford to travel first class? Or does your Mr Snowball pay?'

'I'm taking my custom elsewhere if he doesn't.' David too had his feet up. He had never before paid to travel first class, and he intended to get his money's worth. 'After what I've been through I deserve a little comfort.'

'It was kind of you to let me share it, darling. Does it include food? I'm starving.'

'Presently.' He took a notebook from his pocket and flipped over the pages. 'I'll finish this first; bring the drama bang up to date.' He sighed with smug satisfaction. 'Snowball was tickled pink when I spoke to him on the blower; he's never had a scoop like this. The dailies will be first with the news, of course, but they won't have the human interest stuff behind it. That's all mine. It'll fill the old rag for weeks.'

'You're sure the others won't talk? Journalists can be persuasive, can't they?'

'You're telling me! But you heard them promise, didn't you? All of them. The bare facts to the police, they said; the rest is mine. Exclusive. And it won't cost Snowball a penny.' He grinned to himself in anticipation. 'Apart from what he's going to pay me.'

It might have cost you your life, she thought. And mine. That shot through the porthole had been a very near miss.

'You mean he'll have to raise your salary?'

'Bet your sweet life he will. Plus a big fat bonus. He's mean, but he knows when he's on a winner. And this is the hottest thing ever.'

'I'm glad.' It did not occur to Susan that part of that bonus might reasonably be paid to her. It did not occur to David either. 'What will you do with the money?

Save it for when you marry and settle down?'

'Spend it. I can't see myself settling down.'

Susan sighed. She couldn't see it either.

David was used to writing in trains, and for a while he scribbled industriously. Susan leant back against the cushions and closed her eyes; sleep had had its interruptions on the island. But she found she could not sleep now. The rocking train waggled her head from side to side, and her feet kept slipping from the seat opposite. After a while she gave up and stared out of the window.

What will happen to them all, she wondered, now that their idyll is over? The Baron, she knew, was on the same train as themselves, bent on visits to his solicitor and his bank that were designed to make what restitution he could to his victims. But after that, what? If Olive cared to claim the island, as no doubt she would, he would be homeless as well as penniless. He was also wifeless and (presumably) friendless. Would the new grace he claimed to have found be strong enough to carry him forward, or would he slip back into his former fraudulent ways? According to David they had never brought him much success in the past.

Maurice's immediate future was certain; once out of hospital he would be tried for murder and assuredly convicted, although whether he would then go on to Broadmoor or the gallows was a matter for conjecture. Beryl too was in hospital, but her future was less sure; it was too soon, they had been told by the doctor, to say whether or not her brain had been permanently impaired. Even if she recovers, thought Susan, she will be a soured, embittered woman unless she can find some other forlorn cause into which to fling her restless, unhappy spirit.

The Mackays at least had few problems. Andrew was in no danger; the bullet had passed through the fleshy part of his shoulder. When the wound had healed they would presumably return to their estate in Scotland. Andrew, no doubt, would continue to work for peace in some form or another, and Jutter would be content to be with her husband. Jutter,

Susan suspected, was not interested in causes.

The Hampsons had gone back to the island. No one had queried their decision; they had no other home, and the livestock had to be cared for. To every one's surprise, Harold Myerson had elected to join them. 'I've paid in advance for a month's board and lodging,' he said truculently, 'and what I pay for I take.' Bessie had seemed relieved at his decision, and had gone off with him happily enough. There could be several reasons for that, Susan decided on reflection, perhaps the chief of them being that it meant a postponement of what Bessie might fear to be inevitable — the break-up of her marriage. Whether she loved her husband or not, marriage meant security to a girl in Bessie's position.

David broke into her thoughts. 'Bessie did say she'd seen her husband with Jan's cigarette-case, didn't she?'

'Yes. But she didn't know whose it was. Or so she said.'

'I believe her. That's why she was so on

edge that first evening, when Grevas produced it from his pocket and she learned it was Jan's. She must have thought her old man had been engaged in a spot of dirty work. Not murder, of course; there was no suspicion of murder then. They all believed Jan's death to have been accidental. Even Myerson.'

'Why did he talk of suicide, then?'

'To increase the general tension, of course. It was all part of the plan.' He shook his head. 'But I don't see why Bessie should worry. She doesn't love him.'

Did he say that hopefully? Susan said, 'Perhaps she does. In any case he's still her luncheon voucher.'

He looked at her then. 'You don't like her, do you? Why? Because she's coloured?'

Susan shook her head. She had no aversion to colour, and she did not dislike Bessie as a person. But she feared her as a rival. Now that she had made up her mind about David she mistrusted his interest in any other woman, white or coloured. That might be greedy, but it was common sense.

'Nonsense,' she protested. 'And hurry up, darling. I'm still hungry.'

He grinned at her. 'Gutsy little beast.'

Susan leant back in her corner. What would become of the Myersons, she wondered, when they finally left the island? They both had their problems. Harold had dedicated himself to hatred and revenge; now that the hate had been satisfied and the revenge accomplished, what could he find to take their place? She had fancied that in saving the Baron's life the hate might have turned to forgiveness and compassion, but Myerson had quickly dispelled that fancy. He would cease to hound, but he would not forgive. Compassion seemed to be lacking in his make-up. Even his championing of herself and David, when they had been suspected of stealing Olive's jewellery, had had a selfish aim. He had admitted that. For the theft to achieve its purpose the islanders themselves, not an outsider, had to come under suspicion.

Would he have compassion for Bessie? He had married her solely to obtain access to the Baron. Now that Grevas had been destroyed, would he discard her?

David closed his notebook with a whoop of triumph, disturbing her reverie.

'Well, that's that. Now let's eat.'

As she stood up she said, 'Will you publish the whole story? I'm thinking of the Myersons. They might object to having their dirty linen washed in public.'

'That's their worry. And Snowball's. He and the legal johnnies will decide what to cut.' David chuckled. 'It'll be the laws of libel, not their tender hearts, that govern the decision. Snowball hasn't got a heart.'

Susan wondered if he had a heart himself. Nevertheless, she felt suddenly cheered. If he could so happily throw Bessie to his readers, careless of how it might hurt her, he could hardly be harbouring a secret longing for her society.

They went out into the corridor. As they started down the swaying train to the dining-car Susan clutched David's arm.

'Look!' she whispered.

David looked. In the compartment next

to theirs Olive and the Baron sat facing each other. Grevas held the woman's hands in his, and on her plump face was an expression of happy contentment. The Baron was smiling gravely, tenderly.

'I suppose she's the marrying kind,' Susan said, as they staggered on. 'She just never gives up trying. Well, maybe it's a good thing for both of them. He'll get her money and she'll be a Baroness. And they can share the island.'

'All that lovely lolly!' David sighed. 'Why didn't my old man leave me a title?'

THE END

We do hope that you have enjoyed reading this large print book.

Did you know that all of our titles are available for purchase?

We publish a wide range of high quality large print books including:
Romances, Mysteries, Classics
General Fiction
Non Fiction and Westerns

Special interest titles available in large print are:
The Little Oxford Dictionary
Music Book, Song Book
Hymn Book, Service Book

Also available from us courtesy of Oxford University Press:
Young Readers' Dictionary
(large print edition)
Young Readers' Thesaurus
(large print edition)

For further information or a free brochure, please contact us at:
Ulverscroft Large Print Books Ltd.,
The Green, Bradgate Road, Anstey,
Leicester, LE7 7FU, England.
Tel: (00 44) 0116 236 4325
Fax: (00 44) 0116 234 0205